Dear Reader:

Close Quarters by Shamara Ray is a delightful, thought-provoking romance novel about how the laundry list of desired traits in a mate can fall short to the list of what is truly needed to make one happy. When a man and a woman become roommates out of financial desperation, needing to split bills, they have no idea that they are about to embark on a journey together. Melina is engaged to Ellison, a seemingly perfect man, but sometimes perfection is overkill and a man with flaws provides more excitement. Such is the case with her roommate, Malik, who embodies every trait that has always repulsed her in a man. Funny how life throws you curveballs.

I am sure that many of you have found love in the most unusual places and when you least expected it. Ray does a wonderful job of making readers question their own decisions, or giving them newfound confidence that they made the right choice the first time around. I hope that you enjoy *Close Quarters*. As always, we appreciate your support of all of the Strebor Books authors and we strive to bring you powerful, cutting-edge literature from the most vibrant voices on the current literary scene.

You can follow me online at www.facebook.com/AuthorZane or on Twitter @planetzane.

Blessings,

Zane

Zane
Publisher
Strebor Books International
www.simonandschuster.com/streborbooks

CLOSE QUARTERS

CLOSE QUARTERS

SHAMARA RAY

SBI

STREBOR BOOKS
NEW YORK LONDON TORONTO SYDNEY

Strebor Books
P.O. Box 6505
Largo, MD 20792
http://www.streborbooks.com

ISBN 978-1-59309-443-0
ISBN 978-1-4516-7908-3 (e-book)
LCCN 2012933944

First Strebor Books trade paperback edition December 2012

Cover design: www.mariondesigns.com
Cover photograph: © Keith Saunders/Marion Designs

10 9 8 7 6 5 4 3 2 1

Manufactured in the United States of America

For information regarding special discounts for bulk purchases, please contact Simon & Schuster Special Sales at 1-866-506-1949 or business@simonandschuster.com

The Simon & Schuster Speakers Bureau can bring authors to your live event. For more information or to book an event, contact the Simon & Schuster Speakers Bureau at 1-866-248-3049 or visit our website at www.simonspeakers.com.

For Shinda

CHAPTER ONE
MELINA

The sound of scurrying feet and giggling trailed off down the hallway as I entered my darkened apartment. I braced myself and marched toward the source that suddenly illuminated the hall. Malik was bent over in front of the refrigerator, clad only in his boxers, shoving something onto the shelf. The picture became clear when he turned around and slyly grinned at me. Traces of whipped cream were all over his face and hands, some on the floor. I shook my head and stormed to my room, slamming my door behind me.

My flight from Atlanta was full of turbulence and the cab ride home from the airport wasn't much better. I was supposed to arrive at LaGuardia at eight p.m., but all planes departing from Hartsfield-Jackson were delayed. We didn't touch down in New York until midnight. After waiting another twenty minutes for my luggage, I finally got in a cab headed for Brooklyn. As the driver hit every pothole on Atlantic Avenue, I concentrated on the soothing bath I planned to take once I reached home.

Malik's flavor of the week raucously laughed, pleading with him to stop doing whatever was causing her such pleasure. Our two-bedroom apartment was too small for their folly. I could hear everything. The bathroom separated our rooms, but sound traveled easily through our paper-thin walls. We lived on the second floor of a renovated brownstone in the Fort Greene section of Brooklyn. I had called this apartment home for three years. For two of those years I used the other bedroom as a home office, but the steady increases in rent caused a sister to reevaluate her living situation.

If I knew a year ago what I know now, I would have never placed an ad for a roommate. The string of characters that replied to my listing was frightening. I hoped to share my space with another woman, young and progressive like myself, but when Malik showed up at the door, I breathed a sigh of relief. I had met with too many unsavory, unemployed, uninspired losers trying to haggle with me on the amount for the monthly rent. Malik came with his resume, a three-month deposit, a great smile, a firm handshake and made a convincing case for why I needed to consider a male roommate. A week later, he moved in. A month later, the honeymoon ended.

Music started pouring out of Malik's room, the bass vibrating the walls. I understood it was Friday night—the start of the weekend—but this was intolerable. I snatched my Coach weekend tote from the closet and tossed in a couple of outfits. I changed into my velour sweatsuit, grabbed my bag and headed into the crisp, autumn night. I saw the ticket on my windshield before I even made it to my car. Damn alternate-side-of-the-street parking. I asked Malik to move my car for me while I was out of town at my conference, but apparently he couldn't even do that.

I hopped in my BMW 335i Coupe and put on Jill Scott. Her voice relaxed me as I raced down Fulton Street toward the Brooklyn-Queens Expressway. Traffic was light to Manhasset. I cruised off the exit and navigated the familiar winding roads, the moon casting barely enough light through the trees. I turned onto a private road, slowing down as the gravel popped underneath my tires. Dimming my high beams, I approached the secluded home at the end of the road, pulled into the circular, cobblestone driveway and parked behind the Hummer. I stood on the doorstep, riffling through my bag for keys. I rested the bag on the top step and knelt down, digging my hand beneath the clothing.

The wind kicked up, sending leaves scraping across the ground. I looked over my shoulder at the dark thicket of trees, into the shadows. I lifted the tote and shook it from side to side. I was dreading the possibility of ringing the doorbell when I heard a faint jingle emanating from a side compartment.

I hadn't bothered to call Ellis on my way over because I knew he was already asleep. He didn't believe in staying up late, not even on weekends. According to Ellis, as long as there was work to do and money to be made, it paid to rise before the sun. He'd be up and running a couple of hours after my head hit the pillow. I was not a morning person and usually didn't get up until after noon on Saturdays.

I passed through the marble foyer and ascended the spiral staircase. The double doors at the end of the hall were slightly ajar. I slipped into the room and padded across the floor to the bed. Ellis was on his side, sound asleep. I kicked off my sneakers, climbed on the bed and snuggled up next to him. He rolled over and clicked on the lamp.

Ellis sat up, frowning at me. "Melina, you're on my bed with your clothes on?"

I turned away from him and retreated to the bathroom to undress. "Good to see you, too," I mumbled.

Voices in the hallway stirred me from my sleep. The clock on the nightstand said it was two in the afternoon. Ellis entered the bedroom, his mother filing in after him. I sprang up and quickly put on my robe.

"Mother Harlow, I didn't know you were here," I said.

"You wouldn't, dear, since you've been in here snoozing the day away. Just like Sleeping Beauty," she said wryly.

I finger combed my hair, which I was certain was all over my head, and cut my eyes at Ellis. Why his mother was standing in the middle of his bedroom—at that very moment—made absolutely no sense to me.

"Mother is staying the weekend. She arrived yesterday evening. We just came back from North Shore Hospital. The dedication of the pediatric wing in honor of my father was today."

His mother pulled a handkerchief from her purse, right on cue. "God rest his soul," she said, dabbing her dry eyes.

I went over to her and patted her back. "I miss him, too, Mother Harlow."

She whipped her head around and glared at me. "You could never know the pain I feel. I spent forty years of my life with that man." She straightened her posture and smiled stiffly. "And I told you, call me Bebe."

She pivoted on her Manolos and left the room, her expensive perfume lingering in her aftermath.

I sat on the edge of the bed and shook my head. "Ellis, why didn't you tell me the ceremony was today?"

"I thought I mentioned it to you."

His nonchalant behavior told me otherwise. I would have remembered something as important as a dedication ceremony for his father. Ellison Harlow II was a beautiful man. One of the most respected pediatric surgeons in the country. Three months ago, he died of a heart attack. It was so unexpected—he was the picture of perfect health.

"You *thought*? Never once did you mention today was the dedication," I said.

"Are you sure, Melina?"

I had a sinking feeling in my gut. "You also didn't say anything about your mother being here. You could have at least told me this morning."

Ellis came and sat next to me on the bed. "You know how much you hate to be disturbed in the morning. You appeared so peaceful, I wasn't sure if I should wake you."

"Of course you should have. You know how much I loved your father."

He kissed me on the cheek. "I'm sorry, Lina. I wasn't thinking. Mother and I finalized our plans last night and my schedule was hectic this morning. I had a breakfast meeting, and then I had to pick up Daniella—"

"Great. So Daniella thinks I was a no-show, too."

"I told my sister and my mother you've been out of town all week. They understand you arrived home in the wee hours of the morning. Forgive me?"

He was missing the point. I could not care less about being tired. I would have never missed such an important event.

"So how was the ceremony?"

He shrugged. "Kind words. Everyone touting the noble Dr. Ellison Harlow's many accomplishments. A few requisite tears. Just what I expected."

Since his father's death, Ellis had been extremely cynical when talking about him. He always showed his father tremendous respect. I chalked his recent behavior up to grief and the anger that sometimes came along with a sudden loss.

"I would've really liked to have been there."

"I'll take you to see the new wing next weekend." He walked toward the door. "Get dressed. Mother is having a small reception downstairs."

"I don't have anything appropriate to wear for one of your mother's gatherings. I only packed jeans."

"Just put your jeans on, Melina."

"Right. I'll stick out like a hooker in church. I'm going to head back to Brooklyn."

"That's ridiculous. Stay up here if you want. The guests will be downstairs for an hour at the most."

"Spend the day with your mother. I know this is a hard time for her. I'll call you later on."

I didn't appreciate that Ellis neglected to inform me about the dedication and then invited me to the reception as an afterthought. If the truth be told, I wasn't interested in being around *Bebe* or her snobby friends, anyway.

I showered and dressed, then made a covert departure through the back door, walking around to the front of the estate. Daniella waved to me from the window as I put my bag in the trunk. I smiled and waved back. I had always liked Daniella—she was cool—it was her mother I could do without.

I drove away from Ellis's mansion wondering how I'd possibly fit in there.

CHAPTER TWO
MALIK

It took a while, but Cinnamon finally got the message and took her ass home. When she stopped by last night with her six-pack abs and a can of whipped cream, a brother could not resist. Cinnamon and cream—oh so tasty. But like most sweets, you pay the price later. I used to hook up with Cinnamon regularly, but she started to get attached. I had to cut her back. But every once in a while we'd get together because the sex was banging.

I broke out the mop and busted a move on the kitchen floor, then cleaned the bathroom and straightened up the living room. I knew Melina was going to be bitchin' when she got back and I refused to give her the satisfaction of complaining about the house being a mess.

It was a good week. No nitpicking. I watched what *I* wanted to watch on the TV in the living room, and best of all, the honeys kept a brother company without Melina scaring them off with her dirty looks. She needed to go out of town every week. Melina could be wound a little too tight, but we got along all right. She was an only child and it showed. Everything had to be her way. Nothing out of place. When I moved in, she told me to make myself comfortable, this was my home now, too. I wouldn't have known it. Shortly after moving in, I slightly repositioned the angle of the couch and she almost evicted me. I knew then that although she said *mi casa es su casa*, what she really meant was—you may pay half the rent, but this is still *my* apartment.

My boys were ringing my phone off the hook, trying to convince me to come down to our favorite watering hole to watch the MLB playoffs. On any other Saturday evening I would have been down, but thanks to my unexpected visitor last night, I didn't have a chance to work on my project that was due Monday at work.

I placed the package of sanitary napkins on the coffee table and gaped at them. How was I supposed to come up with a catchy ad for pads with designer scents? Did women really want the scent of Chanel No. 5 permeating from their panties? I opened my folder and read the product profile. Feminine products scented with essential oils, not designer perfume. Fragrant oils with therapeutic benefits designed to energize, relax or alleviate stress. The concept wasn't as bad as I thought, but still not my ideal assignment.

The projects assigned to me lately had been tumbling downhill, but no matter how bad the product, I managed to outshine the fair-haired boys at the agency. Regardless of my performance, I got stuck with the crap no one else would touch—the bottom of the barrel. I called a meeting with my boss to discuss the prospect of getting a crack at some of our larger clients and he had the nerve to tell me that I had to prove I could handle the responsibility. I'd spent six years at the company and could honestly say I was the most talented, not to mention creative, account executive they had at Newport and Donner. My multi-concept campaigns had never failed to appease the client and, despite my portfolio of unusual products, I had the highest ad acceptance rate. Since my next step at the firm didn't seem to be up, it would have to be out—the door.

My bank accounts were swelling, my investments were growing and I was entertaining the idea of starting my own agency. I'd hit the glass ceiling at Newport and Donner and starting over at another agency was not an option. I'd only shared my plans with one person, my father. He'd been helping me with my business plan and, if our projections were correct, I'd be opening my own agency within the next year.

Tupac's classic, "I Get Around," rang out from my cell phone. I checked the caller ID. Cinnamon. I let the call roll over to my voice mail. This would go on for the next couple of days until she realized nothing had changed between us. One night of good sex does not equal a relationship. No matter how upfront I was in the beginning, women always expected more than I was willing to give. I wasn't ready to settle down. I thoroughly enjoyed variety and in the immortal words of R. Kelly, "I don't see nothing wrong with a little bump and grind."

The cell phone rang again. Melina.

"Meet me at Night of the Cookers," she said.

"Bet."

CHAPTER THREE
MALIK

I found Melina at the bar drinking her usual—a glass of Riesling. Annoyance flashed across her face when she saw me coming. I sat on the barstool next to her and signaled to the bartender.

"What's up, Roomie? How was your trip?" I asked.

"You know I got a ticket while I was gone, right?" she asked tightly.

"Don't sweat that. I'll take care of it."

"Damn right, you will."

"Mel, let me get a drink before you rip me a new asshole." I impatiently signaled to the bartender again. I ordered a Johnnie Walker Black and then told her to make it a double. It was going to be one of those nights. The bartender poured but not fast enough. I should have told her to give me the whole damn bottle. I took a healthy swig of my drink and then turned to Melina. "I know you asked me to move your car, but I didn't come home Thursday night. I apologize."

She nodded; her long reddish-brown ponytail bobbed up and down. Silence was never good when it came to Melina. It either meant she was pissed or extremely pissed. She raised her half-filled glass to her lips and polished off the wine. Extremely pissed.

"Malik, if you had a girlfriend—which we know is a ludicrous thought—but *if* you had a girlfriend, and she neglected to tell you about an event that she knew would be important to you, what would you think?"

This wasn't about me after all. The golden boy pissed her off. I eased back in my chair and took a more leisurely taste of my drink. "Well…it depends."

"On what?" she questioned.

"Her explanation."

She motioned for a refill. "Forget it. It doesn't matter."

I went back to guzzling my scotch.

"All I'm saying is," she abruptly continued, "if your girlfriend said 'I thought I told you,' wouldn't you think it was a lame excuse?"

That time, I nodded. She apparently was talking to herself anyway and what I said probably wouldn't matter much.

"Is it me?" she asked.

I didn't know what the hell she was talking about, but I shook my head.

"Ellis knew I wanted to be at the dedication ceremony for his father. I think his mother had something to do with it."

"What are you doing with that tight-ass anyway?" Five-foot-five with booty for days…she could have any man she wanted.

Melina swiveled her stool around and leaned toward me. That did it. I went too far.

"You know I was thinking the same thing as I bolted out of there today," she said.

Now I genuinely wondered what had happened because Melina didn't bite my head off like she usually did when I insulted her stuffed shirt of a man. "Mel, wassup? Talk to me."

"I love him, Malik. That's why I'm with him. It's simple. He's everything I want in a man and more."

I yawned and peeked at my watch. Just that fast, my interest had waned. I should have met the fellas at the bar for the game instead of sitting there listening to *The Young and the Restless*. "Then don't read into anything. If the man said he thought he told you, take his word for it."

I learned a long time ago, sometimes it's easier to tell a woman what she wants to hear. She won't listen to a word you say if it ain't what she wants to hear.

Melina smiled. "You're probably right."

I knew it.

Her whole aura changed in less than a millisecond. The scowl dropped from her face and her body relaxed. "You want to have dinner?"

"All right. Let's get a table."

We were seated and the waitress left us with our menus. I opened mine and Melina placed hers on the table.

"So, who was the tart last night?"

"Why do you have to insult my company, Mel?"

"It's not an insult, merely an observation."

I wondered how she considered that an observation when she hadn't seen my guest.

She must have read my mind. "Any woman who carries on as boisterously as she did, when she knows others can hear, doesn't have much respect for herself."

"It has nothing to do with respect. She was enjoying herself. I have that effect on women."

"Malik, please."

"You know, Mel, some of us actually like living on the wild side. Hot, freaky, uninhibited sex is something to be embraced. You're so used to stuffy, mechanical, blue-blood sex that you can't imagine how the other side lives."

Melina rolled her eyes in disgust. "You know nothing about what goes on between Ellis and me...and I'm not about to tell you."

"You don't have to. I can tell it's real neat and quiet and *tasteful*. You probably don't break a sweat and I bet your hair never falls out of place."

I laughed when she glared at me. I had struck a nerve. That would teach her about making assumptions.

She shook her head. "Do you have to be such a pig?"

"Oink oink, baby."

"Grow up, Malik."

"Loosen up, Mel."

"There's more to life than sex."

"You're right, there's great sex. You should try it someday."

"Let's just order," she said wearily.

I laughed again, knowing I'd won the day's round. That's how it was with Melina; daily debates and you had better be prepared for the challenge.

CHAPTER FOUR
MELINA

I climbed into bed, wondering why I had let Malik get under my skin. He baited me and I fell for it time and again. Ellis and I had a wonderful relationship and my sex life was just fine.

I rolled over and reached for my cordless phone on the nightstand. I dialed Ellis's number. He picked up on the first ring, sounding groggy.

"What are you wearing?" I whispered into the phone.

"What? Who is this?"

I repeated my question, the words dripping from my lips like warm honey. "What are you wearing, Ellis?"

"Lina, I was asleep. I have to get up early and I am wearing my blue pinstripe pajamas, if you must know."

"Oh forget it, Ellis. Go back to sleep. I'll call you tomorrow." I slammed the phone down in the cradle—so much for kinky phone sex.

Ellis and I had been together for two years and Malik was right. Ellis wasn't a free spirit, but that's what I loved about him. He was driven, sophisticated, well- traveled and a highly respected businessman.

The day his assistant called my office to arrange a meeting between Ellis and me, I was ecstatic. *Black Enterprise* magazine had recently included my accounting firm on their list of "Rising

Stars" in the accounting industry and Ellis, having read the article, was interested in hiring my firm. Ellis owned a major research-based pharmaceutical company at the forefront of providing breakthrough medicines. An account like his could propel my company to the next level.

A week later, I was sitting in his spacious Park Avenue office discussing business. I thoroughly outlined the specialized accounting services my firm could provide Harlow Pharmaceuticals. My presentation was flawless and I realized Ellis was impressed when he invited me to lunch, under the guise of discussing the increased scrutiny of the S.E.C. on corporate accounting practices. While we were dining, I found myself getting lost in his penetrating gaze more than once, and though we were talking about corporate scandals and accounting fraud, he graced me with a charismatic smile throughout the entire meal. Ellis was six feet of fine. I forced myself to stay focused and *think* business, and when we finally ended lunch three hours later, I rated the meeting a raving success.

Over the next two weeks, I anxiously waited to hear if I had gotten the account. It was a Friday evening and I was in my office packing my briefcase for the day when I heard a tap on the glass. I had already locked the front door and was prepared to tell whoever knocked to come back on Monday morning—until I saw it was Ellison Harlow III. I quickly let him in from the brisk November air.

He removed his Burberry trench coat, unwrapped his scarf and then sat on the antique leather sofa in my reception area. "Ms. Bradford, I wanted to personally follow-up with you regarding the status of our meeting."

My mind raced. Ellison Harlow III was actually sitting in my office. I was certain it was an indication I had landed his account, but I contained my joy. It was the moment I had been waiting for.

I sat next to Ellis on the chair. "I appreciated the opportunity to present the unique services Trinity can provide Harlow Pharmaceuticals."

"Ms. Bradford, while I feel Trinity Accounting and Tax is top-notch and more than qualified to meet our needs, we have decided to go with another firm."

Not what I expected to hear. An uncomfortable silence filled the room as I struggled not to let my disappointment show. I got up and extended my hand. "Well, Mr. Harlow, thank you for the consideration."

He hesitated before standing to grasp my outstretched hand. I pulled back from his gentle grip, but he held on.

Ellis cleared his throat. "Ms. Bradford, this is a bit awkward, but would you consider having a drink with me?"

A million thoughts crossed my mind. There was Ellison Harlow III telling me that my firm failed to secure his account, yet asking me out on a personal level. My head willed me to say no, but I heard a soft voice say, "Sure."

"Great. My car is waiting out front."

"Allow me to collect my things and I'll be right out."

Without Ellison standing in my face, reality settled in. He came down to my office specifically to ask me out. Perhaps that's what the initial meeting was all about. My firm was probably never a real contender. How unprofessional! I wasn't running a dating service. I expected more from a man whose company was voted one of the top ten places for women to work, by *Fortune* magazine the past two consecutive years.

I jerked my briefcase off the desk, turned off the lights and locked up. Ellison's driver opened the door to the sleek black limo as I approached the curb. I slid onto the soft leather seat across from Ellison Harlow III. His smoldering smile greeted me.

Before I allowed myself to get caught up in the moment, I fixed Ellison with an icy grin. "Perhaps you can help me understand something, Mr. Harlow."

"Please, call me Ellis," he replied, not deterred by my tone.

"Right...Ellis. Well, Ellis, if Harlow Pharmaceuticals would be a perfect fit for Trinity, then why is it that we didn't get the account?"

"I don't mix business with pleasure."

"Excuse me?"

"I could have given your firm the account, but it wouldn't have worked out. Now I could sit here and pretend I agonized over my decision, but I didn't. After we had lunch, my thoughts weren't focused on Trinity Accounting and Tax or what your firm could do for Harlow Pharmaceuticals. I thought about you...and how to get to know you better."

What nerve. There I was trying to build my business and run with the big dogs, and this man discounted me because he thought I was cute. "Who *did* you hire, Mr. Harlow?"

"I'm back to Mr. Harlow?" He chuckled. "We went with Sampson Dewer."

"I see."

"Trust me. You were one of our top candidates. And though we won't be doing business together, I've spoken to a business associate of mine about you. Expect a call from Marty Sewell some time next week."

"Martin Sewell?" The chill melted from my voice. "*The* Martin Sewell? CEO of Omega Toys?"

"The one and only. I hope you don't mind."

I smiled on the inside. "Why would I mind? I look forward to receiving Mr. Sewell's call."

If Ellison didn't believe in my ability, he certainly wouldn't have referred me to the toy magnate of the East Coast. I crossed my legs and relaxed back into the seat. I had hit the jackpot—in more ways than one.

I sipped my coffee and flipped through the Sunday *New York Times*. I had every intention of rollerblading in Fort Greene Park, but Mother Nature had something else in mind.

A driving rain pelted the window with such force I was drawn to peer out at the downpour. The wind whipped through the trees, shaking loose the fall foliage. Broken branches and leaves littered the street. I pressed my hand to the glass, and found it to be much colder than I thought. It was the kind of day to snuggle with a loved one and watch old movies.

I returned to the couch and turned on the television. Malik shuffled into the living room, eyes barely open. Last night, we parted ways after dinner. When I came home, Malik went elsewhere.

Malik eased down onto the couch like a man twice his age. He leaned his head back against the pillows and groaned. I glanced over at him...five o'clock shadow...wrinkled tank...sweats...bare feet...hangover.

Malik turned pleading eyes on me. "Please tell me we have Alka Seltzer in the house."

I took pity on him. "I'll get you some."

"Thanks, Mel," he mumbled.

I went to retrieve the cure to Malik's ailments from the medicine cabinet. I dropped two tablets into a glass of water and prepared a cold compress while the medication fizzed and bubbled.

I handed Malik the glass, hovering over him until he finished its contents. I instructed him to lie back on the couch and then placed the compress on his head. "Where did you go last night?"

"I ended up at a lounge on Dekalb. My boys met me down there and we set the party off right."

"I hope it was worth it. You look like crap." His café au lait complexion was pale, almost ashen. "What's the point of partying when this is the end result?"

Malik winced at me through slits. "I'll let you know once I feel better. Right now, I'm not up for being analyzed."

I left him alone and went to the kitchen to pour myself another cup of coffee. I considered heading to the office since my plans for the day were ruined by the weather, but decided that working on a rainy Sunday was a bad idea. I settled on going to a movie and then maybe doing a little shopping. I picked up my mug and started toward my room. A groan stopped me in my tracks. "Are you going to be all right, Malik?"

I walked back to the living room. Malik's lips were moving, but I couldn't hear a thing. I bent down in front of him, trying to figure out what he was whispering.

He took the compress from his head. "Can you run this under cold water?"

I snatched the compress from him and went to kitchen with it. I returned and plastered the compress across Malik's forehead.

"Thanks, Mel."

I turned to go get dressed when Malik called my name. Again, I went to him on the couch. "Yes?"

"Can you rub my back?"

I scowled. "Can I what?"

"I feel awful and I need to fall asleep. Please. Just for a few minutes."

I was the one who groaned that time. I started to kneel in front of the couch, but Malik stopped me.

"No. Sit down right here."

Malik leaned up so that I could sit on the couch. He turned on his side with his back facing me and laid his two-hundred-plus pounds across my lap. I frowned at the back of his head, wanting to slap it.

"Mel, come on."

"Man, you better chill the hell out. Nobody told you to be out all night drinking like a fish."

"Lecture me later. Right now, rub."

I closed my eyes and took a deep, cleansing breath. It took every ounce of my willpower to stay silent. I placed my hand on his back and began to gently make small circles. Malik moaned. I moved my hand up and down his back in a slow, soothing motion.

In a few minutes, his breathing evened out and his head sank deeper into my lap. I stopped rubbing, and when Malik didn't protest, I realized that he had fallen asleep. I sat, thinking about how to move from the couch without waking him. The phone rang. I tried to get up, but Malik was oblivious and did not budge. I had no choice but to let the machine retrieve the call. I slid my hand underneath Malik's shoulder and attempted to lift his six-foot-four frame from my lap. He shrugged me off, tightening his arm around my legs. I leaned my head back against the pillows and sighed. Apparently, I was staying home.

I was roused by the ringing of the telephone again. I leapt from the couch, bumping my shin against the coffee table. Hobbling into the kitchen, I snatched the phone from its cradle.

"Where have you been? I've been calling you for the past three hours."

"Oh…I…I must have dozed off. Why, what's going on, Ellis?"

"I wanted you to have lunch with Mother and me, but we've already eaten now. I just got her settled at home and I'm on my way back from Manhattan."

I smiled, thankful for the reprieve. It seemed Malik's drunken stupor had benefited me after all. "I'm sorry I missed *Bebe*."

"Don't be cute, Lina."

"I'm not being cute. You heard your mother tell me to call her Bebe. I'm only respecting her wishes."

Ellis sighed into the phone. "I'm coming to pick you up and take you back to Long Island. Are you dressed?"

"I'll be ready when you get here."

"Good. Pack enough clothes for the week. I'll see you in twenty minutes."

Before I could respond, Ellis hung up. I glared at the receiver and spoke to no one in particular. "Yes, Master."

I turned to replace the handset and found Malik leaning against the wall, smiling.

I jumped, almost dropping the phone. "Look who's returned from the living dead."

He was dressed in a pair of dark-blue jeans and a bulky, chocolate-brown turtleneck sweater. "I'm feeling one hundred and ten percent better."

Malik took the phone from my hand and returned it to its place on the wall. He leaned over, kissed me on the cheek and then headed straight for the refrigerator.

I stood there, wondering if he was still intoxicated from the night before. "Malik—"

"Thanks for taking care of me, Mel."

"No problem," I said, snickering. "Your condition saved me from a lunch date from hell."

"With your future mother-in-law?"

"How long were you listening to my conversation?"

Malik took a bottle of cranberry juice from the fridge, placing it on the counter. "Don't get riled up. I didn't intentionally listen to your call. I sort of overheard what you were saying to *Master*." He brought the bottle up to his smiling lips.

"Whatever, Malik." I left him standing in the kitchen, enjoying his own joke.

"Mel, I'm kidding," he called down the hallway.

I went into the bathroom, slamming the door behind me. I had to rush to get ready and didn't have time for Malik with his silly taunts. I showered, dried off and smoothed on my lotion. Male conversation greeted me as I emerged from the bathroom. Great. Ellis had arrived already and was waiting on me. His two least favorite things.

Ellis disliked coming to Brooklyn. He always complained about the traffic, the noise, the parking; you name it. And he despised waiting. If you weren't on his time, then your clock must be wrong.

I shouted from my bedroom door. "I'll be right out."

Ellis and Malik both responded. "Okay."

Malik was trying to get a rise out of Ellis and, as usual, Ellis took the bait.

Fast only hinted at how long it took to pack my bag. I threw on my black jeans with a black-fitted turtleneck and a black belt. My high-heel boots made the outfit complete. I pulled my hair back into a tight bun and dotted my lips with a bit of gloss. My summer tan had long faded and the freckles across my nose were prominent against my sugar cookie brown skin. I sprayed on my scent du jour and hurried into the living room.

Ellis and Malik sat across from one another, debating about whether the republicans in Congress were doing a good job or not. Malik was a democrat and Ellis, a staunch republican. They would never see eye to eye and neither could be swayed, yet they insisted on arguing over politics.

I cleared my throat. "Babe, my bag, please."

Ellis stood up, still bantering with Malik. He took my bag from me. I went to the closet to get my light-blue, cropped leather jacket.

"You look nice, Mel," Malik said.

"Her name is Lina. I can't fathom why you insist on referring to her as if she is one of your homeboys," Ellis responded.

"Mel…Lina…it doesn't matter." I moved between them. "Thank you, Malik," I said, warning my roommate with my eyes. "Let's go, Ellis."

"Take care, *homeboy*," Ellis said.

Malik smirked. "Later, *brother*."

CHAPTER FIVE
MELINA

The rain had subsided and the late-day sun peeked through the thick, gray clouds. I was strapped into the passenger seat of Ellis's Porsche, listening to him rant about how ignorant he found Malik. I reached over and turned on the satellite radio. It was tuned to smooth jazz. George Benson was singing about being lost in a masquerade. I started to sing along. Ellis stopped his tirade.

"Am I boring you, Lina?"

"Relax, Ellis. Every time you see Malik, you get upset. The two of you don't share the same viewpoints. Why do you persist in trying to engage him in these political or philosophical debates and then get angry when he disagrees with you?"

"I'm not angry," he said, nostrils flaring.

"You're not? You have been going on about this for the last fifteen minutes. You haven't asked me how I'm doing, about my day, nothing."

Ellis sighed. "I'm sorry." He finally saw me for the first time that day. His eyes traveled from my head to my toes. "You are absolutely beautiful."

I leaned over and kissed him on the lips. "Thank you."

Ellis could be a real pain when he wanted to be, but I loved him. He possessed a raw honesty that I respected, even when I didn't necessarily agree with him. At that moment, staring at his rugged profile, I realized that I wanted to spend my life with him. I got lost in the graceful movement of his long lashes every time he blinked. Thought about the way his strong jaw felt against my cheek when he held me close to him. Pictured his burnished brown skin against my own. I licked my lips, savoring the taste and the memory his full mouth left behind.

He saw me admiring him and touched my cheek. "I missed you last week."

"I couldn't tell."

"Your departure was so abrupt yesterday afternoon, I didn't have a chance to tell you."

My anger flared slightly at the thought of being excluded from the dedication ceremony. I pushed the negativity back where it came from. I didn't want to fight with Ellis. He had just lost his father. Considering the circumstances, I needed to be more understanding. Maybe he did think he told me about the event. Surely, he had a lot on his mind lately. He had his mother and sister to look after and a business to run. Any issues I had with him concerning the weekend could wait.

I rubbed my hand on the back of his head. Ellis always wore a fresh Caesar haircut. I thought a diamond stud would give him a sexy edge, but he would never wear an earring. He considered it unprofessional and ghetto. His words, not mine.

"How was your conference?" he asked.

"Surprisingly interesting. Tons of information on new tax codes. How was your week?"

"Full of meetings. We're launching a new drug trial next week and anything that could have gone wrong practically did. I'm expecting this week to be even more hectic. In fact, I have a few calls to make as soon as we get to the house."

"Make your calls, Ellis, and then that's it. No more work this evening. We are going to relax and enjoy each other's company."

"All right, beautiful. Do you want to dine out tonight?"

"Maybe we can grab a bite at Eden. We can get it to go, if you want."

Eden was one of my favorite restaurants. Unfortunately, Ellis didn't share my sentiments. On rare occasions, he would humor me and take me to Eden, but he'd squawk the entire time.

He touched my face again. "If that's what you want."

Ellis was being way too accommodating; he knew he was in the doghouse.

I turned on the oven in Ellis's kitchen and placed the aluminum pans of food from Eden inside to stay warm while he made his calls. I removed two dishes from the cabinet and set the small oak table that sat next to the fireplace. Yes, Ellis had a gas fireplace in his kitchen. I retrieved a bottle of Chardonnay from the wine rack in the corner and carried it to the island in the center of the kitchen. I uncorked the bottle and poured myself a glass. The aroma of chicken in rosemary butter wrapped itself around me and my stomach responded with a long grumble. The food was calling my name and I almost went to the oven for a little taste. I turned on the fireplace, dimmed the lights, and sat at the table sipping my wine.

Ellis entered the kitchen, talking on the phone. His voice echoed through the room, bouncing off the pots and pans suspended from the ceiling pot rack. He slipped my wineglass out of my hand and drank from it. I took that as my cue to pour myself another glass. He sat at the table and put his feet up in the chair while I carried the food from the oven to the table. Ellis continued his conversation while I plated our dinner. I sat across from him with my elbows on the table and my hands folded beneath my chin. He gave me the signal that he'd be done in a second. After a few minutes passed, I draped my napkin over my lap and proceeded to dig into my food. Ellis spat out instructions to the poor soul on the other end of the phone. Every time I thought he was wrapping up his conversation, he addressed yet another concern. It was apparent he was unhappy with what he was hearing, and though he wasn't quite yelling, he was dangerously close. Ellis got up from the table and left the kitchen with his wine.

I finished my dinner in silence, watching the flickering flame in the fireplace cast shadows across the kitchen. I washed the dishes, covered Ellis's plate, and left it on the counter.

On my way upstairs, I heard him still conducting business in the study. I walked through his bedroom, directly into the bathroom to run water in the tub. I planned on a long, hot soak. I returned to the bedroom to get my facial scrub from my bag then closed the bathroom door behind me, undressed and immersed myself in the deep, triangular-shaped tub.

I closed my eyes and leaned my head back. Was this what I had to look forward to with Ellis? Always business first, family second. I'd spent nights waiting for Ellis to come home from the office and he never arrived. Waited for a call that I never received. We'd cancelled trips, rescheduled evening plans—all in the name of business. Sure, most women would kill to be where I was right then, in a relationship with one of the most successful African-American men in the country. But it was moments like these, moments having nothing to do with success, when you started to wonder. Was this the life I wanted? I cherished quiet time at home. Time spent enjoying and loving one another. I couldn't really complain much. I was aware of Ellis's lifestyle before we became involved. I suppose, somewhere deep inside, I thought I'd come first. Foolish me.

Cool air and barely tepid water awoke me. Ellis was leaning against the granite bathroom countertop, looking down at me. The door was open, allowing a chill to circulate through the room.

"Can you close the door? The warmth is escaping."

Ellis did what I asked. "I apologize for spending so much time on the phone, but it couldn't be helped." He unfolded my towel and held it open for me.

I stepped out of the tub, taking the towel out of Ellis's hands and wrapping it around my body. "You're apologizing an awful lot lately."

Ellis pulled his sweater over his head. I went to the sink and began brushing my teeth, watching him in the mirror.

He unbuckled his belt and stepped out of his slacks. "Lina, I explained earlier the importance of this coming week."

I rinsed toothpaste from my mouth. "Yeah, you did." I walked past Ellis and into the bedroom.

"You're upset." He followed close behind me. "Would you have preferred for me to shirk my duties and ignore my responsibility?"

"Of course not, Ellis." I sat on the edge of the bed, massaging cocoa butter into my skin.

"There are always last-minute problems before a drug trial."

I went to the dresser drawer and removed my silk chemise. "I understand that."

"Then act like it, Lina. I'm going to take a shower."

I opened my mouth to respond, but Ellis had already closed the bathroom door behind him. I grabbed my robe and stomped out of the bedroom. I mumbled to myself all the way downstairs to the theater room. I went into the control booth and inserted my favorite DVD.

Ellis's home theater could seat up to twenty-five people. Five rows of luxurious, smoky-gray recliners, each with a console for cups and snacks, were arranged in true movie theater fashion— albeit more stylishly cozy. Each row was set on its own platform, descending into the room. I went down the stairs, sliding my toes through the plush carpet, and curled up in the center seat in the middle row.

The opening scene from *The Color Purple* displayed across the sixteen-foot movie screen. It should be illegal to view movies at home any other way. I was engrossed in the movie, moved by two sisters being painfully torn apart, when soft lips touched the back of my neck. I turned and Ellis was standing behind my seat wearing black pajama bottoms, tied at the waist with a drawstring. His broad chest was bare. Droplets of water clung to the soft patch of hair between his pecs. I turned back to the screen. Ellis's hands moved to the back of my head and began removing the pins holding my bun in place. My hair spilled across my shoulders. Ellis massaged my scalp, running his fingers from the roots to the tips of my strands. Upset or not, his touch felt good. My shoulders relaxed and my head moved along with his probing fingers.

He walked around the seats and sat in the recliner beside mine, extending his hand to me. No words, not a smile in sight. The intensity in his radiating gaze said it all—he was a man not to be denied. I slid my hand into his and went to him. Ellis pulled me down on his lap, positioning my legs across his own. He buried his face in my neck, kissing gently down to my shoulder. His hand moved up my thigh, underneath my chemise. I felt him stiffen against my leg. Ellis's mouth wandered lower to my breasts. I leaned back, soothed by the sensation of his lips on my skin. I reached for the drawstring on his pajamas, moving to my knees to straddle him.

Ellis stilled my hand. "Not in here. Let's go up to the bed-room."

"I want you right here," I whispered, "right now."

Ellis stood, taking me with him, and led me up the stairs... snapping me out of the mood.

CHAPTER SIX
MALIK

Monday morning. My meeting was a slam-dunk, but I had not expected anything less. Mr. Donner had been perched at the conference table, accepting accolades from my client as if he was the mastermind behind the catchphrase: *AromatheraPad…turning necessity into once-a-month essential therapy.*

I was distracted by a tap on my door. Kai stuck her head in before strutting into my office. She stood front and center on the other side of my desk. I gave her a once-over. Fitted white shirt with French cuffs and just enough buttons undone, tucked neatly into a black wool skirt that stopped several inches above the knees, revealing legs as long as the horizon.

I motioned for her to take a seat in one of the chairs across from me. Instead she sauntered over to the sofa and sat, slowly crossing her legs. I was captivated by the way her foot arched in her four-inch heels and imagined things that I had no business thinking about. I went around to the front of my desk and sat on the corner.

Kai smiled. "Malik, I'm impressed."

I fought the urge to smile back at her. "And why is that?"

"Don't be coy, Malik. You know you were *the man* in the meeting this morning."

Kai Cooper, the finest woman at the agency, giving me my props. Other account execs had come to examine my flow, trying to figure out why my ad acceptance rate was the best in the agency—hoping to steal my magic. That morning was the first time Kai ever sat in on one of my client meetings.

I nodded. "I appreciate the compliment."

"I was thinking maybe we could go for drinks after work today."

Damn. I *was* the man. Kai had every suit at the agency tripping over themselves, trying to get to her. Hot didn't begin to describe this woman. Chic pixie cut, Bambi-like eyes, skin as smooth as melted milk chocolate, tight body with a luscious ass…made me lick my lips. And to top it all off, she was intelligent and could hold her own with the big boys.

Unlike my other colleagues, I didn't sweat Kai. It wasn't my style. I preferred to let the ladies come to me and it seemed like it was finally my day.

"Drinks would be cool. How about we meet in the lobby at five-thirty? We can go to Topaz if you're interested in grabbing a bite to eat."

Kai got up and smoothed her skirt down. She came over to me and began straightening my already perfect tie. "I'll be waiting downstairs at five-thirty on the dot," she said in a hushed tone. She trailed her manicured nails down the front of my suit jacket while rubbing her thigh against my leg.

My assistant buzzed on the intercom. I cleared my throat. "Yes, Renee."

"Your eleven o'clock is here."

"Send him in."

Kai stepped away from me and put her business face back on. As my appointment walked in, she commented on her way out, "Keep up the good work, Mr. Denton."

I spent the majority of the afternoon on the phone with my boys bragging about my plans for the evening. Bets were made as to whether I could get Kai to come home with me that night. I accepted and was in the process of hatching a plan when my boss called me to his office.

After fifteen minutes of listening to Mr. Donner ramble on about the importance of teamwork, I interrupted him. "You're absolutely right. In order for Newport and Donner to reach the next level, we need to be more aggressive and support one another in our efforts."

Donner shifted in his chair. "I'm glad we're on the same page, Malik."

I hated the way he pronounced my name. He said it so that the "Mal" rhymed with "Al." It didn't matter that I had corrected him a million times; he called me what he wanted. Donner patted his gray comb-over and rearranged his glasses on the bridge of his nose. "I want you to partner with Kai Cooper on a new project."

Finally, he had said something interesting. "What type of account will we be working on?"

"We'll all meet tomorrow morning at nine to discuss the particulars. Block at least two hours on your calendar."

"I anticipate hearing the details." I headed to the door.

"By the way, you did a great job this morning. I'm expecting bigger and better things from you. Don't disappoint me."

"I can guarantee you won't be disappointed."

I strode down the hall, speculating on the magnitude of the assignment I was about to receive. I was certain of only one thing—it had to be good for Donner to pair me with Kai. I couldn't say if it was the short skirts or talent, but she managed to secure the best clients. Our pairing ensured that I was about to get away from the trash heap accounts I kept getting stuck with. I'd wait to see how the project turned out and then gauge the quality of my next account before deciding exactly when to branch out on my own, if at all. Maybe both Newport and Donner were finally taking notice of my worth.

CHAPTER SEVEN
MALIK

The hostess led us through the dimly lit restaurant to an isolated booth in the corner. Smooth jazz filtering through the speakers, mingled with the low hum of conversations. Kai scooted into the velvety red, crescent-shaped booth and I slid in after her. I unbuttoned my suit jacket and reclined against the seat, placing one arm on the backrest.

Kai slinked a little closer to me. "I don't know why we haven't met for drinks sooner," she said.

She could pretend she didn't know, but I was fully aware. Until that morning, I hadn't registered on Kai's radar. She considered me a guppy in the shark tank, measured by the quality of accounts I was given. All of that was about to change. I would make sure of it.

"We're here now and the timing couldn't be better. I hear we're going to be working on a project together," I said.

It was almost imperceptible, but her smile faltered. She straightened up, moving from the crook of my arm. I was steering this ship tonight. Business first, intrigues later.

"Yes, Gerry told me he was entrusting us with the Sphere Electronics account."

My mental assistant kicked in and started taking notes. She was on a first name basis with the boss and already had an advantage with information about the client.

"Sphere is the leader in the videogame market," I said. "I recently read they're developing a new racecar game that looks so real it'll make you think you can feel the wind on your face."

"I've seen it and it's amazing." Kai stroked her hand on my leg. "You and I will be responsible for transferring that same exhilarating feeling through our ads."

"How long have you been at Newport and Donner?" I asked, moving my leg out of her reach.

"Seven years."

"Is this your first time working jointly on an account?"

"No. You?"

"Yeah."

"Gerry likes to have two creative minds working on the larger projects. He says it yields a more abundant harvest. When he told me I would be working with you, I knew he had picked the right man for the job."

I smirked. "I couldn't agree with you more. We are about to shake up the videogame advertising market."

I signaled the waiter over to the table and ordered a bottle of champagne. We perused the menu while waiting. The waiter returned with a bottle of Perrier-Jouët. He filled our champagne flutes and left us to decide on our meals.

"A toast is in order." Kai lifted her flute and waited for me to say something.

I raised my glass to her and smiled. "Let the games begin."

We both had the broiled lobster for dinner. Kai was eating crème brulee with fresh raspberries for dessert. I was drinking a beer. We abandoned our work discussion and talked about whether the Yankees would make the World Series this year. Kai's father was a season-ticket holder and she invited me to a game the next week. I couldn't say no—the seats were behind home plate.

Kai dipped her spoon in her dessert and brought it to her mouth. She licked the spoon while she eyed me. The way she flicked the tip of her tongue in the creamy custard… I poured the remaining champagne in her glass and handed it to her. She finished it off with one tip of the glass.

She leaned forward, lips close to my ear. I looked down and caught a glimpse of cleavage straining against her lace bra.

Kai's lips brushed my earlobe as she whispered, "Would you like to continue this conversation at my place?"

No need to ask me twice. I paid the bill and then escorted Kai outside. She linked her arm through mine as we walked to the corner to catch a cab. I had barely closed the door when Kai grabbed the back of my head and pulled me to her. Our lips collided. The smell of champagne, perfume and cologne filled the space between us.

"Kai…" I pulled away from her, grabbing ahold of her shoulders to keep her at bay. "The driver needs your address."

She turned her head and saw the cab driver peering through the divider. His voyeuristic grin made Kai straighten up and back away from me. "West Seventy-Second Street. Take Columbus Avenue."

The driver nodded and then turned around to do his job. I stared at Kai to let her know what I had in mind for the evening. She licked her lips. Great, we were on the same page. We rode in silence. I didn't know what Kai was thinking, but I was wondering if the two condoms in my wallet would be enough. I could tell she was a freak. I figured her to be a two-rounder. The first round hot and wild, the second, a bit more subdued but a lot more kinky.

The cab pulled in front of Kai's apartment complex. I handed the driver the fare plus a ten-dollar tip. It was the first time I was glad a city cabdriver drove like a speeding lunatic. Kai grabbed my hand, luring me inside her building. The doorman put down his newspaper as we entered the lobby and greeted Kai by her first name. We blazed past him and boarded the elevator. It stopped on the fifth floor and what appeared to be six and a half feet of linebacker stepped on. Kai moved closer to me to make room for Big Boy. Call it male ego, but I placed my arm around Kai's waist. She didn't disappoint. Kai melted into me, resting her head on my shoulder. Big Boy pressed the button for his floor and then glowered at us like we were the offensive line and he was anticipating our rush. I rubbed my hand down Kai's back and rested it on her ass.

The doors opened on the eighth floor. I gave dude a smug nod and led Kai off the elevator. I turned back in time to catch Big Boy winking at her as the doors closed. I started back toward the elevator, but Kai yanked my arm and steered me down the hall to her apartment.

She unlocked the door and I followed her inside. I waited in the foyer while she hung up her jacket. She took me by the hand and walked into the living room. The only light in the room came through the open blinds. Kai kicked off her heels and began to unbutton her shirt. I loosened my tie. She posed before me, shirt open, breasts on display. I tugged on her shirt, drawing her closer to me. Kai yanked off my tie, jerked my jacket down my arms, and almost popped a couple of buttons opening my shirt. I spun her around, unzipped her skirt, and let it drop to the carpet. She bent over in front of me in silky panties with garters and stockings. I gripped her hips and rubbed against her. She bumped her ass into my hardness. Then she turned around, faced me and reached for my belt. My pants joined her skirt on the floor. Kai pushed me back on the sofa and straddled me. She had a condom in hand and was ripping open the packet. I should have cared where it was stashed and how she retrieved it so quickly, but I didn't. I took it from her and rolled it on my partner waving through the opening of my boxers. Kai moved her panties to the side and slid down on my dick. I shoved deep inside of her. She clutched the back of the sofa while she bounced up and down, poppin' it while she was droppin' it. I palmed her ass, guiding her, controlling the tempo.

Kai met each stroke with a force of her own. She threw her head back, digging fingernails into my shoulders, panting louder with each thrust. I knew she was about to come. I grabbed her hips and moved her body back and forth, muscles in my arms flexing. I felt her wetness saturate the front of my boxers. I gave her more of what she wanted, provided her with what she had been seeking since stepping into my office that morning. I pumped until she couldn't stand anymore and then I let go. Kai slumped forward. Our sweat-soaked shirts clung to our backs. I lifted Kai off of me. She climbed from my lap and reclined next to me on the sofa.

"Like I said earlier," Kai stated breathlessly, "I knew you were the right man for the job."

"I couldn't agree more."

CHAPTER EIGHT
MELINA

Giselle prescribed a plan of action for how I should handle Ellis. Just like a doctor—always seeking to cure a problem. We walked down 137th Street in Harlem to Charlee's brownstone for brunch. Striver's Row was always beautiful in the fall. Tree-lined streets, with golden leaves dancing in the breeze, provided the perfect backdrop for memorable moments.

Giselle Kensington and Charlee Garrett were my two best friends. My anchors. I went to college in search of sisterhood and found it in them. I had friends in high school, the kind that would smile in your face and stab you in the back before you had the chance to completely turn around. The same girls that I'd invite to my house to hang would talk about me like a dog. I heard it all. I thought I was cute because I had long hair. It wasn't my real hair; I was wearing a weave. I was stuck-up. I used brown eyeliner to put fake freckles across my nose. My freckles were ugly. I was a boyfriend stealer. I couldn't keep a boyfriend. There was no end to the torment I experienced at the hand of the green-eyed monster.

I went away to Cornell University, jaded and leery of friendship between women. I downplayed my looks. Never wore my hair down. No makeup. Sweats and sneakers all the time. Then I met Giselle and Charlee—when a sista had no sisters—they had embraced me. We lived in the same dorm and met during our first dorm meeting. Charlee was in the back, making wisecracks about the resident advisor. Giselle and I were sitting next to her, providing the laugh track. After the meeting ended, we sat in the lounge and talked for hours. Charlee was from Harlem, an uptown girl. Giselle resided in an exclusive section of Connecticut. I was from the suburbs of Maryland. We couldn't have been more different, but we formed the perfect triad. A tight clique. We ate together, studied together and partied together. For the first time, I had drama-free friendship. With them, I was comfortable enough to be myself, and after months of prodding, I shed the sweats, let my hair down and rediscovered makeup. They met the old Melina and welcomed her with open arms.

Giselle and I traipsed up the stairs to Charlee's apartment. Music thudded behind the door. Giselle went to knock for the third time when the door finally flew open. Charlee greeted us with Biggie lyrics and mimosas.

"Were y'all out there a long time?" Charlee asked, bouncing to "One More Chance."

"Long enough to hear you try to spit the first verse," I said, laughing.

Giselle glided into the living room in her camel-colored leather pants, matching boots and a cream pashmina shawl. Her curly hair was blown straight and styled in a long bob, one side tucked behind her ear. "As long as you're around, Christopher Wallace's legacy will always be alive."

Charlee started dancing in front of Giselle, smiling so hard her one dimple was showing. "Girl, you are so uptight...Christopher Wallace... Hurry up and drink that mimosa because I plan to keep your glass filled. I'm gonna have you calling him Biggie by the end of the day."

I joined in on the teasing. "Charlee, I think Dr. Kensington is stuck in work mode."

"Don't worry..." Charlee raised her glass. "These will loosen her right up."

"Let's not forget, I'm the one that showed you two how to party back in the day," Giselle said, setting her drink on the coffee table.

"But we're going to *remind* you how it's done," Charlee answered.

"Fine. Remind me with some current music. Put on some Drake or Beyonce or something," Giselle fired back.

Charlee told us to come in the kitchen, so she could finish preparing brunch. Once a month we had brunch together, rotating between houses. Giselle and I sat on the stools at the island. Charlee shredded cheese for the quiche she was making.

Giselle dipped her hand in the bowl and snatched a pinch of cheese. Charlee playfully swatted her away.

"How's Ellis doing?" Charlee asked.

Giselle spoke up before I had the chance to. "He could be better. I was just telling Melina that she needs to take a break from that relationship."

Charlee stopped shredding. "How come the only one in this room with no man is always giving advice?"

I chuckled. "You know she has a sugar daddy tucked away somewhere. Probably someone old and rich. Giselle does her dirt on the down low."

"That's because a lady doesn't kiss and tell."

"Well, *you* might not have been tellin' back in the day, but the Ques and Kappas sure were," Charlee said.

"Now you know that's a damn lie. I was a virgin in college."

Charlee and I both looked at her and then burst out laughing.

"I was..." Giselle slapped the counter with her hand. "For the majority of freshman year."

"You certainly made up for it over the next three," I said.

"And all through medical school," Charlee added.

Giselle had to laugh. She could not deny that she had a past full of promiscuity. Her first time had been with a senior on the football team. He turned her out—showed her things she never knew were possible to do to the human body. He graduated and left her in pursuit of a partner that could match his sexual prowess. According to Giselle, no one ever came close. "I do believe the question posed was about Ellis, not me," Giselle said.

"True." I recanted to Charlee what I had already told Giselle on our way to brunch. "I spent the entire week at his house and barely saw him."

Charlee pulled dishes from the cabinet. "The man is running a multi-billion-dollar company. Cut him some slack."

"Since when are you so understanding?" I asked.

"I can relate to the pressures of work interfering with your personal life. I meet so many men that are impressed that I'm the head of my own entertainment management and consulting business. I manage some of the hottest music acts in the industry, but as soon as they discover firsthand that I travel nonstop and I'm not home every day to tend to their needs, they have a problem with what I do for a living."

Charlee was a little spitfire. She had known that she wanted to work in the music industry since she was a teen. She started out on the street team at Jive Records in high school, handing out flyers for upcoming albums and artist appearances. In college, she interned at various record labels doing grunt work but making contacts along the way. She graduated from college and took a job as an assistant to a product manager, moved up to junior product manager, got promoted to product manager and then head of the urban music department. It was common knowledge amongst her peers not to be fooled by her petite stature and dimpled smile. Though many meeting her for the first time were deceived—misled by her jeans and T-shirts, cropped haircut and colorful vocabulary—behind those eyes, lurked a shrewd businesswoman that was all about deal making or, if necessary, career breaking. A few years ago, she left the label and formed her own company.

I sighed. "I know, I know. That's why I don't complain to Ellis about his work. I knew what I was getting myself into when we started dating. It's just that...I mean...there are other things."

Charlee stopped sautéing the home fries in the pan and regarded me with wide eyes. "Things like what?"

I looked from her to Giselle. "The other day, Malik said—"

"Malik?" Giselle frowned. "Anything Malik had to say should be taken with a grain of salt."

"He didn't say anything that I wasn't already thinking. I'm not sure anymore if I belong with someone like Ellis. His mother hates me. And we...we..."

Charlee sucked her teeth. "Spit it out already."

"We lack passion in our relationship."

"Is that all?" Charlee resumed cooking the potatoes.

Giselle interjected. "I can see how that may develop into a problem."

Charlee turned, waving her spatula at us. "I don't. First of all, his mother is a rich bitch with a chip on her shoulder. She probably doesn't think Melina is good enough for her precious son and that's all the more reason for Melina to stay with him. Secondly, if Melina isn't getting passion in her relationship, she can find it somewhere else. There are plenty of men out there that can rock her world."

"Charlee, please. Why is that always your answer to every problem…find another man? What she needs to do is find a way to spice things up with the man she has."

My head volleyed back and forth between them. There are times when it's best to deal with your own problems—this was one of them. "Ladies, let's not ruin our brunch with discussions of men. We can talk about this later, after we've eaten."

I set the table while Charlee arranged the food on serving platters. We took our seats at the table, joined hands and Giselle blessed the food. Quiche, bacon, sausage, home fries, sliced tomatoes and toast.

Charlee told us about the antics of her newest client while we ate. I always liked to hear what quandaries the celebrities were getting themselves into. She knew we wouldn't divulge the information she was feeding us, but every time before she told a story, she started with the same clause: "*I'm telling you this in the strictest of confidence; you cannot tell a soul.*" Today's tale was centered around a gay rapper and his transsexual lover. I was firing question after question off, trying to ascertain how Charlee knew what she said she knew.

Giselle wasn't paying us any mind. "Can you pass me some more bacon?" I handed her the platter. "Any home fries left?"

Charlee passed her the bowl of potatoes. "I don't think I've ever seen you eat this much. When's the last time you had a meal?"

"It does seem like you've put on a few pounds, but you wear it well," I said.

Giselle was five-foot-nine and slender, but had the prerequisite junk in the trunk.

Giselle absentmindedly moved food around her plate. "I missed dinner last night. My hours at the hospital are so frantic, I rarely eat a good meal. Besides, you know I love it when you cook."

Giselle piled more food on her plate. I thought there was no way she'd finish it all. I was wrong. She ate that and then some. Charlee and I didn't have room for cheesecake and coffee, but Giselle was on her second slice.

I helped Charlee clean the kitchen while Giselle lingered over her dessert. Our Connecticut Queen wasn't big on domestic duties. Giselle grew up with maids and nannies; housework wasn't her forte. The only girl out of four children, she enjoyed a privileged life. Her grandfather made his fortune in the publishing industry and her father inherited the business and all of his money. Giselle and her brother, Xavier, were the only two that had respectable careers. Xavier was a lawyer. The other two were living off of their trust funds. Giselle owned a home in Greenwich and a condo in Manhattan. We had spent many weekends in the infamous "Gold Coast," basking in Giselle's world. I'd since grown used to it, but when I went to her parents' home for the first time while we were in college, I was astounded. The acres of land, the stables, the pond, the servants...*the mansion*. I was blown away. Giselle's house paled in comparison to the home she grew up in, but it was extravagant in its own right. Five bedrooms, four baths, a formal dining room and many other amenities I was missing in my two-bedroom apartment in Brooklyn. I never knew black people lived such lavish lifestyles until I met Giselle, then I met Ellis. His estate surpassed anything I had ever set foot upon. Ellis's home had a ballroom, theater, full service spa, tennis and basketball courts, two pools and a game room.

We moved our little soiree to the living room. Charlee refreshed my mimosa. Giselle declined. Her glass was still full from the first round.

"All right, you've stalled long enough." Charlee planted herself on the sofa arm, bare feet resting on the cushion. "What are you gonna do about Ellis?"

"I didn't know I *needed* to do anything."

"You come over here whining about not having passion."

"I don't recall whining. Giselle, was I whining?"

"I'm staying out of this."

"Charlee, I love Ellis. Sometimes, I just wish things were a little different between us; that's all. I'm aware that no relationship is perfect, but I'd say our relationship is damn near perfect."

Charlee raised her eyebrows. "Now that's the best backpedaling I've ever heard."

"Malik has me talking crazy. He commented on how happy he keeps his women in the bedroom and then made a few jokes about Ellis and me. It made me start wondering."

Giselle chimed in. "Wondering what?"

"If I'm missing out on something."

Charlee and Giselle exchanged curious glances. "Ellis ain't holding it down in the bedroom?" Charlee asked.

"I didn't say that," I snapped. "Our lovemaking is beautiful."

"But are y'all fuckin'?"

"Charlee!" I shrieked.

Giselle chuckled. "Just answer the question, Melina."

"Not really," I said, reluctantly.

Charlee shook her head. "All that lovemaking is sweet, but every once in a while, your man needs to treat you like a whore behind closed doors. Now that's passion."

"I don't want to be treated that way."

"Hmph. That's what you think," Charlee said.

"Melina, refresh my memory. How many men have you been with?" Giselle asked.

"I've had my share."

Charlee tilted her head. "Exactly how many would that be?"

"You both know I've only been with four men."

"I know, but I like to hear you admit to that craziness. You're almost thirty. That's embarrassing."

I had never been the type of woman to sleep around. I needed more of a connection, preferably a commitment. I'd always been proud of the fact that I could count the number of men I had been with on one hand.

Charlee doubled over with laughter. "It amazes me that you've only had four dicks in your life."

I glared at her and shared the attitude with Giselle, daring her to laugh. "I've only had sex with four men. So the hell what?"

"We're just teasing. You can't blame us. Here you are, almost virginal, and then there's us. I can't even tell you how many men I've slept with. I admire that about you. Sex means something to you. But the point Charlee and I were trying to make is that you have limited experience. Be open to new things. Ellis is your man. You love him. If you act like a slut in the bedroom, he won't think any less of you. If you want more passion, maybe *you* need to create it."

"I didn't realize I was friends with Dr. Ruth. If you two don't mind, I'm done talking about Ellis."

"Fine. We'll talk about me and the sexy-ass man I had over here last night."

Listening to Charlee divulge every intimate detail about her exploits left me feeling envious. I needed more from Ellis. However, our sex life was only part of the problem.

CHAPTER NINE
MALIK

The waitress placed the next round of drinks on the table behind us and waited to be paid. I pointed to Terrence. He walked up the steps and handed her a twenty. Lex was attempting to pick up a spare.

Terrence started talking just as Lex was releasing the ball. "Man, hurry up. The drinks are already paid for, so you can stop pretending to be concentrating on those pins."

We howled as the ball veered toward the gutter.

Lex came off the lane and over to the seats. "I ought to pull my gun out and shoot your bowlegged ass right now for messing up my spare."

That made us laugh even harder. Lex was a New York City police officer a.k.a. Officer Evans. Most people were intimidated by his presence alone; the sight of him with a gun made it worse. Big. Black. Brash. Bald. The only way to describe him. Lex came over and snatched his beer from the table.

Terrence slapped him on the back. "Let me show you how it's done." He picked up his ball and then got into his stance. He extended his arm in one smooth line, brought it forward and let it roll off his fingertips. The bowling ball traveled fast and clean down the middle of the lane. Strike. "I may be tall and bowlegged, but I got skills."

My brother, Amir, and I gave Terrence high-fives. Lex feigned like he was going for his gun. Amir stood between Terrence and Lex, laughing. "C'mon now, fellas. Let's keep the peace. I got the next round."

"Keep the drinks coming," I said. "I'm enjoying the spoils of victory."

"I have to admit, I was certain that was one bet you would never win," Terrence said.

"That's what you get for doubting a true playa. And don't think I forgot each of you owes me a c-note."

Amir nodded his head. "I gotta c-note for ya. In fact, I can give you all the c-notes you want tonight at the club."

That cracked us all up. Amir played the saxophone in a jazz band. After bowling, we were all heading down to the village to catch his late-night set at the Blue Note. I didn't get to hear him play as often as I would've liked, but I showed support when I could. Amir was a year older than me. Music had been his life for as long as I could remember. My father had hoped it was a phase. Amir dropping out of college told him otherwise. He'd become accustomed to our father riding him about getting a *real* job.

My mother never complained and was always there to bail her firstborn out of financial trouble. Her purse remained open for her songbird. My mother understood the plight of a musician. She was the lead singer in a group called The Pageants when she met my father. She joked that if she hadn't met my father and fallen in love, she'd probably be rich, living the high life somewhere.

It was my turn to bowl. I managed to knock down two pins and then got raked over the coals for my poor showing.

"Man, you better leave Kai alone. She's throwing your game off," Terrence said.

"I'm worn out. Three nights this week, and she was trying to get me over there tonight."

"That must be some good stuff. If you can't handle it, Lex Evans will pick up your slack."

"Thanks, Officer, but I don't need any backup on this one," I said, laughing.

Out of my crew, we were all living the single life, with the exception of Terrence. He recently got engaged to a wonderful woman whom he had met about a year ago. I never thought I would see the day that Terrence Forrester would settle down—he was infamous for his women-juggling skills. I barely recognized him, devoted and faithful. Next Saturday, he was having his engagement party at his sister Jade's restaurant. He'd told me to invite Kai. My response: hell no! An engagement party is the last place to invite a single woman that you are not serious about.

"Let's bowl one more game, and then I need to get down to the club," Amir said.

Lex shook his head. "Why don't we skip the next game and get a head start on meeting some ladies? I'm tired of looking at your ugly mugs."

"It sounds like you're tired of losing and want to quit before you embarrass yourself more than you already have."

"I have the highest average out of all of you."

"Yeah, but tonight you're getting your ass kicked."

"Don't get used to it. Every man is entitled to a bad night."

"I hope you have better luck with the ladies."

"You just concentrate on blowing that horn, Little Boy Blue."

Our table was directly in front of the stage. I had to give Amir credit, he was bad on the sax. He seduced the audience with a mellow groove, had us all rocking in our seats. The room was primarily filled with couples. I found myself thinking of Kai a few times, reminiscing on the wild week we had together. I'd call her after the show to see if she would be game for some late-night company.

Lex capitalized on the single women sprinkled throughout the audience and left us to go sit with a chick and her double D's. Terrence was nursing his drink with a far-off expression that said he was ready to go home to his fiancée, instead of hanging out with a group of single knuckleheads.

Amir's female fans were tempting, sexy, hungry, and eyeing him like he was a succulent steak. They were going crazy over him—it must have been his funky style. Where we both had curly hair, he wore his in a bushy Afro and had a close-cut goatee compared to my clean-shaven face. A small hoop decorated one of his nostrils. We were night and day.

I stuck around for a few minutes after his set to peep how he worked his groupies. It made me proud to see my older brother in his element. Music and women. Why would he ever opt for a different career?

It was two in the morning when we stepped out of the club. I collected my three hundred dollars from my boys and did a little gloating. We made plans to get to the engagement party next Saturday, and then I hopped a cab uptown to Kai's apartment.

CHAPTER TEN
MELINA

I arrived at the office at seven with a full cup of coffee and a long day ahead of me. I was immersed in my work when my assistant, Nadia, tapped on my door an hour later. She entered, carrying a pile of files and a notepad perched at the top.

Nadia set the files in the tray on my desk. "You're in early."

"I have to complete the Omega Toys quarterly audit."

"I put on a pot of hazelnut coffee. Do you want a refill?"

"No, not right now."

Nadia sat in the chair on the other side of my desk with her pen poised above her notepad.

"Can you print last year's Form 10-K for Omega? I need to reference the executive compensation figures. And hold my calls."

"What if Ellis calls? You know he doesn't like it when I don't put him through."

"I'm not taking *any* calls. That includes Ellis."

"I hear you but—"

"No calls, Nadia."

"All right. I'll get you those forms."

When Nadia left the office, I shook my head. How did Ellis have my assistant more worried about his reaction than about doing what I asked her to do? I didn't want to probe Nadia about his behavior, but I would certainly inquire with Ellis about his conduct when calling my office. I could only imagine him shoving his sense of entitlement down Nadia's throat.

I managed to get through most of the morning uninterrupted. My only diversions were a few questions from Dave and Heather, two of the accountants on my staff. In total I had a staff of ten, half of them being accountants. Nadia was my assistant and we had two others that divided their time between accountants. A couple of interns were responsible for miscellaneous office duties.

My purse hummed with the vibration of my cell phone. I reached in the bag and checked the number of the incoming call. Ellis. Nadia wouldn't put him through, so he dialed my cell. Typical. I silenced the phone and laid it on my desk. A few minutes later, he called again. I dropped the phone back in my bag. I gathered up my files for Omega Toys and tossed them into my briefcase. I headed down the hallway to the reception area and retrieved my trench from the coat rack.

"Nadia, I'll be back in a few hours. If you need me, call my cell."

I was meeting with Martin Sewell at noon and had to be back in the office no later than three for my next meeting. Martin was a talker and tended to discuss his family and his travels more than our business matters. It would be a hustle, but if I could keep Martin on track, I'd be back on time with minutes to spare.

My bag vibrated as I walked out of the door. I answered the phone, explained to Ellis that I was in the midst of an extremely chaotic day, and promised to call as soon as I found a free minute. I hurried to my car and off to Midtown Manhattan to meet with Martin.

I was in the kitchen preparing dinner when I heard Malik's key turning in the lock. I added a pinch of salt to the shrimp.

"Hey, roomie." Malik stood in the doorway, pulling off his tie. "Something is smelling good up in here."

"I'm making garlic shrimp and rice."

"Damn and a brother's starving, too."

"There's more than enough for both of us. It'll be ready in a few minutes."

"Okay. I'm going to take a quick shower."

I made a tossed salad and then set the table for two. I usually prepared enough food for Malik when I cooked, but our schedules were so different, we seldom ate together. After my day of back-to-back meetings, I was in the mood to throw down in the kitchen. I needed some comfort food. I grabbed my potholder and pulled a pan of hot cornbread from the oven. I slathered the golden brown top with butter and then cut it into hefty squares.

Malik wandered back into the kitchen barefoot, wearing an old T-shirt and a pair of sweats, his short, curly hair still damp. He plated the salad and went to the refrigerator and pulled out a bottle of Merlot. "Do you want wine with your dinner?"

I nodded. Malik reached into the cabinet and retrieved glasses. I scooped steaming spoonfuls of yellow rice into two bowls and ladled on generous portions of shrimp and garlic sauce. I carried the bowls to the table while Malik poured the wine.

We both sat at the table, said silent blessings and commenced to eating.

"I'm glad you cooked. I was going to run out for Chinese food."

"How much of that can you eat? Don't any of your women cook for you?"

"We don't have those kinds of arrangements, Mel."

"Since when is a meal an arrangement?"

"It's simple. The women I see know that I'm not down for anything serious. The more we keep it casual, the better. Once a woman starts preparing meals and doing girlfriend-type things for you, then she starts expecting you to be her man."

"But you miss out on so many things. What about spending time with someone special? Don't you get lonely sometimes? Not being able to share dinner with someone? Not cuddling up to someone at night?"

"That's what I have you for."

I rolled my eyes. "Will you be serious?"

Malik laughed. "Yeah, sometimes I want those things, but most times I don't. I'm not ready for a commitment. There are too many things I want to do first."

"Like what, more women?"

"Funny. No. Like start my own business."

I stopped eating. "I didn't know you wanted to do that."

"No one does, except my dad, and now you. I've been working on my business plan and scouting out locations for my office."

"I had no idea."

"There's a lot more to me than you think, Mel."

Malik explained how he felt stifled at his current job. Told me how, over the years, he had proven himself an irreplaceable asset and yet they had failed to recognize it until now. He was finally assigned a major client and was working on the project with a coworker named Kai.

"What was that I just saw?" I asked.

Malik looked over his shoulder. "What?"

"I saw something in your eyes when you mentioned Kai."

"You better slow down on the wine."

"I know what I saw, Malik. There was something in your eyes that was hardly professional when you were talking about her."

"Damn. You don't miss a thing."

"No, I don't." I laughed. "So you obviously like this girl."

"We've spent some time together."

"Listen to you, trying to be all evasive. If you're working on an account together, I know you spent time together. Have you asked her out yet?"

"We've been out."

"Okay…and?"

"Mel, you and I live two drastically different lifestyles. You do the relationship thing and I don't."

"What does a relationship have to do with taking someone out on a date?"

"You expect me to engage in some olden-day courtship, but for me, life isn't like that. Kai and I went out, we've already fucked, and since then we've fucked some more."

My mouth fell open. I wasn't prepared for that crass declaration. "You mean to tell me within a week, you already slept with her?"

"That's exactly what I'm saying."

"Your coworker?"

"Yup."

"The woman you have to work with on an important project?"

"Yes, Mel."

"Now what?"

"Now nothing. We continue to work together and when we're in the mood, we play together."

I watched Malik's face, observed the glint in his eye and the subtle smile that graced his lips. He could play it cool if he wanted, but something was brewing. I'd let it go for now. "I'm sure you know what you're doing, but be careful. You know what they say about the dangers of dating coworkers."

"For the record, I wouldn't call what we're doing dating. And as a black man, there are a hell of a lot more dangers for me to be concerned about."

"I can't argue with that."

Malik refilled my glass while I fixed him another serving of shrimp and rice. I drank my Merlot, pondering our conversation. Malik was thirty-two years old. He wasn't interested in a committed relationship because of his business aspirations. When would he be ready? Thirty-five? Forty? Fifty? How many men shared the same perception? What about the women who wanted more?

My eyes were transfixed on a spot on the table. Malik waved his hand in front of my face. I refocused on him. "Do you ever plan on getting married?"

"If I meet the right woman. I'm not anti-marriage; right now, I'm just pro-career."

"Can't you have both?"

Malik shook his head. "Women get accustomed to spending a certain amount of time with their man. I have more time to spend with someone now because I'm working for Newport and Donner. Once I start my own agency, my time is going to be severely limited—which equates to instant trouble. The same woman that was living in bliss and completely happy with the relationship will be complaining that her man is never around. Whining that he doesn't have time for her. When all along this man is out there busting his hump trying to do something positive, to make a better life for himself. I'm not going to put myself in that predicament."

When I met Ellis, he was already well-established, his lifestyle set. Admittedly, I accepted his schedule, but the desire to have more time together was still there. Malik was fooling himself. Perhaps the woman wouldn't speak up or complain because she was aware of his lack of accessibility from the beginning, but there are bound to be repercussions when a woman is unfulfilled on any level.

"What about you? Are you planning to marry Ellis?"

"If he asks me."

"You won't be happy."

"Why would you say that?"

"That's not the life you want."

"Since when are you an expert on what I want?"

"I know what you need."

I ignored Malik's smirking face across the table and dared to ask the question. "What do I need, Malik?"

He leaned forward and poured more wine in my glass. "I think we both know the answer to that."

My face grew warm. I cleared my throat. "You ventured to make such a bold comment. Tell me what I need."

"Two things. To loosen up and an open mind." Malik got up and started clearing the table.

I turned in my chair to face him. "That's not what you were going to say."

"Yes, it was."

"I can tell you were thinking something else."

A fleeting smile touched Malik's lips. He turned around and began washing the dishes. If he was thinking something different, he wasn't going to tell me. Maybe he was trying to leave it to my imagination to figure out what he meant.

CHAPTER ELEVEN
MELINA

I rushed home from the office to get ready for dinner with Ellis and his mother. She was hosting an intimate dinner party at her Fifth Avenue penthouse apartment. Ellis was sending a car service to pick me up at seven. I had been to enough of his mother's events to know the appropriate attire. I pulled my little black Michael Kors dress from the closet and carried it to the bathroom. I wanted the steam from the shower to knock out any wrinkles in the fabric. I gave myself a pep talk while I lathered up. I would not let Ellis's mother get to me tonight. Even if she worked my nerves, I would be as sweet as candy.

I performed a final inspection in the full-length mirror on my wall. Hair styled in a tight chignon, dress flatteringly showcasing my curves without being tight, sheer black stockings, three-inch heels and my small beaded bag. Almost perfect. I fished my diamond studs from my jewelry box and placed them in my ears. Perfect.

I turned off my bedroom light and went to the living room to wait for the car service. My stomach was a bit unsettled, a side effect of spending the evening outside of my comfort zone. When Ellis's father was alive, he would compensate for his wife's uppity behavior. I could always count on him to be warm and inviting. We would discuss a range of issues from the state of the black community to White House politics to sports. He would inquire about my business and even referred a few of his colleagues as clients. It was a pleasure to be around him; I looked forward to our discussions. His wife, on the other hand, had one favorite topic—what was going on in her world.

The driver called up to let me know he was outside. I slipped into my mink, a Christmas gift from Ellis, then locked the door behind me. A town car waited at the curb. I had to tell Ellis, in the beginning of our relationship, not to send limousines to pick me up. If we were traveling together that was one thing, but when I was riding alone, I preferred not to be so pretentious. Besides, I felt silly having that much car to myself. It took some time, but he finally relented and obeyed my wishes.

I arrived at my destination faster than I would have liked. I checked my face in my compact before we stopped in front of the luxury apartment building. I placed a tip in the driver's hand as he helped me exit the town car. A doorman dressed in a black suit with a jacket resembling that of the leader of a marching band, held the door to the lobby open as I passed. I walked over to the gentleman sitting at the desk in front of the elevator bank. I gave him my name and he granted me access to the elevator strictly reserved for the penthouse.

Caroline, the Harlow family maid for more than three decades, greeted me as I stepped off the elevator into the foyer.

"Good evening, Ms. Melina," she said.

"How are you, Caroline?"

"Just fine—"

"Lina, you're right on time. Cocktails and hors d'oeuvres are just being served," Ellis said, walking over to us. He kissed me on the cheek and then helped me with my mink, handing it to Caroline. He grabbed my hand and whisked me into the study. I quickly surveyed the room. A small party of eight, including myself and Ellis. I recognized Ellis's godparents from his father's funeral and had met his mother's best friend Vivian and her husband Joseph at prior dinner parties. I was not familiar with the other gentleman in the room. Daniella, Ellis's sister, was nowhere in sight. Light music played in the background. Ellis led me over to his mother, standing next to the fireplace.

She excused herself from her conversation and gave me a brusque hug. "I was beginning to think you weren't going to make it, dear."

I air-kissed both of her cheeks. "There was a bit of traffic on the way over," I lied.

She walked in a circle around me. "Aren't you just stunning?"

My smile mimicked her tone. "Thank you, Bebe."

Bebe slipped her arm around my waist and walked me over to the bar that was set up in the far corner of the room. I looked back at Ellis, who seemed oblivious to the fact that I was being lured away.

"I'll have a mineral water," she said to the bartender. "What are you drinking, dear?"

"The same."

"Come now, have a cocktail. What's the point of attending a party if you don't have a drink or two?"

I reminded myself to play nice. "I'll have a martini."

The bartender handed me the drink. He smiled politely and then clasped his hands in front of him, waiting for his next order. I noted his uniform—black slacks with a crisp white jacket and a bowtie—and the way he unassumingly stepped back a few paces to remove himself from our conversation. I could only imagine the discussions he'd overheard.

Bebe took a birdlike swallow from her water. "Melina, I would like for us to get together one day next week for lunch."

I made a vain attempt to keep the surprise off my face. "I'll need to check my schedule. Did you have a particular day in mind?"

"I'm a lady of leisure, dear. I'll leave it to you to decide. Do let me know as soon as possible."

Bebe stalked across the room to chat with one of her cronies, leaving me alone and bewildered.

A server came around with a tray of salmon mousse on toast points. He held out a stack of napkins to me. I shook my head. I didn't want to fill up on anything before dinner. Ellis walked over and took an hors d'oeuvre from the tray. He offered me a bite.

"I don't want to ruin my appetite."

Ellis shrugged and ate his toast point. "Mother was right. You are stunning tonight."

The compliment elicited a blush from me. Too bad his mother didn't mean it. Ellis leaned toward me and kissed me on the lips. "I love you, Lina."

I touched his face. "I love you, too."

A female server approached us with a tray of more hors d'oeuvres. I took a sip from my martini, not bothering to look at what tempting delicacy she was circulating.

Ellis looked down at me. "You're not going to try one?"

I opened my mouth to say no until I glanced at the tray. The room went still and I could hear my heartbeat pounding in my ears. I looked at Ellis, then back at the tray again. My hands started shaking as I focused on the little, black velvet box in the center of the tray.

Ellis took the martini glass from me and handed it to the server. He lifted the box from the tray, then went down on one knee. I was trembling from the inside out. My eyelids fluttered, blinking back the tears that were clouding my vision. Ellis opened the box. A sparkling Asscher-cut diamond solitaire gloriously beamed at me.

Ellis took my left hand in his right one. "Melina Bradford, I love you and I want to spend the rest of my life with you by my side. Would you do me the honor of becoming Mrs. Ellison Harlow III?"

A shallow breath caught in my throat. I put my hand to my chest and repeatedly nodded my head until I found my voice. "Yes," I breathed out, "yes, I'll marry you."

Ellis slipped the ring on my finger. Clapping filled the room. Ellis stood up and pulled me into the circle of his arms, kissing me tenderly on the lips. I embraced him with all of my strength. He kissed me on the forehead, then brought my hand to his lips. I slowly became cognizant of the other people in the room, all of the smiling faces. Except for one. I couldn't turn away from that one crooked, superficial smirk.

A server handed me a champagne flute. Once everyone had a glass in hand, Bebe raised hers for a toast. Daniella dashed into the room and stood next to her mother. She was tall, slim and towered over Bebe.

Bebe fixed her face with an almost-sincere smile. "Thank you all for being here tonight to share in this special moment. I would like to wish my son all the best and a future full of happiness." Bebe moved the glass toward her lips.

Daniella grabbed the champagne glass from her mother. "We would also like to say welcome to the family, Melina."

Ellis and I tapped our champagne glasses and sealed our toast with a kiss. Daniella came across the room and gave me, and then Ellis, a big hug. She took my hand in hers and examined my ring. "This is what I call an engagement ring. How many carats is this? Five? Six?"

Ellis laughed. "It's something for you to set your standards by in the future."

"Thank you for your toast, Daniella," I said.

"I meant it. I'm so happy you're going to be a part of our family."

One by one, we were congratulated on our engagement. I waited for Bebe to come over, but she never did.

As Ellis drove us back to his home in Long Island, I could not stop gazing at my ring. Every time I looked away, the weight on my finger drew my attention back to it.

Ellis glimpsed at me. "Do you like it?"

"I absolutely love it."

"Were you surprised?"

"Completely. I was prepared for dinner at Bebe's, nothing more."

"We were all anxiously awaiting your arrival."

"Everyone knew about this?"

"Yes, the dinner party was for you."

"A proposal was the last thing I was expecting tonight."

"My parents were married for almost forty years. Since my father's death, I've been thinking about the importance of marriage and family. I want us to share a wonderful life together. And you heard the advice, the words of wisdom, from everyone during dinner. These people have spent years together. They all want the best for us."

"Not everybody," I mumbled.

"You care to elaborate?"

"That was some toast your mother gave."

"Mother wished us a future of happiness."

"Bebe wished you happiness; she excluded me."

"I'm sure it was an oversight, Lina."

"She wants to have lunch with me next week."

"Doesn't that prove that Mother is welcoming you with open arms?"

"I suppose."

Even though I didn't believe that, now wasn't the time to dispute it. I was reveling in the gleam of my diamond and not even Bebe could spoil my high.

CHAPTER TWELVE
MALIK

We decided that I would pitch our first round of ideas to Donner. Kai sat next to me at the conference table, silently observing, while I explained our concept of using both real and animated drivers in the ads.

Mr. Donner scrutinized the last slide on the screen and read the tagline aloud. *"If you're expecting to win a race with him as your driver, then you're playing the wrong game.* Hmm, a famous racecar driver referring to an animated graphic, I like it. I like it a lot. Malik, Kai, I think you're on the right track. We'll meet in two weeks to select the final ad we'll present to Sphere Electronics." Donner patted me on the shoulder, then left the room.

I leaned back in the chair with my hands behind my head.

Kai closed her portfolio. "Someone's content with himself."

Satisfaction was written all over my face. "We're gonna blow them away with our campaign."

"Malik, you have really impressed me. Donner should have teamed us up a long time ago. I could have used you on a few of my other accounts."

"I'm all for being a team player, but Donner should have given me a shot—on my own—at some of the larger accounts a long time ago."

"Well, here's your chance to make a mark at Newport and Donner."

"I don't intend to make my mark at this agency."

"Why not?"

"I've spent a lot of years, too many years, working my ass off to only just now receive a crack at a top client."

"Are you going to another agency?"

"In a way. I've got some concepts that no one has even conceived yet and when I present them, it will be at my own company."

"I'm interested in hearing more about your plans."

"We'll have to hold off until later. Right now, our focus has to be on dazzling Sphere Electronics."

"We're going to have to put in some long nights," she said with a sly grin.

"I'm not opposed to hard work."

"The harder, the better."

"Keep talking like that and you'll get yourself in trouble up in here."

Kai collected her things and got up to leave. She bent over and whispered in my ear. "In case you didn't know, trouble's my middle name." She switched her hips over to the door, looked back and winked.

I walked up behind Kai and placed my hand on top of hers on the doorknob. "I want you at my place tonight. We have business to handle."

"I'll be there, Mr. Denton."

I let Kai leave the conference room first. I went to get my binder from the table and had to laugh to myself. Kai was a vixen behind closed office doors and strictly business as soon as they opened up the slightest bit. She knew the rules of the game. In fact, she could probably teach me a few tricks. The past week had been an enlightening experience. Kai had stripteased for a brother, massaged my feet, bathed me and sexed me. I didn't mind spending time with her. She was a sports fanatic and knew how to kick back and relax with a cold beer. Kai was a lot like me—maybe a little too much.

Kai was nestled against me on the couch. I flicked my tongue around the edge of her ear, entertaining myself during the commercial break. We were watching the Yankees struggle to maintain their lead in game two of the playoffs. Thanks to Kai, I'd be at Yankee Stadium for game three. We were supposed to go together, but when she came over she explained she had to cancel due to a meeting and gave me both tickets. I had to decide which of my boys to bless with the extra ticket, but that could wait. Kai tilted her head up and licked my neck.

I moaned. "Keep that up and you won't see the end of the game."

"I didn't realize I was here for the game." Kai licked her lips.

"What did you have in mind?" I slipped my hand beneath her sweater. "Whatever it is, I can accommodate you."

Heeled steps echoed outside in the hall, halting my exploration. Melina's keys jingled in the lock. She glided through the door, sporting her fur and a pair of jeans. She looked from me, to Kai, to me again.

"Hello, Malik." She turned her attention to Kai. "Hi, I'm Melina."

"Mel, this is Kai."

Her lips curved upward in slow motion. "Kai? Oh yes, you two work together, right?"

I cut my eyes at Melina and her smile grew.

Melina extended her hand to Kai. "Pleasure to meet you, Kai."

"Same here." Kai shook hands with Melina. "That is a beautiful ring."

"Thank you," Melina said, beaming.

I directed my attention to Melina's hand. Leave it to women to compliment each other on every little thing—or not so little. I jerked my head up and met Melina's eyes. "What's up, Mel? Are congratulations in order?"

She nodded. "We got engaged last night."

"Congratulations," Kai cooed.

"Yeah, good luck," I scoffed, then redirected my interest back to the Yankees.

Kai looked at me, her brows wrinkled.

Melina's smile wilted. "Don't mind him. He's anti-marriage, and correct me if I'm wrong, Malik, anti-dating."

"If that were true, I wouldn't be asking Kai to be my *date* on Saturday for Terrence's *engagement* party."

Kai glanced at me and then Melina.

"Then I suppose it's Kai who will be needing the luck," Melina said before walking off and slamming her bedroom door.

I cleared my throat. "I'm sorry about that, Kai. Sometimes Mel can be a little high-strung."

"I think I'd better be going." Kai slipped her shoes back on. "Apparently you have some issues to discuss with your roommate."

I walked Kai to the door. "I hope you won't let what Mel said discourage you from accepting my invitation."

"I'll go with you on Saturday, though I'm not sure about your approach or intent."

"What do you mean?"

"How or why you invited me. Good night, Malik. I'll see you tomorrow."

No sooner had I closed the door behind Kai, did Melina come flying out of her room.

"Don't start, Mel."

"How dare you disrespect me in front of your company!"

"You're overreacting. I didn't say anything that can be construed as disrespectful."

"You make a snide comment to me, in front of a complete stranger, another one of your many hoes, and you don't see why I'm upset."

"You're always upset. Everything upsets you. You walk around here acting like the Queen of England; like I'm supposed to bow and curtsy for your ass. You talk to me any ol' kind of way, but I'm supposed to watch what I say to you? Then you tell Kai I'm anti-this and anti-that, trying to throw a wrench in my program, and you have the nerve to stand there talking about respect."

"You're damn right. You don't care for Ellis and you don't have to. But I expect you to respect me, him, and my relationship with him."

"Take your own high-and-mighty advice. Respect my shit and stop calling my company hoes. You don't know a thing about any of these women."

"And neither do you." Melina glared at me for a moment, then retreated to her room.

I plopped down on the couch and closed my eyes. Melina could slam all the doors she wanted, but nothing could shut out the truth.

CHAPTER THIRTEEN
MELINA

My girls were expected to arrive at any minute. I invited them to lunch to share the news of my engagement. I was already seated with my hands concealed on my lap when the hostess escorted Charlee and Giselle to the table. They were chattering back and forth, barely stopping to acknowledge me while settling into their chairs.

I interrupted their banter. "Hi, ladies."

Charlee grinned. "Sorry, Melina. How you doin', sis?"

"Well," I said with a sigh, "I don't know."

That got their attention. Charlee and Giselle were watching me with tentative eyes.

"I'm..."

"What's wrong?" Giselle asked.

"I'm... I'm...engaged!" I thrust my hand forward, showing off the proof to my claim.

Giselle screamed. Charlee grabbed my hand and inspected my jewel. My litany spilled out of me. I provided them with a play by play of the evening and then ended the story with a wiggle of my ring finger and grandiose smile.

"Obviously, I don't need to ask if you're happy," Giselle said.

Charlee frowned. "I do. Are you?"

"I want to marry Ellis. So, yes, I'm happy."

"What about his mother?"

"Unfortunately, she's part of the package."

"And you're sure you're ready for this?"

"Charlee, I'm ready, I'm happy and I'm in love. What more could I ask for?"

Charlee raised her hand to signal the waiter. "A bottle of champagne to celebrate."

We shared a collective giggle. Leave it to Charlee to have us returning to work tipsy. I couldn't wait to tell them the news, but I wanted to do it in person. It took every ounce of restraint for me to hold it in for almost two days. I had called my mother in Maryland immediately after the dinner party. She put me on the speakerphone, so my father could listen at the same time. They were overjoyed. After extracting the details of the proposal from me, my mother told me to put Ellis on the phone. My parents congratulated him on our engagement and said they'd be thrilled to have him as a son-in-law.

Giselle reached across the table and grasped my hand. "Congratulations, my sister."

The waiter brought over our champagne and three chilled glasses. He poured our nectar and then left us to our celebration.

Charlee delivered the toast. "Wishing you *all* the happiness you deserve."

I clinked glasses with Charlee and we peered into each other's eyes for a beat. I averted my gaze to Giselle. She tapped our glasses and then sat her champagne down on the table.

I stopped short of taking a sip from my glass. "Why aren't you drinking? You're not on call today, are you?"

"Whatever she ain't drinking, I got covered," Charlee said.

Giselle fidgeted with her utensils. "I also have something to share with the two of you." She inhaled and released a shaky stream of air.

"Don't keep us in suspense, damn it."

I put my hand on top of Charlee's to silence her.

"I'm fourteen weeks pregnant."

Charlee and I sat, gaping at Giselle. I could feel my eyes bulging out of their sockets and forced myself to blink a couple of times. "Gigi, when did this happen?"

Charlee rolled her eyes at me. "If she's fourteen weeks pregnant, you do the math."

"I mean how or with who?"

"I've been wanting to tell you for a few weeks. I found out about a month ago."

"You've known for a month and didn't say anything?" I asked.

"Actually, I've known for longer than that, but I was confused about what to do and wanted to make a decision before I told you. I have my career; I'm not married. I didn't even know if I wanted to be a mother."

"What about the father?"

"A colleague of mine." Giselle looked down in her lap. "He's pretty much out of the picture, so it was solely my decision to make."

I moved my chair closer to Giselle and gently rubbed her back. "Are you all right?'

"I will be. I have no choice but to be all right, and I'm going to have this baby. Things will change for me. My life is going to change drastically, it already has, but I'm having this baby."

And I thought I had news to share with my friends. Giselle, pregnant. I had so many questions, but I refused to inundate her at the moment.

Giselle straightened her back a bit and then picked up her menu. "Let's eat. I know I'm famished." She glanced at Charlee and myself and then back at the menu. "Girls, I'm pregnant. It's not the end of the world," she said, not raising her eyes from menu.

"Anything you need, we're here for you." I figured I had better speak for both of us since Charlee was still observing Giselle like she was a specimen in a Petri dish.

"The only thing I ask is that you be the great aunties I know you will be."

I hugged Giselle tight. When we separated, she wiped a tear from her face. Charlee hugged her next. "It takes a village and you've got one right here. Don't worry about a thing."

There was no way I was going back to the office after lunch. I was a bit buzzed from the champagne and extremely numb over Giselle's news. I tightened the belt on my cream wool coat and walked down Madison Avenue. Rich, golden sunlight streamed across my face. My hair whipped in the breeze, the tips getting stuck on my glossy lips. I kept tucking it behind my ears to no avail. Giselle weighed heavily on my mind. Three months pregnant and planning to raise a child on her own. Financially, she wouldn't have a problem, but the day-to-day responsibility of being a single mother, balancing baby and career, would be difficult. I wanted to know why the father was not involved. I didn't know that Giselle was seeing anyone. She inquired whether I was happy—I should have asked her the same. If the situation held any joy for her I surely didn't see it. The giddiness of my announcement was overshadowed by the reality of Giselle's.

After about ten blocks, I threw my hand up for a cab. I slid into the backseat and instructed the driver to take me to Brooklyn. Thankfully, it was a brother driving the cab. He didn't give me an attitude about the trip or complain that he may have not been able to get a return fare. I planned to give him a big tip for that reason alone.

I gazed at my ring, the way it sparkled. It truly was beautiful. I smiled to myself. I was going to be Mrs. Ellison Harlow III. I was going to be a wife. I was going to take vows that committed me to another person for the rest of my life, regardless of what we went through, good or bad. My stomach churned. I took a deep breath. It was a little early for pre-wedding jitters—I just got engaged, for goodness sake. We hadn't even set a date yet. My breathing sped up with the thought of the road ahead. I had to start planning. I needed to pick the perfect day, find a church, a dress, a place to have the reception, a cake, gifts for my guests and the dreaded guest list and seating chart. It hit me, right there in the back of a cab; I was getting married and had tons of work to do. I needed to call my mother later to start brainstorming with her about my special day.

I put my key in the lock. The door opened, taking my keys along with it, before I had the chance to turn my wrist. Malik stepped to the side, allowing me to pass by him. I took my time hanging up my coat, stealing a glance over my shoulder to see if Malik was standing in the living room. I closed the door and leaned my back against it.

Malik rubbed his hands together, then cleared his throat. "I want to apologize for last night, Mel. I made an unnecessary comment and I was wrong."

"I think you made more than one comment that was inappropriate," I said, joining him in the living room.

"We both said some things that we shouldn't have."

"You're right," I reluctantly admitted.

"I don't know about you, but it bothered me all night. I didn't really sleep."

"I'm sorry for what I said about your choice in women."

"And for trying to mess up my night with Kai?"

"That too."

"Well, if you can admit to throwing wrenches, then I can say congratulations on your engagement."

We stood two feet from each other, wearing contrite smiles. Malik opened his arms for a hug. I shook my head, then stepped up to him and encircled his waist with my arms.

He kissed my forehead. "Friends?"

I nodded and then pulled away. "What are you doing home?"

"I took a half-day. I'm going to the Yankees game tonight."

I started toward my room. "Oh, well have a good time."

"I have an extra ticket. You want to go with me?"

I scrunched up my nose. "I'm not really a baseball fan."

"Come on, it'll be fun. It's the playoffs. You can't turn down the playoffs." He came over to me and placed his arm around my shoulder. "To make amends for last night, hot dogs and beer are on me."

Malik flaunted one of his best smiles, one that had probably convinced many women to do many things.

I relented. "Sure, why not."

"All right, cool. I need you to do me one favor."

"Oh yeah, what's that?"

"Observe my attire." Malik got into male-model stance. He pretended like he was posing for an ad in a magazine. "Now please go into your room and try to dress accordingly for a baseball game. Don't come out here in one of your high-class get-ups."

I laughed. "I'll see what I can do."

CHAPTER FOURTEEN
MALIK

The crowd roared. The Yankees scored a homerun, giving us a three-run lead in the bottom of the fifth inning. Melina sat to my left, clapping her hands with the rest of the fans. She was wearing a Yankees baseball cap, which I purchased for her, pulled down low on her head. I told her she wasn't a true fan unless she donned a hat like the rest of us. I glimpsed at her studying the game. It was unusual to see Melina sporting a hooded sweatshirt with tight jeans and sneakers. In the midst of all the hoopla she fit right in with everyone else. Earlier in the game she asked a few questions that demonstrated her lack of familiarity with baseball. Among other things, I explained who was who on the team and why the pitcher would purposely try to walk a player.

I shouted over the incessant cheering. "Do you want another beer?"

"Okay, but three is my limit."

"I'll keep that in mind, but this makes four."

"I guess I lost track." She started giggling. "Well, four is my new limit."

I called the hawker over and bought two more beers. I handed Melina a cup along with a lighthearted warning. "Last one."

"Thanks for inviting me, Malik."

"No problem. As long as you're having a good time."

She nodded.

Melina directed her attention back to the game. I checked the centerfield scoreboard and then found myself gazing at Melina again. She looked exceptionally cute with her hat covering most of her eyes. I followed the movement of her lips as she brought her cup up to her mouth. She had a sexy innocence. I shook my head to rattle those thoughts from my mind. The beer was beginning to affect me.

Melina tilted her head, unleashing her light-brown eyes on me. "What are you thinking about over there?"

I choked on my beer. "Work. I just thought of an idea for the Sphere account."

She smiled. "Umm hmm. Were you contemplating work or Kai?"

"Kai is the furthest thing from my mind. Trust me." I turned away from her doubtful eyes.

It probably wasn't a good idea for Melina to meet Kai. She already had notions about my feelings for Kai. Some of them may have been correct, but most of them weren't. What I did like about Kai was that there was no pressure from her. Our primary goal was to work together and produce a stellar campaign. The time we spent on extracurricular activities was the icing on the cake. Would I consider Kai as someone I could eventually settle down with? Yeah, I would. She was fine as hell, catered to me sexually and stimulated my mind. Did I plan on making that happen? Highly unlikely. Our current set-up was better than cool. Fun and sex. Fun sex. No strings attached.

My last real relationship ended over four years ago. I met Angelique at the annual auto show at the Jacob Javits Center. She was sitting behind the wheel of a Jaguar XKR convertible, checking out its features. I slid into the passenger seat and joined her personal tour. We sat in the car for over an hour, talking and laughing, while others got annoyed that they couldn't get a closer peek at the latest model. Eventually, we exited the vehicle and ditched our friends, spending the rest of the afternoon cruising the Javits Center together. That evening I took her to dinner. I had never clicked with any woman the way I did with Angelique. She was my girl from the moment we met. We moved in together after dating for only two months. My mother was counting on me to make Angelique her daughter-in-law. I wanted to make that happen. Angelique's parents frequently commented on our living situation and alluded to our making things official. I was in complete agreement. Angelique wasn't. A year or so into our relationship, Angelique left the law firm she had been with for years and went into business with a friend from law school. Her time at home diminished and her time spent in the office, with him, increased. Accusations flew from my mouth to her ears. Turbulent months passed with Angelique trying to reassure me that she was faithful. I began to resent her and she began to resent me. I resented how the dynamics of our relationship shifted. Hated how her career took precedence over me. She resented me for not being supportive, hated me for not trusting her. We tried to make it work, but I wanted more than she was willing to offer. Angelique wasn't prepared to settle down. Wife and mother were not at the top of her list. According to her, we had all the time in the world to get married and start a family. I felt that we needed to seize the day, the minute, the moment. We split two-and-a-half years after our love affair began. I moved out, angry and rejected. The woman I loved enough to make my wife was content with being my girl. I took it personal, thought she didn't want me as a husband. We parted bitterly. In retrospect, I realized that Angelique needed to complete herself before she could complete me. Angelique taught me a vital lesson. Relationships don't belong at the top of your list.

Melina fished her cell phone out of her knapsack. She put the phone to her ear, spoke a few words into it, and then shoved it back into her bag.

"The Stuffed Shirt Patrol got an APB out on you?" I asked.

She sighed like a balloon losing air. "Reminding me to make a call."

"That's new. You're becoming his wife and secretary. Interesting concept."

"Ellis didn't want me to forget to contact his mother about a lunch date."

There was a dimming in her eyes that prevented me from taunting her like I usually did. "Is it that bad, Mel?"

"His mother can't stand me."

"C'mon, now. You're exaggerating."

"Believe me, I'm not. No matter how nice I am to her she always snubs me. Makes me feel like I don't belong with her son."

Seeing her so vulnerable made me feel protective. "What does Ellis have to say about this?"

"I don't think he notices and I haven't mentioned it."

"Don't be naïve. He knows."

Melina twisted the ring on her finger back and forth. She looked over at me and gave me something that resembled a smile but didn't quite make it. "I'll just have to handle Ellis's mother on my own."

I tugged on the bill of her hat. I should have offered words of reassurance that everything would work out for her. I didn't—not because I didn't have any—but because I didn't want to.

CHAPTER FIFTEEN
MELINA

Ellis kept me on the phone the entire ride from Yankee Stadium. He must have asked me ten times why I was at a baseball game and why with Malik. I couldn't answer half of his questions because Malik was next to me, driving us home. I tried to get off the phone, but he kept talking. Kept right on talking as if he did not hear me ask to call him later. Though I was hesitant to believe it, I had to. Ellis was jealous. Jealous that I was out with Malik.

Ellis was still in the city at his office. After he heard that I had spent the evening with Malik, he said he'd meet me at my apartment. Surprisingly, Malik spared me the smart comments when I got off the phone. We had a pleasant conversation about nothing and everything. One of those chats that in a few days you won't remember the details, but when you reflect back, it makes you smile.

Malik went straight to his room and closed the door. I was in the kitchen getting a bottle of water when the buzzer sounded. I went to unlock the door and left it slightly open for Ellis, then returned to the kitchen.

I heard the door close, and called out, "I'm in here."

He strode into the kitchen. We met in the middle of the room and shared a brief kiss. Ellis slowly pulled the baseball cap from my head and tossed it on the table. He caught my eyes and held them hostage under his glare. "Did you enjoy the game?"

"It was my first baseball game. I've never been to one before. I had a really nice time."

"How about Malik?"

"It was a playoff game. What man wouldn't enjoy that?"

"A man that knows there are more important things in life than baseball. Someone who works hard, and if necessary late, to be successful."

"Malik works hard, Ellis. And since when is it illegal to go to a game? Most people take time for recreation or haven't you noticed? Probably not because *you're* always working."

"So now you're defending him?" he said a bit louder than necessary.

I backed up a step and crossed my arms. "Lower your voice. I didn't realize I needed to defend Malik."

"I don't like his influence over you," he said in hoarse whisper. He looked me up and down. "Look at how you're dressed."

"They're called jeans and a sweatshirt. How would you have preferred I dress for a baseball game?"

"I would have preferred if you didn't go. I would also prefer that you don't live with another man."

This was a first. Ellis had never complained about my living situation. I wasn't particularly interested in having that conversation in the kitchen. I led him to my bedroom and closed my door behind us. "Listen, Malik and I have been roommates for over a year now. Why is it a problem all of a sudden?"

"You're about to be my wife." Ellis sat down on the bed. "It isn't appropriate for you to be living with another man."

"We're roommates—that's all—appropriateness isn't an issue."

"I want you to move in with me."

"Why now?"

"Why not now? There's no point in waiting until after the wedding."

I sensed the cement drying on Ellis's plan. I had no intention of living with him before we were married. The problem with Ellis was that the more you resisted him the more persistent he would become. I went to him and sat on his lap. "Sweetie, how was your day?" I began rubbing his shoulders. "You seem tense. Let me give you a massage and we can talk about this later."

Some of the tension drained from his face. I kissed his forehead. He exhaled heavily. I kissed the tip of his nose and he closed his eyes. I unbuttoned his shirt, then slid it down his arms. Ellis pulled his hands out of the sleeves, dropped the shirt on the bed and then took off his undershirt. I knelt down and slipped off his shoes. "Lay back," I said.

He did what I asked. I straddled him and then began massaging his temples. I leaned over and nuzzled my cheek against his, whispering in his ear, "Turn over, baby."

I sat on Ellis's firm ass and used the palms of my hands to knead his lower back. I worked my way upward, applying pressure in the right places.

"Saturday night we're going to Le Cirque for dinner," he said with his face partially buried in the pillow.

I kissed his shoulder. "I'll wear something sexy." I trailed butterfly kisses down his back. I pulled my sweatshirt over my head, unhooked my bra and pressed my naked breasts against his back. I inched upwards and kissed Ellis on the neck. I sucked his earlobe into my mouth. Ellis moaned. There was a knock at my door. I groaned.

Ellis rolled over and put his hands behind his head. I had to rise up slightly to avoid rolling with him. We were shirtless and silent.

Malik knocked again. Instinctively, I wrapped my arms around my breasts.

"Answer it," Ellis said through clenched teeth. "See what he wants."

I put my sweatshirt back on and then climbed from the bed. I opened the door a crack and slipped into the hallway, pulling the door shut behind me. "What is it, Malik?" I said, struggling to speak low enough for Ellis not to hear us.

"Have you seen the key for the storage room?"

"What? You're disturbing me over a key?"

"Disturbing you—"

"Yes," I hissed. "Ellis is in there."

"My bad, Mel. I thought he left."

"Yeah, okay, Malik."

"Seriously. I didn't know. But since you're out here, can you tell me where to find the key?"

I rolled my eyes. "It's on the damn hook where it always is."

I went back inside my bedroom. Ellis was getting dressed. "Don't go, Ellis."

He stopped buttoning his shirt. "Lina, you're moving out of here."

I slinked over to him and tried to undo his buttons. "Fine. We can discuss it later."

He caught my hands, then leaned over and kissed me on the cheek. "There's nothing to discuss. You're moving. That's it." Ellis opened my bedroom door and I followed him down the hallway.

Malik was standing in the kitchen, holding the key up for me to see. "You were right, I found it." He nodded at Ellis. "Hey, man, what's up?"

Ellis barely acknowledged him with an aggravated grunt. Malik opened his mouth to say something, but I shook my head, warning him to keep quiet. I trailed Ellis out of the apartment and down to the front door of the building.

I grabbed his arm and stopped him before he stepped outside. "Ellis, wait a minute."

He paused with his hand on the doorknob. I wrapped my arms around his waist from the back and rested my face against him. He put his arms over mine.

"I'll think about it, okay?"

He turned around and faced me. "My future wife does not belong in a two-bedroom brownstone, in Brooklyn, with a thug."

"There is nothing wrong with Brook—"

"I'm not going to debate this."

He opened the door and went down the stairs.

I stood in the doorway. "Can I at least have a good-night kiss?"

Ellis lingered at the bottom of the stairs for a moment, then smiled. He came back up the stairs and kissed me long and deep. He pulled away and gently chucked me under the chin. "I love you."

"Love you too."

"I'll pick you up at six on Saturday."

"I'll be ready."

Ellis kissed my hand and I held on to his.

"Call me when you get home." I reluctantly released his hand and watched him walk to his car.

He called out from the sidewalk. "Go back inside before you get mugged."

I waved him off. Mugged. Ellis ascribed to every negative stereotype about life in Brooklyn. He tooted his horn as he drove by. I locked the door behind me and went upstairs.

Malik was in the living room, sitting on the couch with his feet propped up on the coffee table. "You wanna watch this movie with me?" He held up a DVD case for some horror flick.

I wanted to be mad at Malik, but I wasn't. It was his nature to be an annoyance on occasion. There was no point in letting it get to me. "Only if you're going to make some popcorn with lots of butter and I don't mean the microwave kind."

"Damn. First I have to get you snacks and beer at the game and now I have to actually pop you fresh popcorn? You're a high-maintenance date."

I raised my eyebrows. "Date?"

"You know what I mean." Malik brushed past me and went into the kitchen to make my popcorn.

CHAPTER SIXTEEN
MALIK

I poked my head in Kai's office. She was at her desk, talking on the phone. She mouthed for me to come in. I went over to her bookshelf to inspect her menagerie of advertising and marketing guides while I waited. Her walls were covered with framed posters of some of her accounts.

"Mr. Denton, to what do I owe this early morning visit?"

I turned around. "Good morning, Ms. Cooper. I stopped by for a sugar fix to start my day."

Kai pursed her lips. "The vending machine is down the hall in the break room."

I laughed. "I went there first, but I couldn't find what I needed."

She seductively eyed me for a moment. "I have what you need right here." Kai reached into her desk drawer, then tossed a Hershey's Kiss at me.

I scrambled to catch the little piece of chocolate candy.

"That ought to take care of your craving," she said, giggling.

"For now." I winked at her. "I really came in here to tell you that I'll swing by your place at five tomorrow evening."

"I'm glad you brought that up. If it's okay, I'd rather meet you at your place. I have an earlier engagement and won't be returning home. It would be easier if I just met you, instead of you picking me up."

"Works for me."

"I'll be at your apartment no later than five-thirty."

"See you then." I walked to the door, unwrapped the candy and popped it into my mouth. "Thanks for my sugar."

Kai's laughter bubbled out as I shut the door. A couple of the fair-haired boys walked by as I exited Kai's office. I straightened my tie, then smirked at each of them. I'd let them speculate until they got up the nerve to confront me with whatever they were about to start gossiping over. But I wouldn't tell them a damn thing. The same competitive guys that barely wanted to speak over who was getting what account, would break their necks to talk to you in order to get in your business.

I headed to my office, pleased with the recent dynamics of office life.

CHAPTER SEVENTEEN
MELINA

Charlee and I weaved our way through Bergdorf Goodman in search of an outfit for my dinner at Le Cirque. I didn't have to bend her arm too much to get her to meet me after work for a little shopping. Charlee was trying to push a long georgette dress on me, but I was leaning toward a short silk, strapless tiered dress. I was carrying it around like a child carries a teddy bear, forming an attachment. I hadn't seen anything that compared to its vibrant coral color.

"How much is that dress, Melina?"

"You don't want to know."

Charlee lifted the dress from my hands and peeked at the price tag. "Fifteen hundred dollars?" she said, her eyes wide enough to fall out of their sockets. "You're going to pay fifteen hundred dollars for this dress?"

"Yeah, why not? I work every day. If I want to buy something nice for myself, then why shouldn't I?"

"Girl, you will probably wear this dress one time and then forget you even own it."

"You may be right, but as long as I'm fabulous in it tomorrow night, that's all that matters."

"Spoken like a woman engaged to a millionaire."

"You know better than that. Ellis's money is Ellis's money. I spend my own money on me."

Charlee gave me a dubious look. "You told me yourself that Ellis deposits money in your account every month."

"Yes and I also told you that I have never touched that account."

Charlee looped her arm through mine and spoke in a hushed tone. "So how much money is in there?"

"I don't know. I don't keep track of it."

She yanked down on my arm. "Stop lying. You know how much is in there."

"I don't," I said with amusement in my voice.

"If I guess, will you tell me?"

"Perhaps."

"Okay, is it more than ten thousand dollars?"

I nodded and kept perusing the racks.

"Is it more than fifty thousand dollars?"

Again, I nodded.

"Seventy-five thousand?"

"Yes."

"Is it more than—"

"There's five hundred thousand dollars in the account, Charlee."

Charlee stopped walking, which tugged me backward since her arm was linked with mine.

"Close your mouth and let's go to the fitting room, so I can try this on," I said, dragging her along with me as I crossed to the other side of the store.

Charlee sat on the chair in the dressing room while I changed. "If you have that much money sitting in an account, why haven't you used any of it to grow your business? You have been talking about expanding your firm for years. More than anything, why did you let Malik move in if you didn't have to?"

"Because I need to maintain my own identity. My own sense of self. The money Ellis puts in my account is a drop in the bucket for him. He doesn't miss it. But it's a way for him to have influence over me and my life. I like working hard to make my business a success and I'll take the bumps and the bruises that go along with it. I never set out to have a cushion or a safety net for the choices I make. I don't want Ellis's money to influence my decisions. I decided that I needed a roommate so that I could free up more money to invest back into Trinity. I don't want to live my life knowing that my achievements are a result of Ellis's money, and not my own blood, sweat and tears."

"You are one crazy chick. I would be all up in his pockets."

It was comforting to know that I'd be well taken care of as Mrs. Ellison Harlow III, but my life as Melina Bradford was my own. I was responsible for my own well-being. I didn't expect everyone to understand or even agree with me, however, I could hold my head high knowing I hadn't relied on the success of someone else to get by.

I wasn't sure what I'd do with the money in my account, but two things were for certain. It wouldn't be used until I married Ellis and it'd be used for a good cause. Maybe I'd use it as a college fund for our children; I didn't know. All I could say was it wouldn't be used frivolously.

"Zip me up."

Charlee slid the zipper closed. I did a slow spin in the mirror, and then I turned toward Charlee. "Now tell me this dress isn't worth every penny."

"Well, now that I know just how many pennies you have…"

I turned back to the mirror. "Unzip me." I was taking my teddy bear home. I put my clothes back on and we went to find a pair of shoes to match the dress.

I held up a pair of Christian Louboutin heels. Charlee shook her head. I put them down and kept hunting.

"Have you spoken to Giselle?" she asked.

"Not since lunch the other day. You?"

"Last night. She was okay. A little tired."

"I still can't believe she's pregnant."

"Me neither. She spent the entire conversation trying to convince me how excited she was about the baby. I thought she sounded as if she'd been crying."

"I'm sure it's a lot to deal with," I said.

"What about you?"

"What about me?"

"How excited are you about your upcoming nuptials?"

"They're hardly upcoming. We haven't even set a date yet."

"Not quite what I asked you."

"Charlee, you are so exasperating. I'm excited already, damn."

She dropped the shoe she was holding. "I don't know which of you chicks is worse. The one crying her eyes out or the one biting heads off. If this is excitement, then you had better get me a dictionary, because obviously it means something other than I thought."

I sighed. "I'm sorry. I didn't mean to get snippy with you. I *am* excited about the engagement, but I'm nervous at the same time. I've been engaged less than a week. Give it time to settle in and I'm sure you'll see me bouncing off the walls from being deliriously happy."

"Umm hmm," she mumbled.

"Let me pay for this dress, and then we'll go have a couple of martinis. My treat."

"I know you're treating, Ms. Moneybags," she said, sauntering over to the register.

It's a good thing I didn't tell her about the stocks. She would have really lost her mind.

CHAPTER EIGHTEEN
MELINA

I looked at my watch for the third time in five minutes. I was perched on the couch, legs crossed, temperature rising.

"What time is it?" That was Malik. He was sitting across from me, sharply dressed, in a black suit and gray shirt, with an abstract black and gray tie.

"It's six-thirty."

He reached for the phone.

"You're not going to call her again?"

"Hell yeah. She was supposed to be here by five-thirty."

The phone rang in his hand. He answered before the first ring stopped. Malik frowned and then passed the phone over to me.

"Hello... Yes... Of course I'm dressed already... Why, what happened... No... I understand... Okay... Bye." I hung up the phone and looked at Malik's inquisitive face. "Well, I'm going to get out of this dress and get comfortable."

"What happened?"

"The usual. Work."

I got up and started to go to my room.

Malik stopped me. "Don't change. Come with me to Terrence's engagement party."

"I don't know."

"C'mon," he sang more than said. "You look too fine not to be shown off."

That earned him a smile. "I do, don't I?"

Malik went to the closet and got my fur. He held it open for me.

"What about Kai?"

"Do you see Kai?"

I walked over to him and slid my arms into the sleeves. He offered me his arm, and then we left the apartment—on our way to a party.

Malik escorted me through the main dining room to the lounge area in the rear of the restaurant. The room was filled with people milling around, talking and laughing, while jazz played in the background. Food and drinks were in abundance. It was a dapper group, men in suits and ties, ladies draped in stylish dresses and pants suits.

Malik spotted Terrence and his fiancée a few feet from the bar. He grabbed my hand and led me through the crowd. They greeted each other with a masculine bear hug. Terrence had spent enough time at our apartment that no introductions were necessary. We kissed each other on the cheek and I congratulated him on his engagement. He introduced me to his bride-to-be, Dru. She was stunning—tall with flawless skin. She reminded me of Iman. I shook Dru's hand and offered my well-wishes, then we commenced to complimenting one another on our rings. Malik and Terrence wandered off while Dru and I struck up a lively bridal conversation.

I liked Dru—she was someone I could see myself hanging out with. We agreed to get together for lunch someday soon. It would be nice to have another bride-to-be to consult with on wedding plans.

I strolled around the room, sipping champagne and catching snippets of conversations here and there. I spied Malik sitting on the sofa with his cronies, Amir, Lex and Terrence. They were a handsome bunch. Lex was saying something that had them enthralled. I stood watching their interaction. They appeared so at home with one another. So brotherly. Not just Malik and Amir. All of them. Lex patted Terrence on the back, then they saluted him with raised glasses. A private toast among partners. Malik took a swig of his drink and then caught me staring at him. He paused for a moment, then a smile crept across his lips. He said something to the fellas and before I knew it, I had eight eyes peering at me. I turned abruptly and bumped into a woman carrying a platter of hors d'oeuvres, sending the platter toppling to the floor.

Apologizing profusely, I bent down to help her pick up the spilt food. She reassured me that it was no problem as we tossed chicken satay skewers back onto the tray. Malik appeared next to me and joined in the cleanup.

"Hey, girl. I asked Terrence where you were."

I thought Malik was going crazy. He just saw me gawking at him a few seconds ago. Then I realized he was talking to the woman with the tray.

"You should have known I was in the kitchen," she said, standing up with the tray of wasted hors d'oeuvres.

Malik assisted me up from my crouching position. "Mel, this is Jade, Terrence's sister. Jade, meet Mel—my roommate."

"I think we met when we collided, but it's nice to finally put a face with the name," Jade said.

"I'm so sorry about that. I didn't see you behind me."

"Not to worry. There's plenty more in the kitchen."

Jade handed the platter to a waiter and told him to dispose of the skewers. He traipsed off in a hurry. Now that her hands were free, she hugged Malik. They exchanged mischievous glances, then burst into a fit of laughter. I laughed along with them, though I didn't know what was funny.

Jade put her arm around Malik's waist. "Malik, you and Terrence have been keeping secrets. You never told me that Mel was so pretty."

He cleared his throat. "Yup. She's gorgeous."

They both stood there admiring me like I was a piece of art in the museum.

"In fact," she said, looking at me with amused eyes, "I thought Mel was short for Melvin."

"Actually, my name is Melina," I said with a smile of my own.

"Well, Melina, I am pleasantly surprised to meet you. Forgive me if I seem a bit tickled, but whenever I see Malik, he never fails to amaze me."

"I live with him, so I know what you mean."

She eyed Malik. "That must be fun."

Malik jumped into the discussion. "So, Jade, what's up with you? Are you still happily wrapped up with your man, what's-his-name?"

"Cain, his name is Cain. And, yes, we are marvelously happy."

A waiter came over and whispered in Jade's ear.

"Excuse me, but duty calls. Funny how I can't even enjoy my brother's party because I have to work. I'll catch up with you two later."

Malik started talking a mile a minute. "Jade is a trip. She's like a sister to me. Her man, Cain, owns a restaurant, too."

"Ironically, I know who he is. Cain Cadman. Owns Eden. Ellis and I eat there on occasion. What I don't know is what you and Jade found so amusing."

"It had nothing to do with you."

"I think it did."

"Jade thinks it's funny that my roommate is a woman. She was under the impression that I lived with a guy named Mel. I never told her you were female and I can only guess that she thinks there's something between us."

"In other words, Jade's familiar with your reputation."

"What reputation?" he said with a crooked smirk. Malik took me by the hand. "C'mon over and say hello to my brother and Lex."

I scooted between Amir and Lex on the sofa, feeling like a sheep in a wolf sandwich. Malik unbuttoned his jacket, then sat on the low cube-like table in front of us. The guys were talking about football season and which teams they would like to see make it to the Super Bowl. I half-listened to their musings, unintentionally tuning them out. Malik was making a case for the Jets. My eyes were drawn to his Adam's apple—the way it moved up and down as he spoke. My gaze traveled to his lips. They were full and looked soft. He laughed and brightened the room with his perfect teeth. His nose was straight but not too slim, prominent but not overwhelming. I slowly looked up and found myself gazing directly into his eyes. Heat crept up my neck. Malik studied my face and then voyaged downward, lingering at my cleavage. I shifted in my seat, but it failed to distract him. My legs held his attention captive.

Amir and Lex excused themselves, claiming to need a refill on drinks. They got up, leaving their half-filled glasses behind. Malik sat in Amir's vacated spot on the sofa. His proximity made me fidgety and I wasn't sure why.

"Isn't this better than staying home alone on a Saturday night?"

I nodded. "It's a nice affair."

"It could be."

"Malik—"

"Come dance with me."

A few couples were dancing to a Sade tune on the other side of the room. I hesitated.

"Don't bother saying no. I'll just drag you kickin' and screamin'."

He stood up and held out his hand. I relented with a sigh. We located an open space amongst the other dancers and Malik stepped closer to me. He slipped his right arm around my waist, drawing me near to his body. I rested my left hand on his shoulder and placed my right in his. We moved to the rhythmic bass and Sade's mellow voice. Malik was a good dancer. His cheek vibrated lightly against mine as he hummed along with the song. Malik tightened his hold on my waist, eliminating the ever-so-slight gap between our bodies. Though I should have, I didn't protest. We danced to a few songs until the music was interrupted for a champagne toast.

Friends and family toasted the happy couple. The future in-laws said things to Terrence and Dru that I knew I would never hear from Bebe. It made me feel sad that I would probably never have a good relationship with Ellis's mother.

Malik and I spent the rest of the evening eating, drinking and conversing with his friends. It was the most fun I had had in a long time. Dru and I exchanged numbers and vowed to contact each other. Jade's boyfriend Cain showed up later and was surprised to see me. I think he was even more surprised that I wasn't with Ellis. He always chatted with us when we visited Eden. He unsuccessfully attempted to conceal his puzzlement as he looked from me to Malik. I commented that it was a small world, then explained that Malik was my roommate and his connection to Terrence. Jade finally finished in the kitchen and joined the party. Malik and I didn't stumble out of Rituals until two-thirty in the morning.

I climbed the stairs to our apartment, holding onto the rail for balance. Six glasses of champagne and I was flying high as a kite. Malik held me by the elbow to make sure I didn't tumble backward down the stairs. I tripped on the top step and started giggling. Malik shushed me, which made me laugh louder. He ushered me into the apartment and helped me take off my fur. I kicked off my shoes in the living room. We walked down the hallway, side by side, to our bedrooms. I leaned against the door, resting my head on the frame.

Malik loitered in front of me. "We should do this more often," he said.

"You know where to find me. All you have to do is ask."

"Is that all it takes?" he whispered.

I nodded. Malik glided to me, closing the distance between us. He positioned one hand above my head on the door and slowly leaned into me, his lips hovering dangerously close to mine. He moved closer. I closed my eyes. I could feel his breath on my face. The buzzer sounded. My eyes popped open. We peered at each other. It was as if time stopped. No one moved a muscle. We waited in silence. The buzzer rang again. Malik went to the intercom and buzzed the door open. A moment later there was a knock at the door. Malik went to answer it.

Kai came through the door with a bundle of apologies and excuses. I slipped into my room and shut the door behind me. A few moments later I heard two sets of footsteps pass my door before Malik's door closed behind them.

CHAPTER NINETEEN
MALIK

Kai was sprawled across my queen-size bed in her bra and panties. Morning sunlight streamed through the open blinds. I was sitting up with my back pressed against the headboard. Kai showed up last night, copping a plea. Rattled off an intricate tale about a family emergency, a hospital visit and no cell phones allowed. She attempted to make atonement through oral means and I let her. I was mad, but I wasn't a mad fool.

"What's your schedule like tomorrow?" she asked.

"Meetings in the morning, but my afternoon is open."

"I'm flying out to San Francisco on Tuesday. I thought we should try to finish as much as we can for the Sphere presentation before I go. Unless..."

"Unless what?"

"Unless you care to join me in California."

I thought about it for a moment.

She crawled up beside me. "If you come along, we wouldn't have to rush the final product when I get back on Friday. It would give us the entire week to polish our pitch. I don't want us to have to scramble over the weekend. Next Monday morning we meet with Gerry and then we're meeting with Sphere Electronics the following week."

"Donner's going to approve my joining you on a business trip?"

"He wants this Sphere account. He'll support whatever it takes to make it happen."

"All right. I'll talk to him first thing in the morning."

"No, let me."

I raised my eyebrows.

She quickly added, "If I tell him I need you in San Francisco for Sphere *and* to assist with my other meetings he can't refuse."

"I hate corporate politics."

"Ahh, but you won't have to deal with them for long. Once you start your own agency corporate politics will be a thing of the past."

"My deadline is eight months."

"That soon?"

"I have an aggressive strategy. If I could do it sooner, I would." I sprang from the bed and paced the room. "I get excited just thinking about my own agency. You know when you have a plan and you feel within your soul that it can't fail? I already have ideas to woo some of the biggest companies out there, specifically in the automobile and cosmetics industries."

"But those are two of Newport and Donner's primary markets."

"Newport and Donner can withstand the competition."

"Do you intend to lure away our clients?"

"I'll have the hottest ad agency in New York. I won't need to lure anyone. Clients will be knocking at my door. I have concepts ready and waiting for Nissan, Revlon and a whole host of others."

"Malik, I would have never imagined that you had all of this going on."

"You know what they say…never underestimate the power of a black man."

I spent the majority of the morning showing Kai another source of my power. It was almost noon when I threw on some sweats and walked her outside to her car.

Melina was in the kitchen making breakfast when I came back upstairs. She looked over her shoulder at me, then turned back to the sausage sizzling on the stove. "I had way too much champagne last night. I could barely get out of the bed."

I walked into the room and sat at the table. Melina rummaged through the refrigerator, pulling out an onion, green pepper, and a couple of red potatoes. A potato dropped from her hand and rolled across the floor near my foot. I leaned over and picked it up. I held it out to her. She grabbed it from my hand, avoiding my eyes.

"Mel, we didn't do anything."

"I know we didn't."

"There's no reason to start acting strange."

"I'm not."

"We both had a lot of drinks—"

"Was that Kai I heard leaving? I think you two make such a cute couple."

Okay, so we were pretending like nothing had happened. Fine with me. It shouldn't have been too difficult, since I really didn't know what had happened other than, I almost kissed my roommate. It was a good thing Kai showed up when she did. In that instance, *better late than never* had never been more true.

"Yeah, she just left."

"Did she explain what happened to her last night?" she asked, dicing her vegetables.

"Family emergency."

"I see."

"What are you making?"

"An omelet. Are you hungry?"

"I'll take one."

I made small talk while Melina cooked. She concentrated on the frying pans as if her life depended on it. I went to the fridge to pour myself a glass of juice and she stepped to the side, giving me more room than necessary. "I'm going to San Francisco on Tuesday for business."

Relief washed over her face. It was definitely a perfect time for me to go out of town. My being away would give Melina a chance to realize that nothing had happened between us.

"When will you be back?"

"Friday or Saturday. Kai's going, too."

"Wow. Taking business trips together…"

"It ain't like that. Kai and I have a lot of work to do for our presentation."

"Mmm hmm."

"I'll take my omelet without the side of cynicism."

After breakfast I went to lie down. What did happen last night? One minute I was about to kiss Melina, the next I was with Kai. Maybe it was the alcohol that made me react to Melina that way. I wanted to kiss her. I could taste her on my tongue even though I hadn't touched her. What baffled me more was knowing that Melina wanted to kiss me back. Although, she did have a lot of champagne. It was divine intervention. That was the only way to explain what had transpired last night.

CHAPTER TWENTY
MELINA

Caroline led me into the study to wait. Bebe thought it would be better if we had lunch at her penthouse. I was hoping that this meeting would be quick and painless—I needed to get back to the office.

Bebe sashayed into the study, wearing a pair of black wide-leg pants and a flouncy cream blouse with a double strand of pearls. She came over and air-kissed both of my cheeks. Her perfume was so strong and floral, it gave me an instant headache. Her cheeks were accented with rose-colored blush that didn't quite match her pale skin tone. Ellis and Daniella got their beautiful bronze complexions from their father.

She sat in the leather club chair across from me. The inspection process was underway. Bebe took in my tweed pencil skirt and matching jacket, my brown leather boots and even my purse sitting on the table. Her icy smile cooled the room. She rested her elbow on the arm of the chair, pressing her finger to her temple. "Let me start off by saying that being a Harlow comes with a wealth of responsibility. I have to believe that my son chose you for a reason."

I gritted my teeth, and took a deep breath, while trying to maintain a neutral expression.

"Everything you do," she continued, "from this point forward is a reflection of this family. I beseech you to conduct yourself in a manner suitable of the Harlow name. I realize you may find it a tad difficult living up to the standards of someone of Ellison's caliber, but you must find the resolve within yourself to make it so."

I leaned forward. "Well, let me say this—"

"Lunch is served, Mrs. Harlow," Caroline said from the doorway.

"Come, dear, we don't want the lobster bisque to get cold."

Bebe waited for me to get up from my chair. I sat for a moment, eyeing her in disbelief. The audacity of this woman. I slowly rose up, straightened my jacket and then followed her to the dining room. The long table was set for two. One setting at the head of the table, the other to the left. I sat and spread my napkin across my lap. Wesley, the Harlow family butler, ladled bisque into our gold-etched bowls. I studied the way Bebe dipped her spoon in her bisque and stiffly brought it to her lips . I scrutinized the baubles on her fingers and her well-manicured hands. This woman wasn't living in the same world as I was. In her mind, she owned the world.

"Have you given any thought to when we'll have this wedding?"

"Not as of yet."

"Fine. An April wedding will be perfect. Of course you will get married in my church on Fifth Avenue."

"I'd like to discuss it with Ellis before I commit to anything."

"Ellison has already agreed, dear."

"Oh, he has? He's made no mention of it to me."

"I plan to make this as effortless for you as possible. Your wedding will be the crème de la crème. Leave everything to me."

"Bebe, I would like to make the decisions of when and where my wedding will take place. I may want to get married in Maryland, where I was raised."

"Maryland?"

She uttered Maryland as if I said I wanted to get married in the depths of hell.

I nodded. "My family is in Maryland. My mother and I will most likely plan to—"

"I will not hear of it," she said, waving me off. "Maryland is unequivocally out of the question."

I wanted to strangle Ellis. How could he tell his mother that she had free rein over my wedding? Now I had to do battle with this titan and he wasn't around to have my back. I wasn't even sure if Ellis would have my back. At that moment it certainly seemed that his mother had his support.

"Bebe, this is all so new. I need a moment to decide what I would like to do. We both want the wedding to be perfect and we have time—"

"We will not have a thrown-together affair that reeks of shabbiness. What we will have is a wedding in April in New York. It will be a grand affair in the customary Harlow tradition."

I could barely swallow my soup. Ellis's mother was infuriating. Wesley entered the dining room with two plates covered with silver lids. He placed my dish in front of me and uncovered it. Filet mignon, baby carrots and potato galette. I wasn't hungry and didn't want to endure another minute with Bebe. All I wanted was for lunch to be over.

Bebe cut into her steak. "Who will be in your wedding party? Besides Daniella, of course."

"My two best friends. Though, I just found out that one is pregnant."

"We can have Ellison's cousin, Daphne, substitute for her."

"I'm not substituting anyone."

"Think of the photos. An enormously pregnant woman will ruin the symmetry."

"Excuse me?"

"I suppose the photographer can work around her. Perhaps exclude her from some of the shots."

"I think we need to table this discussion until a later date. I would like to speak to Ellis about a few things. I also need time to talk to my mother."

She ceased eating her food, wiping her mouth with her linen napkin. "I can remember what I was like before I married Ellison's father." She focused on an empty chair at the other end of the table as she spoke. "I was young. Naïve. Impressionable. Consumed by idealistic fantasies of romantic bliss. It took many years for me to learn that marriage was not what I had imagined it to be. It was hard work. Trying, even. Much like a business." Bebe turned her glare on me with burning intensity. "You can't function in a marriage on whims and notions. In marriage you need a plan, a blueprint, so to speak. A map to navigate you through the years. But most importantly, marriage is about appearances. It's about presentation. It's all about how you represent yourself as a couple to the world. You may have had the most horrific fight of your life with your husband, but when you step outside of the door, your best face had better be in place. No one should be able to detect the slightest fissure in your façade. Presentation is key. The sooner you embrace the concept, the better. You, my dear, will represent the Harlow family. Starting now. Think of your relationship with me as an extension of your marriage. If you are to be a part of this family, know that nothing comes easy. I hope that we understand each other." She tossed her napkin next to her plate, then pushed her chair back from the table. "When you call your mother, let her know that we've settled on April in New York. I have an appointment with my manicurist, but I'll send Wesley in with your dessert. Stay as long as you like, dear."

Bebe paraded out the room, leaving me at the table in a literal stupor. My eyes welled up with tears. Unfortunately, she may have predicted one thing accurately—Ellis and I were about to have the fight of our lives.

Ellis agreed to come by my apartment after he finished at the office. With Malik out of town, I didn't have to worry about being interrupted. I waited in the living room, posted at the window, for his arrival. His mother's behavior was inexcusable. I needed to hear directly from Ellis whether he knew what Bebe had planned for *our* wedding. I barely wanted to address the other issues she harped on. I fought the urge to cry again. This was not the time for weakness.

I was completely out of my element with the Bebe situation. Every relationship I'd been in I had gotten along with the mother. I was the girl that mothers rooted for. I was the one mothers wanted their sons to marry. I had always been good enough, no, make that perfect, for their sons. In some instances I'd been too good. Now I had a rich witch to contend with that felt I wasn't worthy to shine her son's shoes.

Ellis's driver double-parked the limousine in front of my brownstone. Ellis stepped from the vehicle. He didn't bother to wait to have his door opened for him. I went to buzz him into the building.

He walked into the apartment and leaned in for a kiss. I craned my neck to the side, avoiding his lips. Ellis backed off. I closed the door behind him and led him into the living room.

"Your mother and I had lunch today and it was very enlightening. I have been informed that you and I will be married in April at your mother's church. Do you know anything about this?"

"Mother merely made a suggestion."

"A suggestion? Your mother practically rammed my own wedding plans down my throat."

"Lina, my mother wants to be helpful. She made it clear to me that she is excited about our wedding and is willing to assist you in any way possible."

"Bullshit!"

Ellis narrowed his eyes at me. "Watch your tone."

"You have no fucking idea what your mother put me through today. She's controlling, manipulative and obviously has you wrapped around her finger."

"I'm only going to say this once. We will not continue this conversation if you don't calm down. Now I'm willing to hear what you have to say, but I expect you to be respectful of my mother."

"Respect your mother, Ellis? She doesn't fucking respect me."

"I'm warning you…"

"Your mother told me that I wasn't good enough for you."

"Don't be ridiculous. Mother would never say such a thing."

"She may not have said those exact words, but she insinuated, and she made sure that I got the message loud and clear. Do you know what else *Bebe* had the nerve to say to me?"

"Lower your voice."

"*Bebe* told me that one of my best friends should be booted from the wedding party because her presence in the photos will destroy the pictures."

"I'm certain this is a misunderstanding that can be rectified."

"I understood your mother perfectly. I'll have no input in my own wedding because, according to her, it's about putting on airs and treating marriage like a business. She totally discounted the fact that I want my own mother involved in the planning."

"Lina, I doubt Mother discouraged your family's involvement. In fact, why don't all three of you arrange a meeting to plan everything?"

"I would never subject my mother to your mother's wrath."

Ellis came over to me and coaxed me down onto the couch. He sat next to me. "I can see you're upset. I want you to try and calm your nerves. I'm sorry that your lunch with Mother did not fare so well. I know she has the best intentions. Apparently something went wrong somewhere. We don't have to make any decisions today. Right now, the only thing I want you to do is relax. I'll send the limo off for the evening and order some food."

"But why would you agree to a date without consulting me first?"

Ellis put his finger to my lips. "That's enough of this for tonight. I'll talk to Mother in the morning. Go relax."

I headed to my bedroom—not because I thought resting was a good idea—I went because I had to get away from Ellis. He could weasel his way out of an explanation for now, but this was far from over.

CHAPTER TWENTY-ONE
MALIK

I was getting dressed to meet Kai at Silks, one of the restaurants in our hotel, for dinner at seven. I was staying in a cool city view room at the Mandarin Oriental. The hotel was nice, I couldn't complain, but Kai was posted up in a suite with two bedrooms, a private terrace and a view of San Francisco Bay. She chalked up our difference in accommodations to my last-minute reservation.

We arrived yesterday afternoon and went from the airport straight to Kai's first meeting. She briefed me on the plane and I co-pitched her client, a major bank headquartered in San Francisco. We secured the account, headed back to the hotel, then went to our respective rooms. I settled in, ordered room service, watched a little television and was asleep by ten.

The next morning, I accompanied Kai to two of her three meetings. I spent the remainder of my afternoon on the ferry tour to Alcatraz. I walked through the cells of some of the most notorious prisoners in history. As I toured the cellblocks I felt claustrophobic, trapped. I thought about how a trip to a prison should be mandatory for all young black males. Maybe a glimpse into a life of confinement would be a deterrent to a life of crime. The only thing that kept me out of trouble was my father. He made sure I knew that if I got into any trouble I didn't need to worry about the cops, the judge or being locked up. He swore that he would kill me before it ever got that far. I believed him. I kept my nose clean, studied hard, went to college and was now on the cusp of starting my own business.

I sprayed on some Gucci cologne and then put on my striped button-up shirt, tucking it into my slacks. I slipped on my black loafers, grabbed my wallet and my room key, and then went downstairs to meet Kai.

I had the waiter bring me a Johnnie Walker Gold while I waited at the table for Kai. I was finishing up my first drink when she strutted into the restaurant. Her legs, bare and oiled, mesmerized me as she approached the table. The sparkle in her short, glittery dress reflected the light from the chandeliers. I pulled out Kai's chair for her.

I settled back into my seat. "You shouldn't be allowed to be that damn sexy."

"I thought we could check out the nightlife after dinner."

Our waiter came back to take Kai's drink order. She asked for a dirty martini. I ordered another Gold Label.

"Make that Johnnie Walker Blue," Kai said. He waited for my consent. I nodded and he went off to do his job. "Why skimp?" she asked.

I laughed. "I usually reserve the Blue for special occasions."

"You don't consider this special? You and I in a beautiful city… me in this dress…the entire night ahead of us…"

I reconsidered. "Definitely a Blue Label night."

"If you think about it, you and I have the best of both worlds. We work well together and we play together even better. I wanted you with me in California because I knew we'd have a good time."

"And we have a project to complete."

"Let's keep it real. Either one of us can finish that project with our eyes closed."

She wasn't lying. The majority of the presentation was completed. "I understand," I said, imitating like I was buffing my nails on my shirt. "You couldn't resist bringing the man along."

We both laughed. Our waiter returned with our drinks and I ordered for myself and Kai.

"Okay, that was smooth."

"What?"

"Ordering dinner for me. Most men don't take such liberties."

"It's a neglected art form. And I think you already know I'm not most men."

Kai nodded slowly. "You're good, Malik. You must have legions of women enamored by you."

I had to laugh at her assessment of me. "It's the small things that men fail to do that makes one brotha more appealing than the next. If I order for a woman and that one thing turns her on, and as a result she endears herself to me, then who am I to deny her affections?"

"What other methods are you employing to entice these women?"

"It wouldn't make much sense for me to reveal my arsenal of tactics—though something tells me with you it doesn't matter."

"Are you saying I'm not worthy of your seduction?"

"I'm saying that I don't think my tactics would work on you. See, you have your own little games you play and you'd be the one to recognize mine."

"Let's make a deal. I promise not to use any of my romantic devices on you and you can't use any on me. Agreed?"

"Romantic devices? If you mean sex toys, then I can't agree to those terms."

"Well, since you're resorting to jokes I'm going to assume you can't handle me or what I'm offering you."

I put my game face on and got down to business. "Exactly what are you offering, Kai?"

"I haven't come across many men that aren't intimidated by me. I know what men think of me. I'm an exploit, something to be conquered. I see how the guys in the office act when I'm around and how they whisper when they think I'm not paying attention. In fact, I like it. I take their constant tongue wagging as a compliment. And then there's you—so unlike the rest. The one man in the office that's able to get my attention but never tried. Malik, I'm giving you my full attention and I want yours."

"You've got it."

"What do I have to do to keep it?"

"Be creative."

"I'm asking what it takes to get closer to you."

I tasted my Blue, let it slide down my throat. You have to be careful with Blue. It goes down smooth and easy. I'd seen a lot of brothers get drunk off the Blue by drinking too much, too fast. Blue was meant to be savored, not guzzled like a cold beer. I peered into Kai's waiting eyes. I had no idea what to tell her. My usual speech about not settling down didn't seem appropriate. She wasn't like the women I typically dated. I intentionally dated women that tended to go along with my program. That wasn't Kai. She had a program of her own—of which I had to admit to having a certain curiosity. "I don't think anyone can truthfully answer a question like that. I can tell you anything. I can run down a list of likes and dislikes, but in the end, the only thing that brings two people closer is interaction, and there's no guarantee that you'll want to be close to them once you really get to know 'em."

"I'll take my chances."

I awoke the next morning in Kai's king-size bed, in her expensive suite, with her face in my chest and her legs tangled with mine. We hit a few of the local hot spots after dinner, so she could shake her ass all over the dance floor. Our last stop was an after-hours lounge. I was chillin' on the sofa while Kai danced in front of me, working her body like a pro to the music. She was bouncing and bending, giving me an exclusive two-for-one package of cleavage and thong action. When she began to bless me with a scorching-hot lap dance, I dragged her out of there and back to the hotel to hose her down.

Kai stirred, rolling her body away from mine. She turned on her side and pulled the covers over her head. I crept from the bed, went to the living room to throw on my clothes, and then made a stealth-like exit. It was only five a.m. when I got back to my room, but I showered and shaved anyway. I sat on the edge of the bed in my towel and used the phone on the nightstand to check my messages at the office. I grabbed the notepad from the table and scribbled down the important numbers that required an immediate response. It was after eight in the morning in New York, an ideal time to get my calls out of the way.

I checked in with my assistant after I wrapped up my business calls. She filled me in on what had transpired in my absence. Not much. I told her to expect me in the office on Friday afternoon, pushed the button to disconnect our call but held on to the receiver—temporarily lost in thought. I hazily punched in the numbers for my last call. The phone rang until the voicemail picked up. Melina's voice on the message declared that neither of us was home to take the call. I hung up, declining to wait for the beep.

CHAPTER TWENTY-TWO
MELINA

Nadia buzzed my phone to ask if I wanted to take a call from Charlee. I was grateful for the break and told her to put the call through. Charlee was in L.A. taking care of business as usual. She called to tell me that she was worried about Giselle. She had been calling her for a few days and had been unsuccessful in reaching her. Earlier in the afternoon, she called the hospital and they told her Giselle was on vacation for the week. Neither of us was aware that Giselle was on vacation. I agreed to go by her apartment after work to check on her.

I had been so wrapped up in my own drama lately, that I hadn't reached out to anyone. After my disastrous lunch with Bebe last week I sort of went underground. I didn't want to tell my girls there was trouble in paradise. I knew Charlee would go off on an overblown tangent, egging me on to kick Ellis and his mother to the curb, and Giselle would try to persuade me to work it out at any expense. Wasn't it enough that my problems with my future husband and his mother were plaguing me; why infect anyone else?

At five-thirty I packed my briefcase and left the office. I drove over to Giselle's at the height of rush hour. Thankfully, Giselle had a parking garage underneath her building and owned two spaces with her condo. I pulled into her guest spot and then went inside. The desk attendant called upstairs, spoke briefly to Giselle and received clearance to send me up. I stepped inside of the mirrored elevator and pressed the button for the twenty-third floor. I fluffed my loose curls in the mirror while singing along to the light music coming from the speakers. "Wrapped Around Your Finger" by Sting, actually The Police, was playing. I owned a few CDs by Sting. He was one of those white boys I could groove to when relaxing at home alone. I loved his melodic voice.

I walked down the corridor and found Giselle waiting for me at the door. I gave her a hug and kiss as I entered the apartment. She was wearing a pair of baggy sweat pants and a fitted tank with thin straps. I rubbed her small bulge of a tummy.

The television in the living room was muted and open magazines littered the coffee table. I went over to the sofa and picked up the magazine closest to me. *Parents Magazine*. I scanned the others. *Pregnancy Magazine. Fit Pregnancy. Working Mother. American Baby.*

I smiled up at Giselle. She sat next to me on the sofa and sighed. Her hands instinctively went to her stomach and started rubbing.

"How are you feeling?" I asked.

"Tired, but good."

"You know, Gigi, we're here for you if and when you need us." She nodded. "I know."

"Are your parents excited about becoming grandparents again?"

"I haven't told them yet."

"You're almost four months pregnant and you haven't shared the news with your parents?"

"They've been in Florida for the past few weeks. I'm waiting until they return to break the news to them."

"I can't imagine them not being excited."

"I can. I don't think this is the path they had in mind for me."

"Giselle, you've done everything right in life. You have a wonderful career, two homes and you will be a great mother."

"This wasn't how things were supposed to turn out. I wanted the whole package. I didn't want to be a single mother. My child," she gripped her stomach, "this child, deserves better than this."

"You are being way too hard on yourself. You're going to give that child the world."

"Yeah, everything except a father—the one thing that no child should be without."

"If you feel that strongly about it, then maybe you should get the father back in the picture."

"It's not that easy."

"Why is it so difficult? Is it because he's a colleague of yours?"

"Melina, believe me, I wish the situation could be different, but it can't. Trust me when I tell you I have to do this alone."

I didn't want to push it. I had to take Giselle at her word. I suppose it wasn't an ideal situation if she had other plans, but she would be fine. She wasn't the first and she wouldn't be the last single mother. Thankfully, she had friends and family who loved her and were ready and willing to help in any way. Right now I needed to get Giselle to remember that she wasn't alone. "Charlee told me that she's been trying to contact you for a few days."

"I know, I need to call her back. I've been catching up on some much-needed rest."

"You've been spending your vacation pent up in this apartment?"

"I've been out."

I studied the dark circles under her eyes. Her hair was curly and hadn't been blown straight like she usually wore it. "Where?"

"Melina, don't grill me."

"I'm not. Have you eaten?"

"I had breakfast."

"It's almost seven p.m. What happened to lunch and dinner? You're a doctor. You should be the last person that needs the *you're eating for two* speech."

I got up and went into the kitchen. I washed my hands, then opened the refrigerator to see what I could fix Giselle to eat. At least it wasn't empty. I was surprised to see that it was filled with food. Fruit, vegetables, juice and milk cluttered the shelves. I found a package of ground turkey in the meat compartment. I took a box of linguini and a jar of pasta sauce out of the cabinet, then busied myself, preparing dinner.

Giselle stayed in the living room, flipping through the pages of her magazines, while I made linguini with turkey meatballs and a tossed salad. I set the table and summoned her over. She said a silent grace before picking up her fork to eat. I poured oil and vinegar dressing on my salad, then offered the bottle to Giselle.

She shook her head. "I have red wine in the wine rack in the den."

"No, thanks."

"Just because I can't drink doesn't mean that you shouldn't."

"I'm driving, remember?"

"I know you and that isn't why you won't have a glass of wine." She smiled. "I appreciate the gesture."

That was the first smile I got since I showed up at the door. "How's the pasta?"

"Delicious. Thanks, Melina."

"Eat. We want a healthy baby."

Giselle's eyes misted over. She laid her fork on the table. "I really am excited. I know it doesn't seem like it, but I am. The idea that there is a little life inside of me makes me so happy. It's the extra baggage that accompanies the reality of the pregnancy that scares me—my career, my parents, being a single mother."

I tried to imagine what Giselle was feeling. I wondered what I would do if I were in her position. Financially I would be all right, but emotionally would I have the resolve? I didn't know. "I can't tell you that at times raising a child won't be rough, but that holds true for all parents, whether they're single or married. I *can* tell you not to let fear dictate your future. This pregnancy is a beautiful beginning for you. Accept the beauty in this situation and reject whatever has the potential to have a negative impact on you and this baby."

"Just promise me that you'll be here for me…no matter what."

"No matter what," I repeated. "Now eat your dinner before it gets cold."

Giselle ate everything on her plate and even had a second helping. After dinner, I washed the dishes and then joined her in the living room. We paged through her magazines and talked about her plans to have two nurseries, one in each of her homes. Even though it was still early in the pregnancy Giselle admitted she had been out shopping for baby furniture. She showed me a picture of a mural she wanted to have painted on the wall in the baby's room. She assured me that she would hold off on decorating for a few months.

I did see Giselle's excitement peek through when she talked about the baby and everything she needed to do to prepare for its arrival. She said all she really wanted was a healthy baby, but she'd love to have a girl. I could only imagine a little Giselle running around in pink from head to toe, acting like a little lady. Unfortunately, Giselle wasn't planning to find out the sex of the baby in advance. I'd have to wait until the first week of May to find out whether I was getting a niece or nephew.

When I left Giselle's, it was close to midnight. I sped to Brooklyn in record time, but it took more than twenty minutes to find a parking space in my neighborhood. I finally found a spot two blocks over from my brownstone. I parked the car, then started my walk home. It was a mild night for mid-November.

The weatherman had forecasted daytime highs in the low sixties for the rest of the week but was expecting a severe drop in the temperature by the weekend. I gratefully accepted Mother Nature's temporary bout of kindness but woefully anticipated the forty-degree weekend.

I called Charlee when I got home and told her I thought Giselle was going to be okay. Charlee and I agreed to take turns checking on her until we were certain that she was out of her slump. I had even invited Giselle to go to Maryland the next week with Ellis and me for Thanksgiving. We were spending the holiday weekend at my parents' house and I thought Giselle might like to get away on a quick jaunt. She said she couldn't make it because her family was having a big dinner in Connecticut and she was planning to tell them all about the pregnancy. I hoped that once she told her family a large chunk of her stress would dissipate.

Charlee and I chatted about a baby shower before we got off the phone. It was a bit premature, but we couldn't help ourselves. Between the two of us, Giselle could expect a baby shower extraordinaire.

CHAPTER TWENTY-THREE
MALIK

Kai brought me another beer. We were at her house chilling with a college football game—Syracuse vs. Florida State. She made wings and potato skins and we were kicked back with our game food and drinks. I dunked my potato skin in sour cream and ate it in two bites. Kai put a few more wings on my plate and handed it to me. She wanted to switch to the Notre Dame game, but I had money riding on this one. I bet my brother fifty dollars that Syracuse would win. Since I refused to let her turn the channel she started rooting for Florida State.

"Cheer all you want. You and Amir are going to be disappointed when Florida gets their butt whooped," I said.

"Are we watching the same game? Syracuse is trailing by ten points."

"Sit back and watch. My team is gonna make a comeback." I bit into a wing. "Amir is probably watching this and talking much junk like you."

"Can you blame us? There's two minutes left in the third quarter. Your team doesn't stand a chance."

"You sure my brother didn't pay you to jinx my team?"

"Sort of impossible since I've never met your brother."

"You're better off not knowing him," I said, laughing.

"Is it just the two of you or do you have more siblings?"

"Me and Amir, that's it. But if you ask my mother she'll include my father and tell you she has three kids."

Kai laughed. "I think most women consider their husbands as one of the children at times. It has to do with the maternal, nurturing care they give to their spouses."

"My father gets pissed when she refers to him as one of her kids. You want to see an otherwise mild-mannered man lose it? Call him a child."

"Sounds like a classic temper tantrum to me."

"You got jokes."

"Stick around, I'm just getting warmed up."

"Don't quit your day job."

"I won't. You've already got that covered."

"Not yet, I'm still working on it."

I had taken my father to breakfast, and then scouted out office locations, before I landed at Kai's place. I wanted to show him an office I was considering in the Gable building on Lexington Avenue. The location was optimal—Midtown—right next to Grand Central Terminal. My father inspected the suite and thought it would be fine, but suggested I consider New Jersey or Brooklyn for an office with comparable space and less rent. I explained to him that I needed to be in the city if I intended to have a leading advertising agency.

Kai stopped smiling. "Are you sure you want to leave Newport and Donner? I know for a fact that Donner was extremely pleased with our presentation when we returned from San Francisco. His only suggestion was that we co-present to Sphere Electronics on Wednesday. If Sphere is impressed, which I know they will be, we're both guaranteed sizeable bonuses."

"Kai, our meeting with Donner was on Monday. Why are you just now telling me on Saturday that he wants you to co-present?"

"I didn't think it was a big deal. We have three days to work out the kinks."

"Yeah, but we could have had over a week to get our act together."

"I know you're not worried about this meeting with Sphere?" she asked.

"This is a major account and we can't afford to be slacking on it."

Kai put her plate down on the table. "The presentation is complete. It's perfect. You have been pitching it on your own, but now I'll be co-presenting with you. This is not my first major account. All of my accounts are large and lucrative. I can assure you that I will not be *slacking*. I wanted you to do the presentation on your own, but Gerry asked me to co-pitch."

"*Gerry*," I scoffed. "Donner's already seen this presentation twice and both times I've presented it. Why the change?"

"He feels if I share the presenting, I can subconsciously show Sphere Electronics that our ads also target women. He wants Sphere to get the sense that female consumers will also play their racing game."

"Right."

"You think there's another reason Gerry wants me to co-present?"

"Hey, listen, it's his company and what he says goes, right?"

"Gerry believes in our campaign and feels one minor change will clinch the deal for us."

"Kai, I don't have a problem with you pitching Sphere. My concern is the last-minute notice and the fact that Donner didn't tell me about the change."

"I apologize, that was my fault. He asked me to tell you and I never got around to discussing it with you. I hadn't anticipated you would want more time to prepare."

"And you ask am I sure I want to leave Newport and Donner.

I'm positive. I'll be able to avoid all of this when I'm my own boss."

"I wish you would reconsider. Gerry likes you. He has you in mind for quite a few large clients."

"I'll get larger clients but at my own agency. This morning, with barely any thought, I came up with a great ad for that new twenty-four-hour lipstick by Peck Me. They recently fired their advertising agency and they're conducting a search for a new one. Picture a housewife giving her husband a chaste kiss before he goes off to work every morning. He always leaves wiping her lipstick off his lips with his handkerchief. Then, she tries Peck Me twenty-four. This time when she kisses her husband the kiss is passionate and steamy and they're still kissing when the kids return home from school. They pull apart from each other and her lipstick is still perfect and he isn't wearing any. The slogan will say, 'Spend your day seeing if it lasts a full twenty-four hours.' Donner took too long to throw me a bone. I'm taking my own advertising agency straight to the top."

"There's no denying you're talented. I only wish you would consider staying with Newport and Donner."

Kai's telephone interrupted us. I went to the bathroom while she answered her call. When I came out she was in the kitchen adding more wings to the platter.

She turned to me. "That was my friend Justine and her husband, Ira. They were running in Central Park and decided to drop by. They're on their way up." She handed me the wings. "Can you put those on the table for me?"

I brought the wings into the living room. The doorbell rang. Kai shouted from the kitchen for me to answer the door. I went to let her friends in. I opened the door, then paused. Justine was five-feet-eight inches of fine—hair pulled back in a ponytail and ebony skin glowing, from the run I guessed. Her fitted running suit showcased her tight-bodied curves. The lips…I caught myself and remembered that Kai said Justine was married. I looked to the right, then down. Ira. Six inches shorter than his wife. Round. Balding. White. I shook my head and then extended my hand to him. I introduced myself to the couple and ushered them inside. Justine smirked at me as she followed her husband into the living room.

I relinquished my seat on the sofa and went to sit in the armchair. Kai glided into the room and greeted her friends. She sat on the arm of my chair and draped herself around my shoulders. I glanced at her, but it went unnoticed.

Ira reached for a chicken wing and Justine slapped the back of his hand. "Your diet," she scolded.

Ira recoiled from the platter. "You're right. I almost forgot."

"You're always forgetting."

His lips twitched nervously. Ira didn't bother to respond to his wife. I instantly knew what was up with those two. Justine fixed a plate with wings and potato skins and chowed down while Ira salivated.

Kai offered to get him some fresh fruit from the kitchen. He declined, then glumly took a celery stick from the wing plate. I tried to concentrate on the game and not Ira's piteous face while he gnawed on his celery.

"So, Malik," Justine started, "you're the one occupying Kai's time. We haven't seen her in weeks."

Kai ran her hand over my hair. "I told you I've been putting in a lot of hours at work." She leaned over and kissed my cheek, then trailed her fingertips along my jaw.

Kai was saying one thing, but definitely attempting to send a different message.

Justine sucked the tip of her chicken bone, hypnotized by Kai's performance. Ira reached for another celery stick, drawing Justine out of her trance. She looked at him and then patted him on the knee like a good dog.

Kai chuckled, then asked me if I wanted more to eat. I told her no; I had enough.

"Malik, you work with Kai, right?"

"Yeah," I said.

Justine glared at Kai. "That must be pretty uncomfortable huh, Kai?"

"Not at all," Kai said, sneering at Justine. "Ira, I think I have some low-fat yogurt in the fridge. Come with me, I'll get you some."

Ira went with Kai into the kitchen and Justine scooted down the sofa, closer to my chair.

"I bet your wondering what I'm doing with a man like Ira," she said.

"Actually, I wasn't."

"Sure you were. I saw it in your eyes when you opened the door."

"You got me. The thought crossed my mind."

"It's simple. Above all, a woman should always choose three things in a man: wealth, power and security. If you don't believe me, ask Kai."

Justine slid back down the sofa as Kai and Ira returned. He had a container of yogurt in one hand and an apple in the other. Ira plopped down next to his wife and took a bite of his apple.

"Who's winning the game?" Ira asked.

I looked at Justine and then Kai. "I don't know. I wasn't paying attention."

CHAPTER TWENTY-FOUR
MELINA

I told my mother I would bake a red velvet cake and bring it to Thanksgiving dinner. It was the only cake I had mastered and every holiday it was my responsibility to have one on the dessert table. Thanksgiving was two days away and I didn't have any of the ingredients in the house. I had come home from the office, changed my clothes and was heading down the brownstone steps, on my way to the store. Malik was walking up the street on his way from work.

"Wassup, Mel. Where are you off to?"

"The supermarket."

"Hold up. Let me throw on some jeans and I'll go with you."

"Malik, I don't have all night to wait for you."

"Five minutes."

"Hurry up. I'll be waiting in the car. It's down the block in front of the brownstone that's being renovated."

I went to the car and let it run a minute before turning on the heat. The mellow sounds of Les Nubians piped from the speakers. I was too busy acting like a non-French speaking third member of the group to see Malik come down the street. I jumped when he opened the door and slid into the passenger seat.

"Don't stop singing. You were tearing it up, literally."

"Shut up," I said, laughing.

"Damn. You got the heat pumping in here."

"You know I can't stand being cold and I really hate being in a cold car, sitting on cold leather seats."

Malik closed the vents nearest to him. I pulled out of my space and drove us to the supermarket, massacring the smooth French lyrics of Les Nubians. Sorry, ladies.

Malik pushed the cart as I tossed items for my cake inside. He periodically grabbed items from the shelves—a box of Captain Crunch cereal, microwave popcorn, a bottle of Coke.

"How do you survive on that junk?"

"I supplement it with your good cooking."

"Once I get married I won't be there to cook for you."

"I have some time before that happens and even though you don't think so, I can cook."

"I wouldn't know it."

"What?" Malik stopped pushing the cart. "Are you questioning my skills?"

"Malik, please."

He stepped around the cart and came to stand in front of me. He crossed his arms over his chest. "You saying I can't burn in the kitchen?"

His question was met with a blank expression. He walked behind me and spoke into my ear. "You doubt my skills?"

His mouth so close to my ear tickled. I started to laugh. Malik lifted me up from behind and put me in the cart. My legs were dangling over the side.

I started screaming. "Malik! Stop playing! Get me out of here!" I said between laughs. An elderly woman scrutinizing the boxed cake mixes frowned at us. Malik nodded at her, then proceeded to push the cart down the aisle. He passed the old woman and started pushing faster. I struggled to pull myself up and out of the cart. Malik made a sharp turn, throwing me back into the cart. He started running down the aisle. I was laughing so hard, tears were streaming down my cheeks. We were met at the end of the condiment aisle by the store manager. Malik slid to a stop before barreling into him. I attempted to stifle my laughter as Malik pulled me from the cart. The store manager turned around without uttering a word.

"I'm going to beat your ass," I said, wiping tears from my face.

"If you do, then I won't be able to make you dinner tonight."

"Why are you insisting that you can cook?"

"Are you going to make me throw you back in the cart?"

"All right, fine. What are you going to cook for me?"

"Don't worry about that. Finish getting your stuff and I'm going to get what I need to make you the best dinner you've ever had."

Malik bustled around the kitchen while I did paperwork in the living room. He refused to let me come in there. He had brought me a glass of wine and told me to stay out of his work zone. Whatever it was he was cooking did smell good.

He finally came into the living room an hour later and held out his hand. "Dinner is served."

I pushed his hand out of the way. "This better be good. I'm starving."

Malik had a small candle burning in the center of the table. He pulled out my chair for me. I sat down, looking back at him over my shoulder. He refreshed my wine glass and then placed garlic bread on the table. I sipped my wine while he plated our dinner. He put my dish in front of me and I was pleasantly surprised.

Chicken tenderloin sliced into medallions, topped with mushrooms, red peppers and garlic in a cream sauce. It was accompanied by herbed rice and sautéed broccoli. Malik sat down with his plate. He observed me with a prideful grin.

"Okay. It looks good, but it's the taste that counts."

He reached over and turned off the kitchen light. The flickering candle filled the kitchen with a warm glow. I cut a piece of the chicken and put it in my mouth. Tender and garlicky. I tried the rest. Everything was very flavorful.

My surprise leaked out. "It's good. You *can* cook."

"That's what I said." Malik started eating his food.

Every time I looked up from my plate Malik was watching me. He was eating too, but if he looked down in his plate at all, I didn't see it. Maybe it was an illusion of the candlelight, a trick of shadows. Perhaps his eyes weren't gazing at me. I started to say something but stopped myself.

"Go ahead. Ask me," he said.

"Are you watching me?"

"Yeah."

"Why?"

"Why not?"

The feather ruffler was about to get started. I was not taking the bait this time. I kept eating my dinner. I left him hanging with his question unanswered.

"I was thinking about how I like it when we get along," he said.

"We usually do," I said, then confessed. "No, we don't."

"But when we do, it feels real cool to me."

"We live together—we should be able to get along with one another. You and I have a few rough days here and there, but mainly we're fine."

"Yes, you are."

"Malik."

He smirked. "What?"

"Obviously it's too late to tell you to go easy on the wine."

"I can't give my roommate a compliment?"

"In case you didn't know I'm immune to your mackin'."

"Mel, why would I try to mack on you? You're my roommate. You're engaged. And you wouldn't go for it, now would you?"

There was my face getting hot again. At least in the candlelight Malik wasn't able to see that he had embarrassed me, or rather, I embarrassed myself. "I don't need to answer that. You know I wouldn't go for it."

"Right. Like I said, it was just a compliment."

I sipped my wine. "How are you spending Thanksgiving?" It was better to shift gears than to be stuck in neutral.

"I'm having dinner at my parents, then Kai invited me to have drinks with her friend Justine and her husband."

"Hmm. A holiday with Kai..."

"Since when did having drinks with someone become such a big deal?"

"For you it is. And don't play naïve. It's not the drinks; it's the fact that you're doing it on a holiday and with her friends. This is a big step for you."

"Maybe it is. I haven't thought about it."

My smile froze. I was enjoying teasing him, but his last response prickled me. Malik was getting serious about Kai. He may not have taken the time to recognize it, but I had. "Well, whatever you do, have a good time. I won't be back from Maryland until Sunday night."

"I'll be waiting."

I blew out the candle and Malik flipped on the light.

CHAPTER TWENTY-FIVE
MALIK

Kai and I sat at the mahogany table in the conference room with Mr. Donner gracing us with his slickest smile. The Sphere executives had just left the room; we had hit a homerun. We got the account. Donner paced in front of us, rambling about how proud he was to have such a talented team. I noticed that he spoke primarily to Kai, barely glancing my way. I kept a straight face, observing just how much Donner appreciated *my* work.

Kai was all smiles, however, nodding her head to every word that crossed Donner's lips. She was engrossed, mesmerized even.

"Again, that was great work. Kai, be in my office in five minutes. I want to run a few things by you about how our relationship should proceed with Sphere," Donner said.

Kai grabbed her things off the table and hurried out of the conference room behind Donner.

I sat in the empty meeting room, wondering whether a big shark and a little piranha may have just shared a meal at my expense.

CHAPTER TWENTY-SIX
MELINA

It was no easy feat convincing Ellis that it would be pleasurable to drive to Maryland. He wanted to fly, first class, of course. We compromised by riding in his limo to my parents' house. My mother expected us to arrive Wednesday night, however, Ellis had an unexpected meeting Wednesday evening that prevented us from leaving until Thanksgiving morning.

Ellis's driver, Stanley, loaded my bag into the trunk and I carried the red velvet cake inside the car with me. Ellis was as crisp as ever at six in the morning. He was typing on his BlackBerry, paused long enough to quickly kiss me on the lips, then resumed his work. I sat next to him and removed my jacket.

Ellis handed me the remote for the television. "I'll be done in a minute. I'm wrapping up some business with one of my investors in London."

I pressed the power button and the monitor lowered from the ceiling. I tuned in to CNN. I kicked my sneakers off and curled my legs beneath me on the seat. Ellis rubbed my leg. I took in his version of casual—trousers and a button-down shirt—courtesy of Brooks Brothers.

Ellis tossed his BlackBerry on the seat next to him. He wrapped his arm around my shoulders and pulled me closer. I snuggled against him.

He kissed my forehead. "Did you sleep all right?"

"I didn't get much sleep. Too excited I guess. I haven't seen my parents in seven months."

"I thought I would have to come upstairs and pull you from the bed."

"Any other day you might have, but I was ready at five-thirty."

"Now that is shocking. Lina Bradford up early."

"Anything for my parents."

Ellis sighed. "Thanksgiving without my father. It almost doesn't seem real."

I sat up and faced Ellis. "Are you okay?"

"I'm fine," he said after a moment. "I was worried about leaving Mother, but she assured me she would be all right. She's having dinner at Vivian and Joseph's. I figured she would fare well with her best friend. Daniella went to the Bahamas with a few of her sorority sisters."

If I knew Bebe, and I did, she was not pleased that her son was with me and not her on Thanksgiving Day. I had to admit that I felt a sense of compassion toward Bebe. Her first Thanksgiving without her husband had to be difficult. He'd only been gone four months. Ellis and I rarely talked about him. I followed Ellis's lead. If he wanted to discuss him I did, if he wasn't in the mood, then I didn't mention Dr. Harlow.

On a day like today I had to be the bigger person. I'd make an effort and call Bebe later. There would be no harm in my wishing her a Happy Thanksgiving.

"How has Daniella been holding up?" I said.

"My sister wants to take a semester off from school."

"She only has a year left."

"I managed to bribe her out of it."

"With what?"

"Guess."

"Thanksgiving in the Bahamas."

"With five of her friends. They're staying at the Four Seasons Resort Great Exuma. All expenses paid."

"It'll do her good to get away."

"I told Daniella to enjoy herself, but I also expect her to use the vacation to regroup. I will not have my little sister dropping out of college."

I laid my head in Ellis's lap and peered up at him. In his father's absence, he'd really stepped up his role in Daniella's life. With thirteen years separating them, he was old enough to tell her what to do but young enough to understand what she was going through. I'd observed them together on numerous occasions and appreciated the respect they had for one another. They loved each other as siblings, but interacted more like a mentor to a mentee. If Ellis wasn't instructing her on the importance of education, he was drilling it into her that she needed to be preparing herself for business ownership. He insisted that she work at Harlow Pharmaceuticals during her summer vacations and, if she didn't resist, during her Christmas breaks. Ellis was firm with Daniella but not smothering. Dr. Harlow was the exact opposite. Daniella was his little princess and he treated her as such. He spoiled her, but she never took advantage of him. Daniella adored her father. He didn't need to be stern or cajole his daughter to do the right thing. She did what she was supposed to do just to please him. Daniella did not fit the classic mold of a spoiled rich kid.

Ellis brushed a lock of hair from my face. I put my hand over his and held it to my cheek. I loved his brown eyes. This man was going to be the father of my children. I couldn't help but wonder what kind of father Ellis would be. He had never been overly expressive when it came to his emotions. Ellis had a reserved, slightly businesslike nature. He never quite let go. What happened with me and Malik in the supermarket would have offended him to no end. I chuckled at the thought of me in the shopping cart.

"What's funny?" Ellis asked.

"Oh nothing. Just thinking about something that happened in the supermarket the other day."

"Tell me, what happened?"

"Malik and I were in the store—"

"No need to say anymore. Malik's involvement guarantees some sort of buffoonery occurred."

I wanted to argue, but I couldn't; he was kind of correct. "Take a chill pill, Ellis."

"A chill pill? What, are you borrowing some of Malik's colorful colloquialisms?"

"Do you know how old that phrase is? It was around long before I met Malik. He is not responsible for every bit of slang that passes through my lips. Haven't you *ever* used slang?"

"I try not to. It serves no purpose in business, so why start bad habits that are hard to break?"

"You act as if I said a dirty word. I said chill pill. What's so awful about that?"

"Lina, you cannot go around spouting such nonsense."

"I can't?" I pouted my lips, and seductively whispered, "Chill pill."

"Now you're being silly."

"I know a few more dirty words. You may want to cover your ears."

"Don't be ridiculous."

"Stop hatin', Ellis."

"What kind of way is that to talk to someone? Am I supposed to know what you mean?"

"Fo shizzle my nizzle."

Ellis opened his mouth to say something and then began laughing. I started to laugh with him because I knew I sounded silly. "You see, Ellis, slang can be fun," I said mockingly.

"I still think you spend too much of your time with that hoodlum."

Our feel-good moment evaporated.

"I rarely see my roommate. We're on two entirely different schedules."

"Not good enough. I want you out of there. Have you started making arrangements to vacate your apartment?"

I yawned dramatically, then closed my eyes. "I'm checking into it," I mumbled.

"Lina, I have been very patient when it comes to this matter. I expect you to get your things packed and move to Long Island with me."

"I will," I said, yawning again. "I've just been busy at work."

"Do you need me to send someone over to help box everything up?"

"Don't pressure me, Ellis. I'll take care of it."

"Then take care of it. I mean it, Lina."

I turned on my side, face away from Ellis. He was going to harass me to death until I moved in with him. I wasn't ready to move. I needed a well-thought-out argument to persuade Ellis that my living arrangement was just fine until we got married. I'd mull it over for a few days and then approach him with my rationale for staying put. The motion of the limo and the drone of CNN news lulled me to sleep.

We were crossing the Delaware Memorial Bridge when I woke up. Ellis had dozed off, head back on the headrest. Traffic was relatively light, considering it was a holiday. If we continued at this rate we'd be in Silver Spring in two hours. I reached into my bag for the paperback book I had stashed inside. It was a suspense novel Charlee had passed on to me. She gave me all types of books that she read on her frequent flights to the West Coast. I'd been meaning to start this particular one for the past few weeks.

I was engrossed in the novel when the limo exited the Beltway. We were five minutes from my parents' house. I closed the book and then stroked Ellis's arm, rousing him from his nap. He stretched, then straightened up in the seat. Ellis stared out the window at the neighborhood where I grew up. We passed block after block of modestly sized single-family homes with mani-cured lawns and two cars parked in the driveway. I missed the tree-lined streets that were wide enough for kids to play football, basketball or jump rope on a hot summer day.

The limo stopped in front of my parents' home. My mother was out on the porch, coming down the steps before we had a chance to exit the limousine. She was an older version of me— slender with a splash of freckles and reddish-brown hair. Except her hair was cut short and sprinkled with traces of salt and pep-per. She seemed so vibrant in her skinny jeans and fitted sweater. I opened the door and met her in the middle of the lawn with a big hug. She screamed when she saw my engagement ring, then grabbed me up in her arms again. Apparently my father heard the ruckus and came outside. He was shaking Ellis's hand when I pried myself from my mother's hug. Ellis and I switched. I went over and kissed my father and Ellis went to greet my mother. My daddy was a big bear, tall and solid. He was close to sixty years old and still muscular and strong. There was no sign of him get-ting soft in the middle.

After standing around for a few minutes, talking about our drive to Maryland and how happy we were to see one another, we moved our reunion inside.

Ellis stayed behind to instruct Stanley about our return trip on Sunday. He came in trying to balance our bags and the red velvet cake I forgot in the car. I took the cake carrier and my father helped

Ellis with the bags. They went upstairs to take our luggage to my old bedroom while my mother and I headed to the kitchen. The house smelled of roasting turkey and spices. I walked to the stove and peeked into my mother's pots—collard greens, black-eyed peas and rice, candied yams and string beans. Sitting on the counter was the macaroni and cheese, baked ham, roast beef, extra stuffing and sweet potato pies. She shooed me away from the food before I had a chance to sample anything.

"Everything looks delicious, Mom. I can't wait to eat. We didn't have any breakfast."

"Your father bought fresh bagels this morning. They're on the dining room table."

Ellis and my father had returned downstairs to the living room. I prepared a bagel with a tiny bit of cream cheese for Ellis and took it to him.

"Baby girl, maybe Ellis wants a cup of coffee with his bagel. I just made a pot."

"Ellis doesn't drink coffee, Daddy."

"Then get the man a glass of orange juice."

I went to get the juice and handed the glass to Ellis.

"I like your style, Mr. Bradford," Ellis said.

"Baby girl, I know you better be taking care of this man up in New York."

"Of course, I do, Daddy. Ellis is pulling your leg."

Ellis laughed. "Lina's right, sir. She's the best thing that has ever happened to me. I don't know what I'd do without her."

I pecked Ellis on the lips. "Now stop trying to start trouble, Daddy, before I call Mom in here."

"You let your mother finish cooking our dinner. I don't need her getting on my case. Why don't you go on in there and help her."

"Mom doesn't like anyone in her kitchen, not even me. She sent me in here with you two."

"Are you going to get territorial about our kitchen when you move in with me?" Ellis asked.

"It's about time you moved my baby out of Brooklyn," my father said to Ellis.

I shot Ellis a cautionary look. "Daddy, there's nothing wrong with Brooklyn."

"Maybe, but I'd feel better if you were with Ellis."

"I have been trying to convince your daughter of that for quite some time."

"Melina can be stubborn like her mother."

"I heard that," my mother shouted from the kitchen.

"I'm not being stubborn."

"Another thing she got from her mother—she disagrees with everything I say."

"That's not true, Daddy."

"See what I mean? You sure you want marry this girl?" he said, laughing.

I leaned my head on Ellis's shoulder. "He's sure. I have the ring to prove it." I held my hand out for my father to see.

My father looked at my ring and then up at Ellis. He reached his hand out and held mine in his. "This is my one and only baby, Ellis. You better treat her right."

"Mr. Bradford, I will take care of your daughter to the best of my ability. Lina will want for nothing."

"That's all a father can ask for."

We sat around the dining room table after dinner, nibbling on dessert. I pushed a piece of pie from one side of the plate to the other. As tasty as it was I couldn't manage another bite.

"Dinner was delicious, Mrs. Bradford. I haven't had a meal like that in years."

"What does your mother make on Thanksgiving?"

Ellis and I shared a laugh. My mother waited with slight confusion registered on her face.

"Mother doesn't cook. I can't remember a time when she did. She'll have her chef serve a turkey, but she stays away from Southern fare. Now when my father was living, occasionally he would demand a plate of soul food. But it was rare, and Mother resisted when she could."

"Well, anytime you want some down-home Southern cooking I'll fix it up for you."

"Thank you, I appreciate that."

"I'm just sorry we never had the opportunity to meet your father."

"You would have loved him, Mom. Dr. Harlow was a good man."

Ellis nodded his agreement. "I would like to have you and Mr. Bradford come to New York to meet my mother. I know Lina wants her mother, and her mother-in-law-to-be, to help plan the wedding."

"I was just telling my husband that we haven't been to visit Melina in a long time."

"Why don't we arrange for you to come up in a few weeks? Don't concern yourself with a hotel; you can stay at my house. I'll have Mother come in from the city and we can make a weekend of it."

Ellis called Bebe after we finished dessert to inquire about her availability. I spoke to her briefly and she was actually quite civil. By the time we hung up the phone with his mother, my parents had confirmed that they would definitely be visiting us in New York in a few weeks. I was excited that my parents would get to see my future home; I wasn't so sure I felt the same about my future mother-in-law.

CHAPTER TWENTY-SEVEN
MALIK

I heaved the cooler full of beer from the back of Terrence's truck. Lex poured charcoal into the barbeque grill while Amir and Terrence set up the table. We were at the Jets game at the Meadowlands Arena in New Jersey, getting ready to set off our after-Thanksgiving tailgate party.

The sun was shining, but it was cold outside. I was layered in a thermal shirt, turtleneck, T-shirt, a Jets sweatshirt and a scarf. I also had on gloves with the fingertips cut out. No sooner than I released the cooler did Lex open the lid and plunge his hands down in the ice in search of a Corona.

"Damn, man, it's only nine-thirty in the morning. You're starting already?" I said.

"If I wanted a sermon I would've taken my ass to church. Stop sweatin' me and hand me the bottle opener."

I tossed Lex the opener. "Don't go burning up our food because your ass is too drunk to man the grill."

We started every tailgate party off with a breakfast of steak and eggs. By game time we were on to the burgers, dogs, chicken and ribs.

"I'll cook the food before I let this fool ruin my T-bone," Terrence said.

Amir shook his head. "Yo, y'all brothers eat too much. You

stuffed your faces on Thanksgiving, ate leftovers all day Friday and Saturday, and now y'all are about to pig out on barbeque."

"Man, go blow that hot air in your horn," I said, laughing.

Lex gave me a pound. "I hear that. If Amir don't want his T-bone I'll eat it."

"Y'all Negroes are just greedy. Make my steak medium rare and my eggs over easy. Lex, you can have whatever scraps are left when I'm done," Amir said.

"Keep talking shit and you're going to be using your steak to cover your black eye."

We rolled off of that one. The digs were already underway and we had the whole day ahead of us. I hooked up the portable television to check the reception. Lex brought his TV to the last tailgate party and the picture had so much snow, we thought there was a blizzard inside the stadium. I purchased a new one because I sure as hell wasn't going to struggle to see the game on Lex's snowstorm in a box again.

The lot was filled with fellow tailgaters, grilling and setting up sterno racks filled with trays of food, laying out six-foot subs, salads, you name it. Ticketholders think they're living the life inside the stadium, sitting in their box seats, but there's nothing like the energy at a tailgate party. The real party isn't in the stadium; it's out in the parking lot.

The smell from our steaks hit me as Lex turned them over. He put a cast iron frying pan on the other side of the grill to make the eggs. Lex was our official grill master—and not just at games. At any of our barbeques or picnics you would find Lex behind the grill. He piled the sizzling meat into an aluminum pan and finished with the eggs. We lined up at the table, grabbing paper plates and plastic forks and knives for our breakfast.

"Dru needs to learn how to make a steak from you," Terrence said.

Lex threw a piece of meat in his mouth. "You mean to tell me you're marrying a woman that can't cook?"

"Don't start talking about my girl," Terrence said, pointing his plastic knife at Lex. "She does all right. But sometimes the food is a little bland."

"You better introduce Dru to Adobo—the all-purpose seasoning," I said laughing, almost choking on my steak.

"And when was the last time you had a woman cook for your ass?" Terrence said.

"I have two women cooking for me."

Amir set his plate down. "What two women do you have?"

"That just goes to show you that I don't need no horn to seduce a woman into making me a meal."

"I don't *need* it either, but my sax gets me a hell of a lot of perks that you ain't getting."

Lex leaned forward in his chair. "I want you to get back to your brother's question. What two chicks you got?"

I grabbed a beer from the cooler and took my time opening it. I took a long swallow, making them wait. "I told you all about Kai. Baby doll is doing everything in her power to get Big Daddy to keep her company, including cooking."

"So a brother is getting a little nookie and a hot meal to go with it," Lex said.

They cracked up laughing.

"I always gets mine. That ain't nothing new."

"You're stalling, brotha," Terrence said. "Who's the other woman?"

"Mel," I said. "Mel cooks for me all the time."

"Awwwww man," they yelled in unison.

"You ain't hittin' that," Lex said.

"I didn't say I was. I said I have two women cooking for me— and I do."

"But you wish you were getting a piece of that sweetness, don't you?" Amir said.

"C'mon, man. Mel and I don't get down like that."

"You've never pushed up on that?"

"No."

"Malik, we got the same mother. You can't lie to me." Amir was in hysterics. "I've known you your entire life. I remember when you were hitting on girls in kindergarten. You can't help yourself. Tell the truth. You've never peeped shorty coming out the shower or peeked through her keyhole while she was getting dressed?"

"Nah, man. I respect Mel."

Lex shook his head in disbelief. "I know your ass is lying. Your roommate is too fine for you to be frontin' on the booty."

"Mel's fine, but she's not my type. I like 'em wild like Kai. No inhibitions and always willing to please."

"Kai's all that?"

I nodded. "And some."

Kai was a bad specimen. I usually flaunted my women around the crew, we all did, sort of like a who-has-the-baddest-chick competition. For some reason, I didn't want to bring Kai around—probably because I worked with her. I wanted to keep my personal life private from my colleagues. I lived one way and worked another. It was a way to guarantee that a person never really got to know me. They saw the "me" that I wanted to portray, not the "me" that I really was. At this point, Kai had limited access to a brother. The last thing I needed was for her to see me clowning with my boys, then go back to the office with a negative impression of me, thinking I wasn't serious enough to perform my job. If she had showed up to go to Terrence and Dru's engagement party it would have been all right because my boys were all on their best behavior. But for her to be with us when were just sitting around shooting the shit, that would've been another story. I had already disregarded some of my basic rules by hanging out with Kai and her friends on Thanksgiving night.

After I had the obligatory turkey dinner with my family, I scooped Kai up and drove her to Justine and Ira's home in Scarsdale. Justine met us at the door in a low-cut shirt with cleavage spilling out the top. I moved to shake her hand and she pulled me into a hug, rubbing her breasts against my chest. I pulled away and she winked at me. Kai didn't catch the exchange because she had already gone into the house. Ira was in their living room in a smoking jacket with a cigar clenched between his teeth. He sat in his chair ensconced in a cloud of smoke. He explained that he was only allowed to enjoy his Cubans on special occasions and intended to smoke all night long. Kai told me that Ira was a successful television producer—somehow Justine managed to slip his pants off and start wearing them herself. Kai and I stayed a few hours and had a couple of drinks. We consumed Ira's good scotch and talked about advertising and product placement in television and movies. Ira was an all right guy. He was content as long as he had his cigars and, if allowed, some food. I felt sorry for him, though, as his wife salaciously eyed me throughout the evening. When Kai and I were leaving, Justine hugged me a little too long and a little too tight. Later that night, I found her cell phone number in my blazer pocket.

More laughter snapped me out of my reverie. Lex was running his mouth about making a Kai and Melina sandwich—they could be the bread and he'd provide the meat.

"Chill out, man," I said.

Terrence put his hand on Lex's shoulder before he could respond.

"I think the pre-show is about to start. Turn up the volume on the TV."

We crowded around the little television, but we weren't listening. We conducted our own pre-show commentary on the teams and players. I kept an eye on the game once it started, but I mostly drank beer and talked shit with my boys. The Jets went into the fourth quarter with a twenty-point lead and on to win the game, as expected.

I drove home thinking about how I'd never had a problem popping shit about women with my boys, but today was different. I didn't want Kai or Melina disrespected. These women were off limits. No tasteless jokes. As far as I was concerned, they deserved better than that.

CHAPTER TWENTY-EIGHT
MELINA

Malik wandered into the kitchen and poured himself a glass of orange juice. I hadn't seen him all week, not even a glimpse of him since returning from Maryland. I diced apples for apple cinnamon pancakes.

Malik snatched an apple wedge from the cutting board. "Pancakes. Sausage. Grits. Eggs. What, are you cooking for an army?"

"Charlee and Giselle are coming over for brunch."

"Seems like a lot of food for your girls. I'm willing to stick around and help you eat all of this, so you don't waste it."

"I bet you are. Where are you off to anyway?"

"Kai needs me to go with her to get her car serviced."

"Oh, then you better not keep her waiting." I chopped into an apple and sent half of it flying off the cutting board.

Malik bent down to retrieve the apple from the floor. He tossed it in the garbage and then lingered in the doorway for a moment. "I'll see you later, Mel."

"All right," I said without looking up from what I was doing.

The apartment door closed behind Malik and I immediately started mumbling to myself. "All of a sudden he's all wrapped up in Kai. Meanwhile, I'm taking messages all week from his chicks that couldn't reach him on his cell phone because he's wrapped up somewhere with Kai. Please. I'm not his damn secretary."

"I know you're not my secretary."

I shrieked, dropping the knife onto the counter. "Oh, my God, I thought you left," I said, with my hand on my chest, trying to calm my frantically beating heart.

"You heard me close the closet door. So what's the problem?"

"What's the problem?" I repeated. "I'm…I'm just tired of taking messages for you, that's all."

Malik grimaced at me. "I barely get calls on this phone. But let's skip the debate and pretend you won. You want me to get my own phone?"

"It would be nice."

"Done. Anything else?"

"No, that's it."

"Cool."

The buzzer rang and Malik pressed the button to open the front door. "I'll leave the door open for your girls."

He turned and left the kitchen. I rinsed my hands at the sink. Charlee and Giselle called out to me as they came in the door. I went to greet them in the living room.

"Malik damn near knocked us over on his way out," Charlee said. "You know Malik is a trip."

"What was he so upset about?" Giselle asked, rubbing her stomach.

I touched her round belly and smiled. "Who cares. Let's talk about you and how cute you look pregnant."

Giselle had on a fitted crochet sweater with a pair of faded jeans and some bad high-heel suede boots.

"Do I also look like my back is aching? Because it is."

Charlee rolled her eyes. "Stop complaining and enjoy the ride."

I laughed. "I wouldn't have phrased it that way, but I agree. You're four months pregnant and you're beautiful. You haven't gained an ounce anywhere other than your stomach. What more could you ask for?"

Giselle's smile dimmed. "A lot, but I won't go there. What's to eat? You know you have to keep me and my baby well-fed."

I led them into the kitchen and they sat at the table. I placed fruit salads in front of each of them.

Charlee frowned. "I ain't pregnant. Give lil mama the fruit salad. I'll wait for the real food." She pushed her bowl in front of Giselle.

"Everything will be done in a minute."

"Good because I'm starving. Last night, the finest man I have ever met, sexed me down something proper."

"Aren't you getting a little old for one-night stands?" I asked.

Charlee looked at Giselle and Giselle looked at me. "You're never too old," Giselle said.

They laughed a laugh that said they were in total agreement. I shook my head and continued to pour perfect circles of pancake batter onto the griddle.

"You are such a Pollyanna," Charlee said with a dismissive wave. She turned to her partner in crime and continued her story. "I was at Club Fiasco last night for an album release party for one of my groups and I peeped this dude the minute I walked into the club. He was a dead ringer for Boris Kodjoe. You know I couldn't resist giving him one of my sexy smiles when I strolled by him. I didn't turn around to see if he was scoping me because I knew he had to be. About a half an hour later I was chilling in the lounge area and a waitress brings over a bottle of champagne, a bottle of Patron and a bottle of Remy VSOP. She points to homeboy sitting at the bar and says he wants to buy me a drink and if his selections don't entice me, let her know, and she'll bring me my drink of choice. I told her the champagne was fine and she could take the Patrón and Remy back with her. She tells me he instructed that after I made my selection, the other two bottles were for my friends. I told her to invite him over to have a taste with me."

I flipped the pancakes over and they were a tad past golden. "Girl, I got so caught up in your story I'm over here burning breakfast."

Giselle shushed me like we were in a movie theater. "Go ahead, Charlee."

"So he joined me on the sofa and introduced himself as Torrey Biggs. He's a sports agent. I was relieved he wasn't in the music industry. Y'all know how I hate dealing with men in the industry—always wanting to talk business and always trying to see what I can do for them. Anyway, Torrey and I got acquainted over a bottle of champagne and a couple of dances, then made our way to the W Hotel." Charlee fanned herself with her napkin. "What happened in that hotel room is too raunchy to divulge."

"You better spill it," Giselle said.

"If you insist," Charlee said, giggling. I put a platter of pancakes on the table and sat down to listen. "Torrey had my panties around my ankles, and his face buried in my pussy, before the door closed behind us. I tore his shirt trying to undo his buttons. We were sprawled across the bed in the sixty-nine position, his tongue all in my pussy and my mouth wrapped around his big dick—and I mean *big*. His last name ain't no lie. Girls, he flipped me over and fucked me from the back so hard I was wailing like a banshee. The entire floor had to hear me. And that was only the first session. We fucked two more times."

"I hope you used a condom," I said.

"Shut up, Pollyanna. You can ruin a wet dream. Yes, we used a condom and I'm on the pill. Now what do you have to say?"

"Nothing," I mumbled.

Giselle laughed. "I wish it was me getting done by a Boris look-alike. Keep the stories coming, Charlee. I'll live vicariously through you while this little load has me out of commission. Lord knows Melina doesn't have any exciting tales."

"I'm sure nothing I do would sound exciting to you tramps." Their snickering filled the kitchen while I set the rest of the food on the table. "Do you think you can stop laughing long enough to bless the food?"

We bowed our heads and gave thanks. Giselle was sliding pancakes onto her plate before the word "amen" left our lips. "Smells good, Melina."

"Eat up. I want my god baby to be nice and healthy."

"You must want me to turn into a blimp. If I keep eating like this I won't be able to fit anything."

"Speaking of fitting, what are you guys doing next weekend?"

"I don't have any plans," Charlee said.

"I may be on call at the hospital, but I'm not sure, why?"

"I want you to come dress shopping with me."

"Have you picked a wedding date already?" Giselle asked.

"I wouldn't quite say that, but the wedding will be in April."

"April? I'm due the first week of May. I'll be as big as a house."

"You'll be beautiful," I said.

Charlee narrowed her eyes at me. "That's less than six months away. What's the rush?"

"It's a long story."

"Give us the short version," Charlee demanded.

"The Harlows don't like long engagements."

"And you're okay with this?"

"I'll have a wedding planner doing the majority of the work."

"I meant are you okay with the Harlows calling the shots?"

"No, I'm not, but I don't feel as if I have a choice."

"So, what, you're their puppet now? The Harlows are pulling your strings and you have no control?"

Giselle stopped eating and looked at Charlee with wide eyes. "I'm not anyone's puppet."

"But you're letting the Harlows dictate what you should do."

"Bebe is a little difficult to deal with and sometimes it's just easier to go along with her."

Charlee sucked her teeth. "You can let them run you if you want, but I know one thing, it wouldn't be me."

"You need to discuss this with Ellis. Address the problem before you marry him or it will only get worse," Giselle said.

"It can't get any worse than it already is."

CHAPTER TWENTY-NINE
MALIK

K ai wheeled her car out of the service station. I sat in the passenger seat, keeping an eye the road. Her driving wasn't too bad, but she got easily distracted while talking. The driver in the car next to us blew his horn as Kai strayed into his lane. I just shook my head. She went on and on about how much she loved the holidays and couldn't wait until Christmas. I was only half-listening when I caught the end of her question.

"So will you?" she asked.

"Will I what?" I said, diverting my attention to her.

"Come with me to pick out a Christmas tree."

"When?"

Kai looked annoyed. "Were you listening to anything I said, Malik?"

"Of course, I was, but I was also concentrating on your driving, since you didn't seem too preoccupied with it."

Kai took a playful swipe at my arm. "I said that I wanted to get my tree today and wondered if you wouldn't mind going with me. I'll need help getting it up to my apartment."

She had me just where she wanted me. My car was parked at her apartment and if I wanted to go my own way, I couldn't. What choice did that leave me? I relented. "I don't mind."

Kai flashed a cryptic smile that I was apprehensive to interpret.

It probably resembled how a spider must look at a fly caught in its web. Was Kai intricately spinning a web from which she didn't want me to escape? I immediately unraveled that thought. I was not one to get entangled in anyone's traps. Never have. Never will. Kai was on another level, but she was still a woman, and I knew women. Kai was used to men doing what she said, when she said it. She knew how to use her assets to get what she wanted. And, yeah, at that moment I was indulging her. But Kai shouldn't have underestimated Malik Denton.

We turned into the parking lot where the Christmas trees were being sold. Kai and I stepped out of the car and joined the people milling around the aisles, checking out the various trees.

"What size tree do you want?" I asked.

Kai touched the branches on a spruce tree in front of her. "I don't know but not too big or too small. Maybe a six-foot. Don't worry; you'll be able to carry it," she teased.

"Me, worried? I think you know by now that I can lift, flip and carry when necessary. I handle my business."

Kai laughed. "You always manage to make everything about sex."

"Who mentioned sex? I was just letting you know that I won't have a problem getting your tree into your apartment. I guess we know where your mind is."

"Nice try, Malik, but I got your message loud and clear. I'm starting to think you have a one-track mind."

"I thought that's what you liked about me," I said, smiling.

"Oh, I do. But sometimes it's good to know that there's more to it than that."

I kept walking down the aisle, inspecting the trees. So she was going to take it there. I guessed the topic of conversation came along with the activity. We were shopping for Christmas trees together. A very couple-like thing to do. It was obvious that Kai would start hinting at what she wanted from me. She wanted more. Until she decided to broach the subject head-on, I wouldn't either. Kai was an intelligent, articulate woman. If she wanted to talk about what was going on with us, then she would. I could tell that she was only feeling me out at the moment. She wanted to gauge my reactions, wanted to see if I would take her bait and delve into a serious relationship discussion. Kai didn't know that I wasn't fond of fishing and unless she asked a direct question, then she shouldn't expect a direct answer.

The attendants secured the tree to the roof of Kai's car. We drove back to her place in relative silence, with the exception of the radio. She didn't have much to say after her comment about my one-track mind.

I moved to change the station. "Do you mind?"

She shook her head to signify she didn't. It was apparent she wasn't talking to me and I decided that I would cut our day short. I would get her tree upstairs, then take my leave. Hopefully it wasn't too late to catch up with the fellas.

When we arrived at her place, I told her to head upstairs; I would untie the tree and bring it up. She mumbled something and then briskly walked into the building. I took my time removing the tree from the car. The doorman met me out front, guided me inside the building and directed me to the service elevator. The service elevator crept slowly to the eighth floor. The doors opened, letting me out on the opposite end of the hallway from the main elevator. I was few a few doors down from Kai's apartment. She left the door ajar for me.

She was leafing through her mail when I entered. "Can you set it up in the stand over in the corner?"

This time I was the one to silently nod. I set the tree in the stand and removed the cord that bound the branches.

Kai had a box full of ornaments on top of the coffee table. She started rifling through the box, not acknowledging my presence.

I clapped my hands together. "All right, Kai, I'm gonna get out of here and let you decorate your tree."

She looked up at me. "Don't leave, Malik." I stood in place. She came over to me and pulled me toward the couch. "Please."

"What's wrong with you?"

"Nothing's wrong."

I cocked my head to the side. "Really?"

Kai unwrapped my scarf, slinging it over her arm. "I haven't said much since we picked the tree, but I'm cool. Have a seat. Do you want a beer?"

And so it begins, I thought. I sat down on the couch, eyeing her wearily. "Okay. I'll have one."

Kai returned with my beer and a better attitude. She chatted easily while she strung lights on the tree. I spent the rest of the day slouched on her sofa, drinking Heineken and suffering through her decorating the damn thing. Kai cooed over each ornament and then dangled it in front of me before she put it on the tree. I thought my lack of response made it obvious I didn't share her enthusiasm for Christmas bulbs, but she kept showing me anyway.

I must have dozed off because when I opened my eyes, Kai was on her knees in front of me, undoing my belt. She had candles burning in the living room and Ledisi playing softly through her Bose system. Through partially opened eyelids, I could still appreciate what I saw. Kai wore a pair of stilettos and nothing else. I let her remove my clothes and lead me into her bedroom. More candles were burning, illuminating her sexy sanctuary. She crawled onto the bed, pulling me with her. She reached over to the night table and retrieved a pair of handcuffs.

I asked, "Are those for you?"

She smiled at me, pressed her fingers to my lips, requesting my silence, and then gently pushed me back against the pillows. She slipped a silk scarf from behind the pillows and blindfolded me. I was in total darkness, dick standing at attention, impatiently waiting for the action to jump off.

Kai leaned over me, her breasts touching my chest. She raised my right arm over my head. I felt the handcuff enclose my wrist, then heard it click closed. She roughly yanked my left wrist, raising my hand toward the other. She handcuffed me to the wrought-iron headboard.

"Somebody's feeling freaky tonight," I said.

She didn't answer me. I felt her move off the bed. I heard her footsteps cross the carpet toward the bedroom door. I called out, "Kai?"

Ledisi's mellow voice filled the room. Kai must have turned on the speakers near her bed. The deep bass line vibrated through the headboard. I felt movement on the mattress. I sensed Kai hovering close to me.

A warm, thick substance trickled down my chest to my stomach. The sudden sensation made me shiver. Kai straddled me. She licked my earlobe, down my neck, then slowly licked my chest. She moaned as she traced her tongue in what she drizzled on me. She slid her breasts against my chest and then rubbed one of them against my lips. I sucked her nipple into my mouth. Warm honey. I sucked hard, licking all of the sweetness from her flesh. Kai drew her nipple out of my mouth. She resumed her exploration downward…mouth on my stomach…tongue in my bellybutton. She grabbed my stiff dick and sucked its length into her mouth. She worked her mouth and hands like a professional, moaning at the same time. I wanted to see her at work, wanted to grab the back of her head to control her flow. I tugged at the handcuffs, but they were secure. Kai licked and sucked me until I couldn't hold it in any longer. I exploded in her mouth.

Kai removed the blindfold. I squinted at her and she smiled at me. The same smile she gave me earlier in the car.

I tugged my arms. The handcuffs clanked on the headboard. Trapped just like a fly. "Can you unlock these, please?"

She went over to her dresser to retrieve the key, then released me from my bondage. I rubbed my wrists. My arms were beginning to tingle from being suspended in one position for so long.

Kai went into her adjoining bathroom and turned on the shower. I lay on the bed with Ledisi lulling me into a state of complete relaxation. When Kai finally returned, she was fresh and clean, wearing a silky pajama shirt. I got up and went into the bathroom to wash the sticky honey residue from my body. I stood under the hot, streaming water, realizing that Kai had just freaked me. No words. No kisses. No control. Just sex. Kai wanted to make a statement.

I dried off and wrapped the towel around my waist. I stepped back into the bedroom and Kai was under the sheets. I lay on top of the blanket and folded my hands across my chest. I looked over at Kai, sound asleep. She just had me how she wanted me— on her own terms.

CHAPTER THIRTY
MALIK

I hung up the phone with Terrence and threw on my clothes. He was stopping by to pick up a pair of football tickets. I was supposed to drop them off to him the day before, but I didn't leave Kai's until the wee hours. I left there aggravated with myself for getting sucked into her holiday hustle and freaky shuffle.

I checked the fridge for beer. Three bottles. I couldn't have my boy over without a case of Heineken in the house. I had to make a quick run to the store. I knocked on Melina's bedroom door. She answered me through the closed door. I told her I was going out for a few minutes and asked her to listen out for Terrence.

I walked four blocks to the corner bodega. I heard muffled salsa music as I approached the store. I stepped through the doorway and bumped into Cinnamon, almost sending her bag toppling to the floor.

Her eyes lit up when she saw me. "Hey, stranger."

I kissed her on the cheek. "How you doin', Cinnamon?"

"I've been doing fine. Just wondering why you haven't called me."

I led her away from the door, away from the path of traffic. "I've called. A few times. You never answer your phone."

Cinnamon twisted her lips. "We both know that isn't true."

"The truth is," I took Cinnamon's hand in mine, "I've been wondering why you haven't hollered at me."

"I left a message with your roommate last week."

"See there. You can't blame me for not returning your call when I never received the message. Mel is funny about telling me who called and when."

"You need to tell your roommate to learn how to deliver messages."

"I'll speak to her about it." Situation successfully flipped.

Cinnamon's eyes softened. She reached up and stroked my chin. "I expect to hear from you soon."

"You will."

"I'd like to believe you, but for some reason, I just don't." She kissed my lips and then turned to leave the store.

I pulled her back to me and kissed her for real. Deep. Intense. The kind of kiss that she would feel from her head to her toes. I knew I wasn't planning on seeing Cinnamon anytime soon, if ever again, and I wanted her last impression of me to be better than what I had given.

Cinnamon drew away from me with a dreamy look in her eyes, lips parted. She blinked a couple of times, then cleared her throat. "If only you meant that. See you around, Malik."

Cinnamon left me in the store, my mouth agape. A part of me wanted to follow her out of the bodega and back to her place, but I knew that was a bad idea. That was my ego thinking for me. My pride trying to take over. I understood what had just happened with Cinnamon, and even though I didn't want to be involved with her anymore, I wasn't prepared for her to not want to be with me.

I laughed to myself—I was trippin'. I was through with Cinnamon, not the other way around. I grabbed two six-packs from the refrigerator, paid up front at the register, and then hurried back down the street.

I learned a long time ago, when it comes to relationships, keep it casual and no one gets hurt. I don't allow myself to be in a position to be dumped by anyone. Immediately after my breakup with Angelique, I thought we'd get back together. I waited for weeks for her to call me, and when I couldn't stand it anymore, I broke down and called her. I waited for weeks for her to return my call. I spent many sleepless nights waiting for the phone to ring. Waiting to hear her voice. Just waiting. Always waiting.

There were a lot of women that paid for the heartache and despair I was left with after Angelique. I still feel bad about the things I did to those women; it wasn't right. But that was before I had a chance to work past the anger, to get over the hurt. It was before I realized that I needed to tell them relationships weren't for me. I started to be honest from the beginning. Those that could hang, would hang. Those that couldn't, wouldn't. No one could accuse me of being a dog or unfaithful because I didn't make commitments. I liked it that way, and so far, I was doing a damn good job of keeping it that way.

Melina was in the living room fluffing the pillows on the couch when I entered the apartment. She was wearing a pair of cut-off shorts, a tank top and had a scarf tied around her head. She bent over to pick up a pillow that had fallen to the floor.

"Not that I don't appreciate the view, but maybe you shouldn't bend over like that."

"You see plenty of ass on a regular. I'm sure the bit of cheek I'm flashing isn't doing anything for you," she said with her back to me, not bothering to look up from her task.

"What if it was?"

Melina stood up straight and turned around. "I'd say you better call Kai."

I cracked a smile and changed the subject. "Terrence will be here in a minute. Do you want to be seen walking around here resembling the maid or are you getting dressed?"

She brushed past me and went into her room. I followed her down the hall. Her clothes were laid out on the bed.

"You going out?" I asked.

"I thought I would give you and your company some privacy."

I laughed. "Terrence and I don't need privacy. He's picking up some tickets and probably staying for a beer or two. You should stick around. Have a beer with us."

"No, that's okay. You guys enjoy yourselves."

"One beer won't kill you. Do you have plans?"

"Not really."

"So chill with us. But please don't wear those shorts."

"All right, let me get dressed." She pushed me out of her room. "I'll be out in a minute."

Melina wandered into the living room an hour later. What she was doing in her room for that long I couldn't imagine. She was wearing a pair of fitted sweats, with a hole in the knee, and an oversized sweatshirt. Her hair was pulled back in a ponytail, curls bouncing at the ends. She came in sporting a bright smile that widened when she saw Dru sitting on the couch next to Terrence.

Dru stood up and the two women hugged as if they were old friends. The gabbing commenced at the speed of light. I caught every other word as they covered multiple subjects within seconds.

Terrence cleared his throat with a dramatic flair, interrupting their chatter. "Hey, Melina."

"I'm sorry, Terrence. It's good to see you," Melina said, barely pausing her conversation with Dru. She went over to him, kissed his cheek and then led Dru to the kitchen.

I shrugged at my boy. "You know how women are. Either they

love or hate each other from the very beginning. Apparently these two hit it off at your engagement party, which is surprising. Mel can be standoffish."

"I heard that," Melina said, entering the room, holding a beer.

She propped herself on the couch next to me. Dru came in with a bowl of potato chips and placed them in front of us on the coffee table.

"Terrence, I know Malik has probably made you think I'm some sort of anti-social tyrant, but that isn't true. I'll admit I'm not as outgoing as he is, but I'm far from introverted."

"So the tyrant part is true?" I said, jokingly.

Melina was about to respond, but Terrence cut her off. "I know better than to believe anything Malik says, but for the record, he has nothing but good things to say about you."

Melina nodded and sipped her beer from the bottle. I eyed her for a moment, perplexed. Extremely casual clothes—for her—with company in the house, drinking beer without a glass, and chatting it up with a woman she hardly knew. Yet she seemed so comfortable. Not the usual uptight version of the woman I was used to having around. She motioned to me with a wide-eyed expression.

I looked over at Terrence and Dru; they were staring at me, too. "Did you say something to me?" I asked.

The three of them burst into laughter.

It was Terrence who enlightened me. "Yeah, man, I said can I get another beer or do you plan to stare at—"

"Coming right up." I cut him off before he could finish. "Dru, are you set? Can I get you something else?"

Dru looked quizzically at me and then glanced at Melina. "No, thank you," she said, smiling. "Melina, we really need to get together for lunch and some girl talk real soon. I'll call you this week to set it up."

Dru gave me a playful wink as I got up to get Terrence his beer. I didn't know what it meant, but I smiled just the same.

I hadn't seen or spoken to Kai since the night she'd cuffed and sucked me. The joke I made while we shopped for her Christmas tree triggered an interesting response. She tried to prove a point. On Monday, I was glad we managed to stay out of each other's way. I had a lot of work anyway. Tuesday, I thought she'd pop into my office to play a little cat and mouse, but that never happened. By Wednesday, when I heard her having a conversation with a colleague right outside of my office door, I started to get annoyed. I was going to wait and see how far she'd take things. I'd been accused of having a one-track mind many times—that didn't bother me—but hearing it from Kai, rubbed me the wrong way. Kai wielded her sex appeal with authority and used it however and whenever she pleased. I thought that was the one area I wouldn't need to be concerned about with her. If anyone could identify with how I felt about sex and relationships, it should've been Kai. I was surprised when she alluded to wanting something more, especially her roundabout way of doing it.

At noon, I grabbed my briefcase to head out to a meeting. The Sphere account had been taking up a significant amount of my time. While preparing for the final presentation, I had rescheduled a few client appointments and planned to spend the rest of the week off-site.

I was pitching new concepts this week. I was energized. This was all practice for when I opened my own agency. I had enough of a reputation in the industry that I was optimistic I'd be able to secure clients within the first few months, but I wanted the large accounts. That would take a hell of a lot of work and I was ready to roll up my sleeves to make it happen. I hailed a cab and jetted off for my string of afternoon meetings.

I dragged myself through the door at close to ten that night. I ended up having drinks with one of my clients and apparently he didn't want to go home to his waiting family. After three hours of listening to him complain about his kids' tuition and wife's spending habits I told him I had an early meeting in the morning and needed to do some final preparations. I left him sitting at the bar, ordering another drink.

Melina was in the bathroom belting out an Esperanza Spalding tune. Her voice was sultry and filled with passion. I lurked outside the door, listening to her sing about falling in love. She sounded like a woman in love. The stuffed-shirt obviously made her happy. I didn't know why I was so hard on her about her relationship with Ellis. The brother, if I could even call him that, irked me. He wore his wealth like a badge of honor and his attitude stunk. I didn't accept being treated like I was less than anyone, especially not by another brother. I contradicted everything he said just to prove that others have thoughts and opinions and his word was not the gospel. I wondered about Melina's motives for being with a man like Ellis. Was it the money that made her want to be with him? He was all business, no amusement, at least from what I could see. She had basically admitted that the brother was whack in the sack. Other than the money, what did he have going for him?

The door to the bathroom opened. I hadn't noticed that Melina had turned off the shower. She jumped and abruptly stopped singing when she saw me standing outside the bathroom. Her towel slipped, exposing one of her breasts. Her skin glistened. I didn't move. I was a spectator while she clumsily clutched the dangling end of her towel. I absentmindedly reached to help her. She turned away, causing my hand to brush against the side of her barely covered breast.

Her eyes widened. "Malik, what are you doing?"

"Sorry, Mel. I was just...I was trying to help," I stammered.

She tucked her towel and shook her head. "I didn't even know you were here. What were you doing?"

"I just got home; I wasn't doing anything. I was heading to my room. Sorry, again."

I left her standing in the hallway and went into my room, closing the door behind me. I loosened my tie and sat on the edge of my bed. I replayed what had just happened. I reclined back on the bed. Melina was beautiful. Her golden skin was smooth to the touch. Her breasts so full and soft. I imagined what the rest of her body looked like underneath that towel and began to stiffen. I shook my head and sat up. I shouldn't have been thinking about Melina that way. She must have thought I was crazy, standing in the hallway like some sort of stalker. I coaxed my hardhead down and then continued to undress.

I was about to step out of my boxers when I heard a light tap on the door. "It's open."

Melina slowly opened the door and stepped into my room. She had on a long tee that came to her knees, fuzzy slippers and a ponytail perched on the top of her head. I was standing next to my bed, bare-chested. She gave me a once-over and it looked like her face got a little red.

"What's up?" I asked, breaking the silence.

She cleared her throat. "I just wanted to let you know I'll be at Ellis's for the rest of the week. I'll be back on Sunday."

"Thanks for telling me." I waited, puzzled. "Is that it?"

She looked me up and down again. "Oh, no, also the repairman is coming to fix the dishwasher tomorrow evening around seven. Do you think you can meet him or should I reschedule?"

I rubbed my hand across my chest while I thought about it. Melina's eyes followed my hand. I smiled. "I'll do whatever you need me to do."

She opened her mouth, closed it, then shook her head. She went to the door and spoke over her shoulder. "Good night, Malik."

She shut the door before I could respond, but I was sure I caught a glimpse of a smile on her face as it closed.

CHAPTER THIRTY-ONE
MELINA

When I entered the dining room, Ellis was already at the table, reading the paper. His eggs and bacon were half-eaten, the plate pushed aside. I kissed his forehead and then took a seat next to him, where my slice of toast and glass of grapefruit juice sat waiting for me. Sunlight streamed into the room, little rainbows glittered across the table from the chandelier.

He folded his paper and rested it beside his neglected breakfast. "So what time do you expect to be finished with your shopping today?"

I was meeting Charlee and Giselle at a wedding boutique in Manhasset to begin the search for my dress.

I took a bite of my toast. "I expect we'll be out most of the afternoon. Maybe we'll grab a little lunch or go get massages. We should be back no later than four or so."

"That's perfect. Mother is planning to come by, so I figured she could meet your bridesmaids and maybe join us for dinner."

I almost choked on my juice. "I didn't realize that Bebe was coming today."

"She called this morning. When I mentioned that you and the girls were going dress shopping, she thought it would be a great opportunity to do a little wedding planning and to meet your bridal party."

He just didn't get it. I certainly didn't want his mother involved in the planning and if I wanted her to meet my bridal party, then I would have arranged it. I wasn't aiming for a fight, but Ellis needed to get a clue.

"Sweetheart, I planned this day to spend a bit of quality time with my friends and to find the perfect dress. And after our day of shopping, I thought it would be nice if you and I had them over for an intimate dinner." I realized I sounded patronizing, but I couldn't help it. "I wasn't planning on introducing my friends to your mother today."

"You know you like to procrastinate, Lina. Mother wants to know who will be participating in the wedding so that she can plan accordingly."

I firmly set my glass down, causing a bit of juice to splash onto the table. "Plan what, Ellis? What does your mother need to plan that makes meeting my friends a necessity?"

"Maybe a better question is what have *you* planned? Our wedding is taking place in less than six months. What have you done so far?"

"Are you serious? This is *our* wedding. Yours and mine. Not Bebe's, not anyone else's. Do you understand that?"

"My mother is only trying to ensure that we'll have a Harlow wedding in April."

I shook my head. "Oh, I see. The Harlows don't trust that I can plan a wedding suitable to the Harlow standards. Is that it, Ellison? You and your mother think I can't plan my own wedding?"

"Now you're being ridiculous, Lina."

Typical Ellis. He discounts my feelings and then tries to convince me that I'm misreading a situation. "I'm being ridiculous? Anytime I bring up your mother, then I'm ridiculous."

"Yes, you are. My mother has nothing but time on her hands. So what she wants to help you with the wedding? You should be grateful. Do you know how many women wish they had someone to do what my mother is offering to do for you?"

"You mean for *us*, don't you?"

"Don't play semantics with me, Melina. Mother has been nothing but helpful to *both* of us. She knows how busy we are with work and has made our wedding her top priority. She's booked the church, arranged for the same minister that christened me to perform our nuptials, and I know she wanted to tell you herself, but I think she may have found the perfect location for our reception."

I narrowed my eyes at him. "Do you hear yourself? What makes you think I wanted your mother to do *any* of that? Did it ever cross your mind that I wanted to pick my own wedding date and find the perfect church and location for the reception? Did it?"

Ellis leaned forward and pointed at me. "Fine, Melina. You can tell Mother this evening about *all* the arrangements you've made thus far and that she can cancel what she's done." He sat back and tapped his temple as if just remembering something. "Oh yeah, you don't have any arrangements to share because you haven't done anything." He leaned forward again, elbows on the table, fingers laced. "My suggestion to you is that you graciously accept the help that Mother is offering and get involved before there's nothing left to plan."

Ellis stood, appraising me for a moment before kissing my forehead. I opened my mouth to respond and he shook his head. "I'll see you and the girls at four. Have fun shopping."

I watched him leave the room, wondering whether I could stand being married to a man and his mother.

Charlee sipped on champagne in the main salon while I changed into the next dress. Giselle was inside the fitting room with me, buttoning the row of buttons on the back of the dress.

No sooner than I stepped out of my fitting room did Charlee comment, "Too traditional. I don't like it."

"I like it," Giselle chirped.

"You like all of that poof and flounce? Turn around, Melina."

I did a slow spin, so she could see the entire dress.

Giselle straightened out the train. "The detail is exquisite. Do you see the beadwork?"

"Do you see how the back makes it look like she has a beach ball for an ass? I don't like it. My girl is too fly for this outdated frock."

I laughed. "All right, calm down. I still have plenty more to try on and I won't be picking anything until my mother gets here in a couple of weeks to give her input."

I slipped back into the fitting room with Giselle in tow.

Charlee called out, "I think you need something sexier. Form-fitting. Low-cut. Sexy."

"Of course, you do," I said, stepping into the next dress. "I think I may want the flounce that you're not so fond of. I happen to like it."

I always imagined that I would look like a fairy-tale princess on my wedding day, wearing a beautiful gown with a fitted-bodice and a full, flowing skirt. My hair would be done in a glorious up-do with curling tendrils to frame my face. No veil but an ornate headpiece reminiscent of a lavish, diamond-filled tiara. So far, we hadn't come across that perfect dress yet. Although this was only the first dress shop and my first day searching, I hoped I'd be lucky and find a dress quickly. I should have known I'd have no such luck.

I modeled the next dress. It was a classic A-line dress, no beading, very simple. Definitely didn't fit what I had in mind. Surprisingly, Charlee liked it. Giselle didn't. About ten dresses later, with no consensus, we decided to wrap up our shopping for the day. I loved the input from my girls, but I looked forward to shopping with Terrence's fiancée, Dru. We had spoken during the week and made arrangements to meet next weekend. It would be nice to have the perspective of another future bride. I was certain that my outing with Dru would be more easygoing and involve less debate and conflict.

Giselle and Charlee followed me in their car to the Deja Spa. After my morning with Ellis, and the impending evening with Bebe, I needed a massage. Giselle opted for a facial and a manicure instead. She said she wasn't in the mood to have a stranger rubbing on her and her unborn baby. It was obvious her hormones had gotten the best of her because no one loved to be pampered as much as she did.

Soft jazz music played throughout the spa. We were greeted by three smiling technicians, ready to cater to our every whim. Charlee and I were escorted to the changing room to disrobe while Giselle headed off for her manicure.

I stepped inside one of the changing stalls and drew the curtain. Charlee was in the stall next to me, humming along with the song piping through the speakers.

I undressed, wrapped the plush robe around me and exited my stall. I took off my bracelet and slipped it inside my purse, then placed the purse in a locker along with my clothing. I reclined on the overstuffed sofa in the waiting area, flipping through the pages of *Vanity Fair*.

Charlee glided out of the changing room and plopped down on the opposite end of the sofa. "I hope I get a man. I don't like for women to massage me. I want a strong-fingered cutie to dig in to my limbs."

I rolled my eyes. "I guess I should let you know that one more person will be joining us at Ellis's for dinner tonight."

Charlee's eyes brightened. "One of Ellis's fine friends? No, wait. One of his rich colleagues? I won't be mad if he's invited one of his filthy-rich buddies."

"We should be so lucky."

"Well, who is it, then?" Charlee asked, sitting back.

"Bebe."

Charlee's brow wrinkled. "Ellis's mother?"

"The one and only," I said with a sigh.

"Wow. Okay. So his mother is coming for dinner. Based on your expression I can see that you're not happy about this."

"That's an understatement. I don't know if I should subject you guys to her. I was thinking maybe we should reschedule dinner."

"Oh no you don't. We planned to have dinner with you and Ellis and that's what we're going to do." Charlee gave me a mischievous smile. "As a matter of fact, I think it's about time we got to meet Ms. Bebe."

I knew my friend and I didn't like the way that sounded. "Why? What are you going to do?"

A petite female masseuse came in to get Charlee. She frowned before saying, "Don't worry. I'll be on my best behavior."

While the masseuse kneaded my knots, I tried to still my mind. I kept going over and over my conversation with Ellis. No matter how much his mother stepped out of bounds he failed to see any flaw in her behavior. I knew mothers and sons had a special bond, but their relationship was something else altogether. As much as Ellis was his own man, it seemed his mother controlled invisible puppet strings to make him do and say as she pleased. Not that I wanted to control Ellis, but if anybody was going to pull his strings it should've been me. Bebe needed to step aside. She needed to acknowledge that her son was about to be married and would have a wife—a partner—and that maybe she didn't need to be so intrusive. I knew what I had to do. After dinner, I'd sit Ellis and his mother down, together, and let them know from that point on, things would change. I would not succumb to Bebe's tactics and refused to tolerate Ellis's insensitivity. I needed Ellis to have my back. I needed to feel that he'd give me the same type of support that he gave his mother. I needed my husband to be *my* husband.

My masseuse commented that I was really tense and to relax my body. I took a few cleansing breaths and settled into the massage. I told myself to enjoy the moment because later I'd need to channel the calm I was currently experiencing.

CHAPTER THIRTY-TWO
MELINA

Bebe swirled the wine in her glass. I watched as Charlee studied Bebe's every move. I was more than tense, I was on edge. Bebe's typical haughty visage grated on my nerves.

Ellis was seated at the head of the table, his mother at the opposite end. I was to his immediate right, with Giselle next to me and Charlee across from her. We were an interesting group, sipping wine, no one talking.

Bebe cleared her throat. "So, Charlee, is it? What do you do for a living?"

I shot Charlee a glance, trying to catch her eye to issue a warning, but all of her attention was focused on Ellis's mother.

"Bebe, right?" Charlee asked.

"I prefer Mrs. Harlow when I first meet—"

"Well, Bebe, I work in the music industry. I own an entertainment management company and manage some of the hottest artists out there right now."

"That makes perfect sense."

Charlee tilted her head slightly. "In what way?"

"Oh, I can tell a lot about a person upon first sight and I thought you had a particular manner about you."

"And what manner would that be?"

Bebe set her wine glass on the table. "Well, your style immediately told me that you probably had some sort of alternative lifestyle."

"Alternative lifestyle?"

"Well, yes. That hippity-hoppety garb you're wearing screams alternative."

Ellis cleared his throat. "Mother."

Bebe raised her hands in a conciliatory gesture. "Yes, son?"

"Charlee is one of the top female executives in the music business."

I was just about to interject when Charlee spoke up first. "Bebe, I'm not sure what about my clothing makes you think I live an alternative lifestyle, but please be assured my life is about as mainstream as they come. I'm well-educated, run my own business, have quite a name in my industry, and oh yeah, I make a helluva lot of money. I work hard. Don't be confused because you don't see me wearing Brooks Brothers. That is not my uniform of choice. I wear what I please, when I please. Oh, and I play hard, too." Charlee picked up her glass and then paused to say, "Now did your *first sight* tell you all of that?"

I concealed the smile that was threatening to spread across my face and shifted the focus of the conversation. "Bebe, Giselle is a doctor. She's a cardiologist."

Bebe's face brightened. "A doctor? You know my husband was a pediatric surgeon. A cardiologist? Now that's impressive."

I registered her slight to Charlee but continued calmly. "As you can see, I have been blessed with wonderful friends. Beautiful and successful, but more importantly, faithful and devoted. I don't know what I would do without either one of them in my life."

"That's sweet, dear," Bebe said, brushing me off. "Ellis, what's on the menu tonight? I'm famished."

As Ellis rattled off the menu to his mother, I took a moment to give my girls *the look*. The one that said, *This bitch has lost her mind.*

Charlee chuckled at my unspoken words. Giselle excused herself to the restroom.

Bebe waited until Giselle left the dining room. "Is she all right?"

"I'm sure she's just fine," I said.

"She's expecting, isn't she?" Bebe asked.

It seemed her curiosity was genuine and not laced with any ulterior motives, so I answered. "Yes. I believe I had mentioned that one of my bridesmaids is expecting. That's Giselle."

Bebe nodded. I relaxed a bit when I saw that the first course was coming in. Baby lamb chops drizzled with a maple peppercorn glaze. I was sampling my first bite when Giselle rejoined us at the table.

Giselle had barely placed her napkin on her lap before Bebe pounced. "Are you married, dear?"

Giselle looked around the table to see if Bebe was speaking to her or Charlee. She fiddled for a moment with her utensils and then looked directly at Bebe. "No, I am not."

"Do you plan on marrying before your baby is born?"

"Actually, no."

"Why not, dear?"

"I'm raising my child on my own."

"Where's the baby's father?" Bebe pried.

Ellis stood up, interrupting his mother. He raised his wine glass. "Ladies, this toast is long overdue. I know how important you are to Lina. I recognize that she loves you both like sisters and I'm pleased to embrace you as family."

I stood next to Ellis and tapped his glass. I appreciated his effort to shut down his mother's inquisition of Giselle. I fixed Bebe with a look that told her to proceed with caution. She raised her glass in my direction and smiled a wicked little smile. Charlee tapped Giselle's glass of seltzer water and ignored Bebe altogether.

Considering we still had two courses to get through, I figured we were off to a marvelously treacherous start.

Ellis took his seat and gestured for me to do the same. "Mother, do you want to share your news about the reception with the ladies?"

Bebe dabbed the corners of her mouth with her napkin. "I was going to deliver my good news over dessert but I suppose now is fine. Melina, through no easy feat, considering the lack of time we're working with, I managed to secure the Waldorf Astoria for your reception." She clapped her hands together as if delighted with herself.

I wanted to say something, but my lips wouldn't move.

Ellis turned to me. "Well? What do you think?"

He was beaming. Like mother, like son. Obviously, he was elated with the location and quite pleased with his mother.

Giselle, sensing my discomfort, spoke up. "Melina, Ellis, you are going to have a beautiful reception."

Charlee chimed in, "Wow. The Waldorf. Sounds like a fairy tale. Is that what you had in mind, Melina?"

This was my opportunity to speak up and tell Bebe just what she could do with all of her plans. "Sounds wonderful, Bebe."

"I told you that this wedding will be a grand affair. I'll see to it."

Ellis leaned over and kissed me on the temple. I didn't know what to say. Especially with my girls watching the black widow spin her web. If I didn't know it before, I certainly knew now that she was the spider to my fly. With extreme clarity I felt her wrapping me tighter and tighter to the point of suffocation.

"*We'll* see to it," I said. "This wedding should be a collaborative effort, Bebe."

Bebe frowned at me. "Perhaps I wasn't clear about Harlow family tradition. I have always done everything within my means to maintain Harlow standards and traditions. That includes ensuring that my son's wedding is perfect. I understand that you probably find me meddlesome and feel I'm encroaching on your special day. Maybe I am, but remember one thing. I am the head of this family. I determine how the Harlows do things. This isn't just your wedding, it's *our* wedding. The entire family."

Ellis placed his hand on top of mine. I slid my hand away. "You know, Bebe, I was going to wait until later when we were alone to address this, but since you wanted to discuss matters in front of my friends…"

"You take issue with something I said?"

Ellis spoke up. "Of course not, Mother. As I told you before we appreciate all that you have done. Lina, we'll talk about this later. In private."

I glared at Ellis in disbelief. His expression told me that lines had been drawn and that, as usual, he was siding with his mother. I slowly pushed my chair back and excused myself from the table. I heard someone following behind me, but I didn't turn around. I headed straight toward the kitchen.

"Lina," Ellis called out gruffly. "Lina."

I ignored him, continuing my march across the living room and into the hallway. Ellis caught up to me right outside the kitchen and grabbed my arm. He glided past me and pulled me into the center of the room.

He jerked me close to him. "What is wrong with you?"

"With me? What's wrong with *me*? What's wrong with your mother?"

"I don't know what's gotten into you lately. We're supposed to be a family. These past few months you seem to have launched some sort of war against my mother."

"You are so blind," I said, half-whispering.

"No, I'm not. I can clearly see that you resent my mother's help. I would think that you would defer to her experience and embrace her because all she wants is our happiness."

I shook my head. "Do you hear yourself? Your mother is not concerned about our happiness. All she cares about is putting up a good front and making sure the Harlow image isn't tarnished by me. Your mother does not like me, Ellis. It's obvious to everyone, except you."

"You know, Lina, my patience is wearing thin with all of this you-versus-Mother nonsense."

"It's not nonsense. It's the truth and I can't understand why you don't want to acknowledge it."

"I'm going to say something to you and you better take it for what it's worth."

I walked over to the table and sat down. I was suddenly feeling drained and a little lightheaded.

Ellis grabbed a chair and pulled it close to mine. "I've always been the type of man that doesn't allow diversions of any kind in my life. For many years my life was my company—my work. Then I met you. I let you into my life, welcomed you into my family. There are few people that truly matter to me in this world. My mother and my sister *are* my world. There's nothing that I wouldn't do for them. You know I feel the same about you. I do not want you to be at odds with my mother. I won't tolerate it. So whatever you need to do to get on the same page with my mother, you do it. This little feud you have going with her is a diversion to me. A diversion I don't need. I don't have the stomach for it and I want you to put an end to it right now."

Ellis got up to leave the room.

"You don't even care what I have to say, do you?"

"No." He started toward the door. "Take a moment to get

yourself together, but hurry up. I hope this is the last time we have to discuss this." He left the kitchen.

I leaned forward, elbows on the table, and let my head fall into my hands. I hated Bebe. I was beginning to hate Ellis. How could I hate the man who was supposed to be my husband? I tried to swallow the bitter taste Bebe and Ellis left in my mouth, but I was starting to choke on it.

I'd never forget the first time I met Bebe. Ellis and I had been dating about three months. His father was on the Board of Directors for Lincoln Center for the Performing Arts and they had invited us to join them at a jazz benefit. Ellis and I were elegantly dressed for the evening. He was in a black tux and I had on a long black gown. We arrived at his parents' penthouse for cocktails before the show. Ellis's father entered the study and immediately walked over to me. He was a handsome man. I extended my hand to shake his and he pulled me into a warm hug. He kissed me on the cheek, effusing about how glad he was to meet me. He was so engaging, so interesting to talk to. He took an immediate interest in my business and spoke about how important it was for young, black women to have their own companies. He invited Ellis and me to come to dinner the next weekend and would not accept no for an answer. He made me promise to make Ellis stop working so hard and commented that he didn't think I would have a problem keeping him home a bit more.

We were enjoying a glass of champagne when Bebe floated into the room, her flowing, black skirt billowing out over her shoes. Her white wrap blouse with an upturned collar and revealing neckline, flattered her svelte shape. Bebe appeared to be the epitome of class and grace.

Ellis immediately went to his mother and kissed her on the cheek. She air-kissed both of his cheeks, then captured him by the chin.

She turned his face from side to side. "My, you are handsome. We've created such beautiful children, haven't we, Dr. Harlow?"

Ellis was beaming. His father said, "Let go of that boy, Bebe."

She gave Ellis a quick squeeze and then turned her attention to me. Ellis guided Bebe by her elbow the few steps to where I was seated. "Mother, this is Melina."

I arose to greet her. Bebe air-kissed my cheeks the way she had just done to Ellis. I gave her the sweetest smile I had to offer, the one reserved especially for meeting parents for the first time. "It's so nice to meet you, Mrs. Harlow."

"Same here, dear," she chirped. "Ellis, I'd like a glass of champagne," she said to her son, never taking her eyes off me.

"I appreciate you inviting us to the benefit tonight," I said.

"It's our pleasure," Dr. Harlow said.

"We thought it was time to meet Ellis's latest love interest."

I raised my eyebrows at her choice of words. Ellis handed his mother a glass, then put his arm around me. "Lina, Mother is not one to mince words. You'll never have to wonder what she thinks."

Dr. Harlow looked at me and nodded. "Trust me, Melina. I know better than anyone how true that is."

Bebe playfully swatted at her husband and son as if they were just teasing. They definitely were not.

If I knew what was in store for me with Bebe, I would have thought twice about dating Ellis. I did my best to put that first encounter out of my mind. It wasn't helping my current mood and I wanted to get through the remainder of the evening. I went over to the sink, wet a paper towel and dabbed a bit of cold water on my face. I blotted it dry and then took a deep breath before returning to the dining room.

CHAPTER THIRTY-THREE
MALIK

It took me forty damn minutes to find a parking space. As I walked up the block I saw balloons tied to my neighbor's wrought-iron gate. Damn kiddie party. Just as I reached my brownstone, a car pulled out from a space directly in front. Damn. Seconds later, Melina's BMW zipped down the street and she seized the newly vacant spot. I laughed to myself. It figures she'd have all the luck.

I waited on the sidewalk for her to get out of the car. She popped the trunk and then slowly opened her door. "Hey, Mel."

"Hey, I didn't even see you standing there."

I must have been wearing my invisible suit or she was really concentrating hard on her parallel parking. "You need help with your bag?"

"No, I got it, thanks."

Melina lifted her bag from the trunk. I ignored her, walked over to the car and took the bag from her hands.

She gave me a tired smile. "Thanks, Malik."

I shut the trunk and we went upstairs together. She locked the door behind us, went straight to the couch and plopped down with a loud sigh.

"That good, huh?" I asked.

"It was a long weekend."

"What happened?"

"I don't want to talk about it."

"You look pretty upset."

"I've been better, but don't worry about me. How was your weekend?"

"My weekend isn't over yet. I'm meeting the guys at Rituals for a drink. Lex got a promotion to sergeant."

"Wow, that's nice. Tell him I said congrats."

Her tone didn't match the sentiment. I didn't like seeing her so down. "Why don't you come with me and you can tell him yourself?"

"No, thanks. I'm going to fix a mug of steaming hot tea and settle in front of the television for the evening."

"Is there an opening for a new Golden Girl because you sound like you'd be perfect. Come on out and have some fun. Maybe you'll feel better. Dru might be there."

She reluctantly gave me a weak smile. "Okay, you twisted my arm."

"Be ready in an hour."

I spotted Amir and Lex over at the bar. Melina excused herself to the ladies room and said she'd join us in a second. She reached in her purse before she finished her sentence, so I figured she had to call her warden.

I greeted my brother and my boy with pounds and brotherly hugs. Their faces said they were waiting for an explanation.

"She needed some cheering up, so I brought her along."

"Where's Kai?" my brother asked.

"That's what I want to know," Lex chimed in.

"I put Kai in a time-out. She has a few lessons to learn about Big Daddy."

Amir took a swig of his beer. "Uh-huh."

Melina stepped up and spoke to the guys. Lex pulled out the chair next to him. She sat down and I took the seat on her opposite side.

"Congratulations on your promotion, Lex," she said.

"Thank you. It's long overdue, but I'll take it."

"Where's Terrence, late as usual?" I asked.

"Nah, Dru wasn't feeling well, so he ain't coming down."

Amir laughed. "I never thought I'd see the day when Terrence would be playing nurse."

I joined in. "Why do you have to make the brother a nurse? Why can't he be playing doctor?"

"Because that wouldn't be nothing new. He's been playing doctor for years," Lex added.

We howled, but Melina just smiled.

"We're just kidding, Melina. Don't take anything we say seriously."

"I won't, Amir. You should know I'm used to your brother's antics by now," she said, laughing.

"She does put up with a lot of my shit." I grabbed her hand and planted a kiss on it.

Melina nervously blushed at me holding her hand. The gleam from her rock flashed at me and I released it.

Lex and Amir went quiet, giving each other curious looks.

"I'm used to his antics by now," she repeated. "He keeps me on my toes."

"I bet," Lex mumbled.

"Man, I know you're not talking. Lex, you're a cop and you're crazy. You know you don't know how to act."

Amir gave me a fist bump. "I hear that."

"Amir, you're related to this fool, so you can't say shit to me."

Melina ordered a drink and was laughing right along with me and the fellas. She could adapt when she wanted to. She made it hard for me to convince the brothers she was wound a little tight when every time they saw her she fit right in. My cell phone vibrated. It was Kai. I stepped away from the bar to take the call.

"Ms. Cooper, to what do I owe this honor?"

"Don't get dramatic, Malik. I've been inundated with projects, so I was off the grid this week."

I wasn't buying it, but I didn't feel it was worth debating. "What's good for tonight?"

"Me and you. When can you get here?"

"Give me a few hours."

"Don't keep me waiting."

I hung up with Kai and reinserted myself into the conversation at the bar. Lex, never missing an opportunity to give me flack, started ribbing me on my so-called discreet phone call. "That must've been Big Daddy's star pupil just released from her time out."

Amir wasn't going to miss a chance to add his two cents. "Lesson learned, huh? She must be a quick study."

I turned to Melina. "Ignore these fools. They don't have the sense God gave them."

"Thank goodness I do," she said.

"What's that mean, Melina?" Amir prodded.

"It just means that I'm used to your brother's antics."

"You keep saying that," Amir replied.

I dropped Melina off at home and kept on rolling to Kai's. She was waiting at the door in a pair of heels and strand of pearls. I closed the door behind me and smiled at her nakedness.

"I don't need to ask if you like what you see."

"I like." I shrugged off my coat as I hungrily assessed her *outfit*. I lifted Kai by her ass and she wrapped her legs around my waist.

I carried her to the bedroom while she sucked on my ears and my neck. I dropped her down on the bed and began unbuckling my belt. She stretched out her hand to help and I backed up out of her reach. The last time she took control, not this time. My clothes got tossed into a pile on the floor. I took a condom from the nightstand and covered up my hardhead.

Kai laid back and raised her legs, crossing them at the ankles. I kneeled on the bed next to her and touched her pussy. It was already hot and wet. I dipped my middle finger inside of her and slowly moved it in and out. "Turn on your stomach."

She lowered her legs and quickly rolled over. I grabbed Kai by her waist and pulled her up on all fours. Her big ass was up high and she was moaning before I even touched her. Kai looked back at me, put her finger in her mouth and started sucking. I got behind her and smacked that ass. She moaned louder. I smacked harder and she started backing up into me, rubbing her wet pussy on the tip of my dick. I grabbed her hips and held her still. I played with her, letting the tip of my dick enter her but only the tip. Heat radiated off of her. She tried to reach around and grab my ass to push me inside. I backed up and took my tip out of her. Soft whimpers escaped from her mouth. She stopped reaching for me and grabbed her comforter. I held my dick, rubbed it in her juices, then plunged deep inside of her. She let out a cry and almost collapsed forward. I yanked Kai back up, pulling her into me. I moved her hips back and forth as I plunged and pulled out of her. Kai was chanting incoherently, repeating the same high-pitched phrase with each pump. I hit it harder and faster, drilling deep into her wetness. She tried to lay on her stomach, but I pulled her into me. We were upright on our knees, my chest pressed against her back. I reached around and tugged on her nipples. She popped her pussy with force. I leaned forward, laying her down on her stomach, my dick still up in her. She was pinned beneath my body, arms at her sides, my arms outside of hers. She squeezed her legs shut and raised her ass, tightening her pussy around my dick. I dug deep, as far as I could go and pounded it out. I was hitting her spot. Kai yelped her pleasure. Sweat poured down my face. I wouldn't relent. She shouted she was coming and I pulled her back up on her knees. I managed to ram her pussy twice before she exploded. I finally released my grip and let her collapse on the bed.

Kai rolled onto her back, eyelids fluttering. She was struggling to catch her breath. I stretched out next to her. She turned her head in my direction. "Wow."

I laughed. "What, you didn't know?"

She smoothed her hair down. "Wow."

"You said that."

"Can't talk. Need water." She opened her eyes.

"I'll get it." I got up and slid the condom off.

"You didn't come?"

"Nope."

"Why not?"

"It's about you tonight. You came, right?"

"Like a roaring rapid."

"And I enjoyed the ride."

She was underneath the blankets when I returned with the water. She propped herself up against the pillows. "We make a good pair, Malik. In the boardroom and the bedroom. You and I can be the ultimate power couple."

"Yeah?" I sat next to Kai, leaning against the headboard.

"You don't agree?"

Here we go again and this time she decided on a direct plan of attack. Kai was breaking the unspoken rule of our situation. She was beginning to push me and I honestly didn't know what I thought about us being a power couple. Hell, I wasn't sure about us being a *regular* couple. I'd be a fool not to acknowledge that she was the type of woman a man would want to show off on his arm.

"We definitely got it poppin' in the bedroom and our collaboration at work was a success," I said.

"I feel a but coming on."

"No, you don't. What we got going on is good. A brother can't complain."

"But?"

"But right now I'm focusing on my business prospects."

"I knew you had a *but*."

"I agree with you that our situation works. I'm enjoying you, Kai, but I'm also at a crucial juncture in my life. I've told you I'm starting my own agency. That's not a game to me. I'm about to make a move that will either make or break me."

"So you're leaving Newport and Donner for sure?"

"Yup."

"When?"

"I'm not ready to leave just yet, but I'm on schedule to launch in the next six to nine months."

"Do you have clients lined up?"

"Of course I do. Newport and Donner doesn't recognize my talent, but I've been making a name for myself in the right circles for a while now."

"How many of these companies have officially retained you? I mean you haven't even launched yet."

"If you had the opportunity to commission the hottest designer to make you a one-of-a-kind dress, but her schedule was booked for six to nine months, would you pass up the opportunity or would you schedule the appointment because you know in the end it would be worth the wait?"

"Point taken."

"All I'm saying is that the buzz is building, and when I launch, that buzz is going to turn into a big-ass boom. I've secured eight accounts and I'm already receiving referrals."

"I know your worth, Malik. You don't need to convince me. Sounds like I need to convince you how a powerful man like you needs a powerful woman like me by your side."

I rolled over on my back. "How do you plan on doing that?"

"There are many ways, but how about I start like this?" Kai took my hardhead in her hands and snaked her tongue at me.

She climbed from underneath the blankets and proceeded to make her case.

CHAPTER THIRTY-FOUR
MELINA

I tapped my glass against Dru's. We were having a little wine with our late lunch at Nobu. I wasn't sure she'd be able to keep our date after I heard she was under the weather over the weekend, but she called to confirm when she heard she missed me at Rituals.

"How are your wedding plans coming along, Melina? It's in April, right?"

"With Christmas in two weeks I've been spending most of my time preparing for the holidays."

"You must be inundated with the arrangements. I'm getting angst about my wedding and Terrence and I haven't even settled on a date yet."

"I still have a lot to do, but my mother is coming to visit this weekend to help me with the planning."

"I told Terrence I needed a long engagement, so I could orchestrate the perfect event with as little stress as possible. Between seeing patients and my charity work, I don't have as much free time on my hands as I would like. I'm not going to put any undue pressure on myself. You know what I'm talking about—you run your own business."

Dru was a psychiatrist with a private practice. Malik had told many jokes that Terrence had finally met his match, a woman that could analyze his every move and beat him at his own games.

"Once you set a date are you going to hire a wedding planner?"

"No, I'm too traditional. I don't want someone else to plan one of the most important days of my life. I want to pick that special location to say my vows, choose the perfect flowers, create a divine menu, select the most beautiful cake, the music—everything. Down to the minutest of details, I want to plan my dream wedding."

"You know, Dru, I've always wanted the same thing. Unfortunately, my dream wedding is turning into a nightmare."

Dru knitted her brows. "Why, what's going on?"

I sighed and shook my head. "My fiancé's mother has managed to hijack my wedding. She's acting like she's getting married. And Ellis, well, let's just say that Ellis is his mother's son."

"That does sound like a nightmare. Do you want a little advice? And be honest if you don't because I'll just keep my mouth shut."

"No, I don't mind."

"Melina, this speaks of a broader issue. The wedding is only a component of a much larger dynamic. If you don't have the support of your fiancé before you get married, do you think it'll get better after you say 'I do?' I don't want you to answer that question now. I want you to *think* about it. Give it some serious thought before you take that trip down the aisle."

"I've asked myself that question a million times. My head already knows the answer, but my heart still hopes things will change."

"Have you told Ellis how you feel about his mother taking over your wedding?"

"Ad nauseam and it doesn't make a difference. He views it as his mother providing much-needed assistance. I get that he's trying to make us both happy, but somehow I feel I'm getting the short end of the stick."

"You know how those mother-son relationships can be."

"Yeah, a pain in the ass." We both laughed and tapped glasses again. "How do you get along with Terrence's mom?"

"When we first met, she kept me at arm's length. She was pleasant enough, but she made sure I'd be around a while before she warmed up to me. Thankfully, we get along pretty well."

"I can only pray that Bebe and I come to amicable terms."

"Girl, with each passing day I learn just how important communication is in relationships, especially marriage. Keep trying to get through to Ellis and work on his mother if and when you feel like it. We've only known each other a short time, but if you ever need someone to talk to…"

"I appreciate that, Dru."

Dru's sincerity made me smile. She wasn't the first person to mention how important it is to communicate with your partner, but considering she was a professional therapist, it reinforced what I already knew. I would make a concerted effort to better express myself to both Ellis and his mother. Maybe they weren't understanding what this wedding meant to *me*. Sometimes it's difficult to think about a situation outside of your own viewpoint—I would make them see mine. I had to make them understand that a wedding is one of the most important days in a woman's life. It was a day I had dreamt, fantasized and talked about since childhood. I needed to relay *my* vision for *my* wedding. I had yet to do that.

"Okay, I have to ask," Dru said, interrupting my thoughts.

"Ask what?"

"About Malik."

"What about Malik?"

"I'm just curious, I guess."

"Curious about Malik? In what way?"

"There's nothing between the two of you?"

I erupted with laughter. "Why would you think that?"

"Well, I've seen the way you are together. I mean, I could be misreading things, but I don't think so."

"That's funny," I said with amusement. "We're just roommates. There's nothing going on between myself and Malik."

Dru laughed. "I'm sorry if I'm intruding. Terrence always says I analyze things a bit too much."

"I'm going to agree with Terrence on that one," I said, still chuckling.

"He is a fine specimen though, isn't he?"

"Yeah and he knows it. You can't tell Malik he isn't God's gift to women."

"He'll settle down eventually. He's a nice guy. If you listen to Terrence tell it, there's no one more reliable, honest or dependable."

"Malik knows how to push my buttons, but I know if I need him for anything, he'd be there for me." A smile crept across my lips.

"You see. It's that expression on your face right now that made me ask you about Malik in the first place."

I was puzzled by what Dru thought she saw. "Dru, please."

"I've seen the same look on Malik's face when he's talking about you."

Now *I* was curious. "Malik talks about me? What does he say?"

"Well, your interest is piqued all of a sudden," Dru teased.

"I can imagine the stuff he says about me."

Dru shook her head. "I've never heard Malik say anything negative about you. I'm serious. He doesn't talk about you, per se; he mainly relays funny stories about the two of you. He told us about the shopping cart incident in the grocery store," she said, stifling laughter.

"Malik is crazy," I said, as I replayed the event in my mind. "He does make me laugh and I do enjoy his company. I might actually miss him when I move in with Ellis."

"I hope your marriage to Ellis doesn't mean the end of your friendship with Malik."

"We are friends, aren't we?" I asked pensively.

"I would say so, Melina, if not more."

I playfully swatted at Dru. "Girl, you're just as crazy as Malik."

I went back to the office after lunch with Dru. I sat at my desk, leafing through a few spreadsheets, my mind wandering. I thought it was a little strange that Dru asked me about Malik. True, we had been spending more time together than usual, particularly going out to events. However, I didn't think that we displayed any sort of feelings for one another. Malik was fun, and I loved when we got along, but there was nothing between us. I reflected on a few of our recent moments and smiled. I had to admit that I really enjoyed going to the baseball game, dancing with Malik at Terrence and Dru's engagement party, movies and popcorn at home, and even when he cooked me dinner. I could acknowledge that lately there had been some tension between the two of us, but that's all it was. Tension.

I gave this too much energy. I let Dru get in my head. She must've been really good at her job because if she had an influence on my thoughts after our casual lunch meeting, I could only imagine Dru's impact on her patients that were paying for her expertise.

I grabbed my belongings and told Nadia I was leaving for the day. I had a few errands to run. My parents were arriving in two days and I wanted to be prepared for their visit. I had ordered them plush monogrammed bathrobes and big fluffy slippers that I needed to pick up from the boutique. I was also planning to cook dinner for everyone on Friday night and needed to go food shopping for the ingredients. I had seen a cooking show on television where the chef prepared authentic seafood paella served sizzling in a large cast-iron paella pan. A meal shared family-style, paired with a nice Spanish white wine, would be a great way to stimulate great conversation. We were all staying at Ellis's for the entire weekend, including Bebe. I was fairly optimistic about the visit. I figured since Bebe was all about putting up fronts that she would be on her best behavior for my parents. I wouldn't be surprised if she pretended that she loved me to death. I also knew that if Bebe got the slightest bit out of line, my mother would deftly maneuver her back into place.

After picking up the robes, I stopped to purchase the wine, then for a manicure and pedicure. It was getting late and I still had to pack my bag for the weekend. I decided the food shopping could wait until Friday morning. My parents weren't scheduled to arrive until late afternoon and Ellis would send the limo to collect them from the airport. I headed home. When I stepped from the car, I glanced up at the steel-gray clouds. Rain had to be on the way. I hurried up the stairs and into the apartment, dropping my bags on the living room sofa.

I was in my room pulling clothes from my closet when Malik came through the front door. Moments later, voices from the television in the living room blared through the apartment. The meteorologist on the weather channel was predicting snow, possibly heavy, in the next couple of days. I folded a sweater, placed it in my bag and went out to the living room.

Malik jumped when he saw me. "Shit! I didn't know you were here."

I held in my laughter. "I came in a while ago. They're predicting snow? My parents are supposed to be flying in the day after tomorrow."

"They're forecasting snow for Friday night. They should be all right if their flight gets in before eight p.m. That's when it's supposed to start."

"Oh, good," I said, relief washing over me. "They'll be here in the afternoon."

"So what's the plan? Are your parents staying here with us? Because if you need my room I can sleep on the couch."

"No, thanks. We're staying with Ellis for the weekend. I'm heading to Long Island tonight."

"Sounds nice," he said with zero emotion.

"So I'll be out of your way all weekend. You don't have to worry about seeing me until Monday night."

"Cool."

I returned to my packing and left Malik on the couch flipping through the channels. I sort of wanted to plop down and join him for a while, but I knew Ellis was waiting and would be calling to find out what was taking me so long to arrive.

I zipped my overstuffed bag and placed it by my bedroom door. My phone rang. It was Charlee and Giselle on three-way. I reminded them I'd be at Ellis's and they could reach me over there if they were unable to get me on my cell phone.

I hung up with my girls and grabbed my bag. Malik was exactly where I had left him. Slumped on the couch. Mindlessly focused on the television. "You need help with your bag?"

I opened the apartment door. "Thanks, but I got it. Have a good weekend." I stepped into the hallway.

Malik called out. "Do you need these bags?"

I turned around. I had forgotten about the robes I tossed on the sofa when I came in. I was supposed to gift wrap them.

Malik brought them over to the door. "Are you sure you can carry all of that stuff?"

I hefted my bag over my shoulder and took the two shopping bags from him. "I'm sure. Thanks, Malik."

He smiled, moved in closer and then planted a soft kiss on my cheek. I don't know why, but I returned the favor.

"Have a good time, Mel. See you when you get back."

Malik closed the door before I had a chance to respond. I'm glad he did because I didn't know why he kissed me, but even more strange, I wasn't sure why I kissed him back.

CHAPTER THIRTY-FIVE
MALIK

The first thing I noticed when I opened the door to my office was that the lights were already on. The blinds had been opened and Kai was propped on the sofa, flipping through a portfolio.

She looked up when I came in. "Good morning," she said with a smile.

"Morning." I looked around to see if I could gather clues as to why she was in my office.

Kai puckered her lips and craned her neck in expectation of a kiss. I paused a beat before crossing the room to her. I leaned down and briefly touched my lips to hers.

"That's all you got for me?" she asked.

"What's up, Kai?" I said. It was too early for these games and I was feeling a little short on patience.

She sighed, then patted the sofa next to her. I took my time sitting down.

"I was going over the print ads for Sphere Electronics and found a problem," she said.

I knew those ads inside out and there was nothing wrong with them. "What would that be?"

"The Sphere logos are missing."

"Let me see that," I said with more than a touch of annoyance in my voice. The ads were going live in two days.

Kai handed me the portfolio she had been flipping through. "It's missing on this one and also the one with the animated characters."

I scanned the pages. "These aren't the final versions I submitted. You saw and approved the final ads. Who gave these to you?"

"I know. I saw the final ads and they were correct. I don't know how this happened."

"We better get this rectified."

"Malik, there's no way we can halt a national campaign that's scheduled to launch in less than forty-eight hours."

"Who said anything about halting the campaign? I said let's get this rectified."

Kai's eyes darted around the office. She bit her bottom lip, then started fidgeting with her skirt. "All right, let's meet in an hour in the conference room. I have a few calls to make and then we can try to sort this out."

"Make it fifteen minutes. I want to get ahead of this problem." I went over to my desk and picked up the phone. I was going to find out who was responsible for the imminent train wreck.

Kai turned to me on her way out the door. "Oh, I almost forgot. Gerry wants to see you in his office."

I dropped the phone back into the cradle. "Now?"

She nodded.

"I don't have time for Donner right now."

"I'll see you in fifteen minutes," she said as the door closed.

I straightened my tie before I stepped into Donner's office. He was behind his massive mahogany desk, glasses hanging off the tip of his nose.

"Mr. Donner, you wanted to see me?"

"Malik, sit down." He had copies of the ads spread across his desk.

I took my time getting situated. "I was just reviewing those in my office. I plan to find out exactly how—"

"Malik, I thought you were ready for an account like Sphere. Obviously, I was wrong."

"Mr. Donner—"

"At this level there's no room for mistakes. No room for excuses. Sphere was your project. The ad campaign is supposed to launch in two days. Due to this mix-up, it won't. This has never happened in the history of this company. Effective immediately, you are terminated from Newport and Donner."

"I'm fired? Just like that I'm fired?" I loosened my tie. It was suddenly constricting around my neck. I stood up, my voice rising with me. "After all I've done for this company?"

Donner droned on, staying on message. "Your office has been packed up and security is waiting to escort you out."

A security guard walked up behind me and motioned toward the door. I silently nodded my head at the guard.

Planting my hands on Donner's desk, I leaned over him. "Remember this day. It will end up being one of your biggest regrets."

I followed the guard through the office. The fair-haired boys stared, some poked their heads out of their office doors. I was led out like a common criminal. With each step toward the exit, the more pissed I became that I was providing their entertainment for the day.

The receptionist looked down at her computer screen as I passed her desk. The same woman that greeted me when I arrived in the morning and departed at night, avoided eye contact with me as if I was a stranger.

I was handed my box by another security guard waiting for me next to the elevators. Two security guards for the occasion? Donner must have really thought I was going to turn angry black man on his ass. Instead, I calmly took my box, rode the elevator down to the lobby and exited the building.

The first person I called when I got home was my father. I kept him on the phone for over an hour, venting my frustration and anger. I couldn't believe that I had just been fired. Donner couldn't give a fuck about all of the hard work I had put into the Sphere project. He hadn't given one iota of consideration to all the money that I had made his company over the years. His ass didn't even give me an opportunity to address the problem. He blindsided me, caught me completely off guard, and fired my ass. No questions asked. My dad tried to get me to refocus my energy and concentrate on what the situation meant for my future—that I could move forward unencumbered. Carpe diem and all that shit, but I wasn't in the mood for any pep talk. He wouldn't let me off the phone until I promised that we'd meet up in a few days to rework the timeline for my business strategy. He was trying his best to keep me on track through the storm and as I reached for an unopened bottle of Patron, I was hurtling toward a derailment.

CHAPTER THIRTY-SIX
MELINA

Stray snow flurries blew past the window. I stretched, then burrowed deeper beneath the covers. I stole a few extra minutes of relaxation in Ellis's bed before I needed to spring into action.

The weather was supposed to take a turn for the worse by the evening. I just wanted my parents to arrive safely and well ahead of the snow. Ellis was going to bring Bebe home with him after work. That left me with a couple of remaining hours in the morning and early afternoon to prepare for our "family" weekend. I forced myself from the warmth of the bed and got started with my day.

On the way to the supermarket, I decided to give Bebe a call to make sure she was in a good mood. I figured a little buttering up would set the tone for a pleasant experience during the weekend. I really did want us to get along better. Nothing would make me happier than to have a beautiful relationship with the mother of my future husband. Right now, we were struggling for cordial. When her voicemail picked up, I left a message letting her know that I was looking forward to seeing her later and that I'd have a glass of her favorite wine ready when she arrived. No one could say that I wasn't trying.

I called my mom next. She was in the middle of packaging some sort of delectable treat to bring with her to New York. She refused to tell me what it was and hurried me off the phone. Knowing my mother, she had probably baked a batch of homemade cookies. I had barely managed to tell her that Ellis's driver, Stanley, would be waiting for them at the airport before she hung up.

The clock was ticking and I needed everything to be perfect. I wrapped my scarf around my neck, pulled on my gloves and rushed into the market. The snow was coming down a bit heavier. There was a light dusting on the ground and I hoped it would hold off long enough to avoid impacting flights coming into JFK Airport. I quickly got my shopping done and then headed back to Ellis's to get ready.

I had the entire evening planned. I was going to do away with all the pomp and circumstance that came with entertaining at Ellis's. This was an informal occasion with family. We'd have dinner at the kitchen table, served by me, not in the formal dining room and definitely no staff on hand. After dinner we could all go to the theater room for a movie or maybe drinks and smooth jazz in the study before turning in for the night. I was finally starting to feel that we would enjoy one another this weekend. I was prepared to do everything in my power to bring our families together.

I was standing by the window, arms folded, peering out into the night. As soon as I saw the headlights from the limo pulling into the circular drive I ran to the front door and down the steps. My mother was out of the car and headed my way before Stanley had a chance to open her door.

We hugged each other tightly. "Hey, sweetheart," my mother said. She kissed me on the cheek. "You're going to catch a cold out here."

I laughed. "You just got here and you're already worried about somebody catching a cold."

My father walked up and gave me a hug. "Hey, baby girl."

"Hi, Daddy." I beamed at my father. He towered over me by at least a foot. "Stanley, can you please bring the bags inside?"

"Stanley, let me give you hand." That was just like my father to offer his assistance. He stayed behind to help Stanley as I led my mother into the house.

"Mom, how was your flight?"

"It wasn't bad. I thought the snow would delay us, but thankfully it hasn't started accumulating yet."

My father came into the house. "This is some place Ellis has here," he said, handing me his coat.

"Do you see that Christmas tree, Lawrence? It's beautiful, and so tall. Melina, I know you didn't decorate it."

The fifteen-foot tree sparkled with white lights and gold and ruby ornaments from top to bottom.

"Of course not, Mom. Decorators take care of that." I led them past the living room. "Let me give you guys a tour. Ellis and his mother should be home soon."

"I can't wait to finally meet her," my mother said.

I said a silent prayer for all to go well. "And I can't wait for you to come with me to find my wedding dress."

My mother grabbed my hand. "My little girl is getting married. I'm so happy for you, Melina. You're marrying a wonderful man who loves you and will take care of you. Your father and I couldn't ask for more."

I squeezed my mother's hand. "Mom, don't start getting emotional on me."

She smiled. "I won't. I promised your father."

"It's true. She guaranteed me that she'd leave the waterworks back in Maryland."

All I could do was laugh. She might have made that promise,

but I knew she couldn't keep it. Once we got to the bridal shop and she saw me in a wedding gown, all bets would be off.

I began the tour downstairs, leading my parents from one room to the next. My father couldn't believe there was an Olympic-sized pool inside the house and my mother wanted to make use of the spa. I showed them to their room last, so they could get settled. "Come down to the kitchen when you're done. I'll be making dinner."

It felt so good to have my parents visiting. Sometimes I didn't realize how much I missed them until I had them with me. I went to the kitchen to finish dinner. The fireplace was burning and generating the warmth and coziness I was hoping to have for the evening.

I busied myself at the stove, browning the chorizo and then the chicken for the paella. I cleaned the shrimp, scrubbed the clams and split the lobster tails earlier to make preparing the rest of the dish relatively easy. The salad was already tossed and in the fridge and I also had a loaf of rustic bread that would be accompanied by a nice olive oil. We were having pumpkin cheesecake for dessert— one of my mom's favorites.

My parents joined me in the kitchen. "Do you need any help, Melina?"

"No, I want you to sit down at the table and relax yourselves." I placed a bottle of white wine and two glasses in front of them, then handed my father a corkscrew. I pulled baked brie wrapped in a puff pastry from the oven and arranged it on a cheese board alongside sliced strawberries, apples and candied pecans.

"Dig in while it's hot," I said, setting the cheese board between the two of them. "Here are some plates and forks."

"Looks good," my father said.

"I know how you love brie cheese, Daddy. Let me know if you

like it." Voices and footsteps traveled toward the kitchen. "Sounds like Ellis and Bebe are here."

I placed two more glasses on the table and Bebe's Bordeaux she was so fond of drinking.

"Hello," Bebe sang out, as she entered the room. She walked straight to my mother and gave her a kiss on each cheek. "Cynthia," she said, smiling. Bebe turned to my father as he waited to greet her. "Lawrence. It's so great to meet you both."

She extended her arms for a hug. My father leaned down to accommodate her gesture. I was completely caught off guard by Bebe's warm welcome. I came from behind the counter and approached Ellis and his mother.

Bebe pulled me into a long embrace. "How are you, darling? Something smells delightful."

"Bebe...hi...I'm fine," I stammered.

My mom gave Ellis a hug and my father followed it up with a manly handshake.

"How was your trip?" Ellis asked. He walked over to me and kissed me on the temple.

"It was pretty good," my father responded.

"I apologize I was unable to pick you up from the airport myself. I had a meeting that couldn't be rescheduled."

"We know you're a busy man. I appreciate you sending the car for us."

"Bebe, this meeting is long overdue," my mother said.

"I was just saying the same thing to Ellison. There's no excuse for not doing this sooner."

I pulled Ellis over to the side while our parents continued chatting at the table. "So far so good," I said in a hushed tone.

"What did you expect?" he asked, brows furrowed.

"Honestly? I don't know."

"Let's not make a problem when there isn't one."

I nodded. "You're right." I leaned in for a kiss. "Why don't you pour yourself a glass of wine and get comfortable?"

"Now that sounds like a good idea. The snow is starting to get heavy out there."

"I'm glad you made it in before it got too bad."

"What are you cooking?"

I led him over to the simmering rice and seafood mixture on the stove. "We're having authentic paella," I said with a Spanish inflection.

"It looks delicious," he said, reaching for a fork to dip into the pan.

"It's not ready." I shooed his hand away from the stove. "There's cheese and fruit on the table to hold you over until dinner is served. Now go on over there and wait."

My father patted his stomach. "Melina, everything was delicious."

"I had no idea you knew your way around the kitchen," Bebe added. "The cheesecake was divine. A tad rich, but—"

"Lina is an incredible cook, Mother."

"She learned from the best," my mother said.

I had to laugh at my mother's cheekiness. "Thank you."

"Would anyone like another slice?"

Ellis shook his head. "Maybe later."

"I couldn't possibly eat another bite," Bebe answered. "It seems your daughter will be fattening up my son once they get married."

"This is a beautiful kitchen and I hope Melina plans to use it to keep her husband happy," my mother countered.

"Mother doesn't cook, Mrs. Bradford. She's more concerned about me getting fat rather than being well-fed."

"I'm concerned about my son's health and I'm certain that, as a mother, Cynthia can relate."

I quickly interjected with some levity. "I promise I won't starve him or turn him into a pig. I'll do my best to keep Ellis happily fed *and* healthy."

Ellis raised his glass. "I couldn't ask for a better combination."

"As long as Melina won't be plying you with that heavy, artery-clogging Southern fare she grew up on. No offense, Cynthia and Lawrence. I just know how that type of cuisine can take a toll on your heart."

"The key is moderation," my mother said.

"I suppose, but I never touch the stuff. Fried food dripping in grease and sauces should be avoided at all costs."

"Well, thankfully Lawrence and I are in perfect health."

"I plan to have my chef teach Melina how to cook," Bebe said.

My mother cocked her head to the side. "My daughter knows how to cook as evidenced by tonight's dinner. Melina has been cooking since her early teens."

"Oh, Cynthia, I only meant that my chef can share health-conscious recipes with our children. We certainly want them to have a long-lasting life together."

Ellis interrupted. "That's thoughtful of you, Mother. More wine, anyone?"

My father passed his glass to Ellis. "So where are you two planning to honeymoon?"

"We've narrowed it down to either Fiji or St. Barts," I said.

Bebe shook her head. "That will never do."

"I think either of those places sound absolutely lovely," my mother retorted.

"The Harlows honeymoon in Europe. It's tradition. And we're not going to start breaking tradition with this wedding."

"I can respect tradition, but perhaps the children would like to start a few traditions of their own."

"Ellison knows they'll honeymoon in Europe. We've already discussed it. Plans are being made. Cynthia, trust me. Melina will love it."

"It sounds as if my daughter has other plans for *her* honeymoon and that she and Ellis have some talking to do."

Bebe narrowed her eyes at my mother. "You're right. The children can handle it. I've taken care of all the *important* details. It's good that you're finally here to help your daughter with the few remaining loose ends for the wedding."

I sensed the unmistakable brewing of a storm between my mother and Bebe. I cleared my throat. "Ellis, why don't you take our parents to the theater room and put on a movie? I'm going to clean up the kitchen and then I'll be right in."

My father finished the wine in his glass. "I think I'm going to take a rain check on the movie and turn in for the night."

"Really, Daddy? It's only nine-thirty."

"It's been a long day," my mother said.

"You're going to bed, too?"

"Yes, but I'll be up bright and early tomorrow, so we can flesh out your wedding plans and go dress shopping."

I knew better than to argue with my parents. "Ellis can take you up to your room. I'll see you in the morning."

My father pushed back from the table. "Good night, baby girl. Bebe, have a good evening."

"Sleep well," Bebe replied.

"You, too," my mother answered.

Ellis escorted my parents out of the kitchen. I cleared the plates from the table and loaded them into the dishwasher. Bebe leaned back in the chair and fixed her eyes on me.

"Wasn't that fun?" she said.

That was not the pleasant voice that told my parents to sleep well merely seconds ago. I turned around to face Bebe. "I always love spending time with family." I didn't want to exclude anyone, so I was careful not to single out my parents. "Did you enjoy the paella?"

"It was a little heavy for my taste. I'm not accustomed to eating food prepared in that manner. Sausage and seafood all mixed up in rice. No. No, I don't believe I enjoyed it in the least."

I froze where I was standing. "Wow, okay. Well, I'm sorry you didn't like it."

"Did I offend?"

"Was it your intention to do so?"

"You'd know if I was trying to offend you. I don't understand you young girls. So temperamental."

"Bebe, it's fine." I lifted the paella pan from the table. "You didn't enjoy dinner and that's okay."

"It's not okay. I wish my only issue was with your little dinner. Unfortunately, it's more about class or, should I say, your lack thereof. Your interpretation of entertaining is unacceptable. I will never allow you to host *my* family, serving a meal like that."

"You can't be serious." I slammed the paella pan back down on the table. "I planned a family-style dinner for my parents, fiancé and his mother. Not every occasion is meant for formalities. These are my parents. I don't have to put on a show for them."

"That's obvious and I can see the apple doesn't fall far from the tree, since your mother loved it. But I suppose if you weren't shown better, then you can't possibly know better."

"Bebe, you're crossing the line and I'm trying to maintain some civility between us."

Bebe came over to my side of the table. "You are utterly disrespectful. Who do you think you're speaking to, Little Ms. Melina? I think you better tread lightly."

"You have to give respect to get respect and if you think you can talk about my family, then you're wrong."

"I don't have to respect you or your family." Bebe sneered at me, her disdain displayed on her face. "I can't for the life of me figure out what my son sees in you. The only reason I haven't told Ellison to break off your engagement is because I know he would go through with it just to spite me."

I could not believe what I was hearing. This woman was evil personified.

"Ellis loves me, Bebe. There's nothing more to figure out."

"Don't test me, dear. I can put a halt to this wedding."

"Oh, really? What makes you think you can stop it? This is not *your* wedding. It's *my* wedding!"

"Don't fool yourself." Footsteps approached. "And don't make too many tacky wedding plans with your mother tomorrow that I'll have to undo. Remember, this is a *Harlow* affair."

Ellis came into the kitchen, focusing on me and his mother. Bebe headed to the door, hugging him on her way out. "Good night, son. Melina, thank you for such a delicious dinner."

I didn't say a word to Bebe as she left the kitchen.

Ellis leaned against the island, crossing his arms over his chest. "Lina, did you mean to ignore Mother?"

"Yes, Ellis, I meant to ignore your trifling mother."

"Don't start this foolishness again."

"Your mother is a phony, Ellis. We just had it out right here in this kitchen."

"Why are you always fighting with my mother?"

"Do you ever have my back?" I said, my voice elevating. "Your mother is always fighting me. Why would you automatically think that I'm the catalyst?"

"Because I know how much Mother loves you."

"Get a clue, Ellis. She hates me."

"I'm not going to tell you again to cut it out with all of this nonsense."

"You're not going to *tell me* again?"

"That's what I said and I mean it, Lina. Stop it with the attacks on my mother."

"I'm sick of you, your mother and the warped relationship you two have. You are so blinded by her act and I don't want to deal with it." I pushed past him and stormed out the kitchen. "I need some air."

He followed behind me. "Where are you going?"

"I don't know," I said, hurrying toward the front door. "Anywhere but here right now. I don't even want to look at you." I grabbed my coat from the closet.

Ellis was on my heels. "Are you crazy, going out in this weather?"

"Yup. That's it. I'm crazy, Ellis. And guess who's making me crazy? Your mother—and you're running a close second."

I snatched up my purse, pulled my coat closed and rushed out the door. The snow whipped across my face. Ellis called my name a couple of times before I hopped into my car and started the engine. I turned the windshield wipers to high, to clear off the two inches of snow that had accumulated, and then peeled out of the driveway. I couldn't see out of the rearview mirror, but I left Ellis standing on the porch, watching me drive off into the storm.

CHAPTER THIRTY-SEVEN
MALIK

I sat across from Kai on the living room sofa and waited for her to respond. She crossed her legs and smiled at me. That sexy shit wasn't going to work tonight.

"So why am I just now hearing from you?" I repeated.

"I didn't know what happened until this afternoon."

"Cut the shit, Kai. I got fired *yesterday* morning. You didn't wonder why I never made it to our meeting? What about the ten messages I left on your cell phone yesterday and all day today? Now you show up over here at almost nine at night, acting oblivious."

"I'm telling you the truth. After I left your office I received a distraught call from Justine. She told me that Ira was being rushed to the hospital with chest pains. I just dropped everything and ran out of the office to meet her. I didn't realize that I had left my phone behind until I was almost at the hospital in White Plains. I stayed with Justine until Ira was out of the woods this morning. I went home to freshen up and I didn't get to the office until early this afternoon. That's when I found out what happened to you."

"And still no call."

"I was in shock that they let you go, Malik. I didn't want to speak with you over the phone. I wanted to see you face-to-face."

"So you rushed right over a day and a half later."

"You don't have to get sarcastic with me. I came over as soon as I could."

"So you see me. What's up? What did you want to talk to me about?"

"Are you all right? I mean, what happened?"

"Maybe you can tell me. Donner is *your* boy. What did he tell you?"

"I haven't seen Gerry. He wasn't in when I got to the office this afternoon."

"That's convenient—just like Ira's emergency. It seems your friends and family can't stay out of the hospital."

"I understand you're upset, but I don't understand why you're directing your anger at me."

"Because it's real funny how you go missing when all of this shit is going down. I come in and you're in my office telling me there's an issue with the campaign and the next thing I know I'm fired. I don't hear a peep out of you until you pop up at my door with half-assed excuses."

"I don't appreciate the way you're talking to me," she said as she got up from the couch. She pushed my half-empty bottle of Patrón to the side and sat on the coffee table in front of me. "Tell me what happened."

"What is there to tell? Your boy fired me. I was blamed and took the fall for someone else's fuck-up."

"I'm so sorry."

"Are you?"

"What kind of question is that? Of course, I am."

"You didn't know that I was going to be held accountable for the missing logos on Sphere's ads?"

"No. Gerry had only told me of the problem right before you arrived."

"*Gerry.* It seems *Gerry* kept you abreast of way more shit than he told me. Why is that? What's up with you and Gerry?"

Kai threw her hands up. "I don't like where you're going with this, Malik. I think I better leave and give you time to cool off before we both say some things we might regret."

"Good idea."

Kai leaned over and kissed me on the cheek. "Feel better and call me when you're in the mood to talk."

I reached past her to get my shot glass. "Later."

She grabbed her purse off the couch, then walked to the door without even a glance back.

I refilled my glass and took another shot as Kai let the door slam behind her.

CHAPTER THIRTY-EIGHT
MELINA

The flakes were blanketing the road, making it tough for my tires to get proper traction. I had spoken to Charlee and told her that I was on my way to her place in Harlem. At the rate the snow was falling I would never make it there. I was getting scared as cars in front of me slid across lanes on the parkway. Some cars were scattered along the shoulder with their hazard lights flashing and I saw several stuck in the embankment on the right side of the road. Rushing out of Ellis's house during a snowstorm may not have been the smartest thing to do, but it was too late to turn around now. He had been blowing up my cell since I left. Each time it rang I sent him directly to voicemail.

Two hours passed and at least six inches of snow had fallen. The wind gusts were making it difficult to see anything through the blowing snow. Traffic was at a crawl. My best option was to get home to Brooklyn.

I followed behind an SUV on Atlantic Avenue, trying to drive in its tire tracks. When I finally turned onto my street, the snow was completely undisturbed and too high to navigate. I pulled as close as I could to the curb and parked my car on the corner in front of a *No Parking* sign. I texted Charlee to let her know I wasn't coming.

I draped my scarf over the top of my head and wrapped it around my face and neck. I slung my purse over my shoulder and stepped out of the car and into a foot of snow. The wind whipped past me, pushing me away from the car door. I caught hold of the side view mirror to steady myself. The heavy snow was clinging to my jeans and the wetness was already seeping into my ankle boots. I began the trek to my brownstone. A half block had never seemed so far. With each step my feet grew colder. My fingers were stinging. I couldn't put my hands in my pockets because I needed to balance myself. If was going to go down in the snow I wanted to break my fall with my hands, not my head.

I gripped the rail as I pulled myself up the stairs to the front door of the brownstone. Once inside the doorway, I stomped the snow from shoes, removed my scarf and brushed as much snow as I could from my jeans. I was shivering from the inside out. I made my way up the stairs to my apartment. I tried to unzip my purse to get my keys, but could barely bend my fingers. I banged on the door, hoping Malik was home. I didn't hear any movement inside, so I fumbled with my purse again. It slipped from my hands and dropped to the floor. As I knelt down to pick it up, the door flew open.

"Who the hell is it?" Malik bellowed.

I teetered backward, falling on my ass. "Oh, my goodness. You scared me."

"Mel?" Malik peered down at me "What are you doing out here?" He extended his hand to pull me up. "Your hands are freezing. Get in here."

I followed him inside the apartment. He took my purse from me as I took off my soggy shoes and socks. I unbuttoned my coat.

Malik held out his hands. "Give me that stuff. I'll put it in the bathroom."

I peeled off my jeans and passed everything to him. "Thanks, Malik."

He paused and looked me over. I stood in the doorway, shivering in little more than a shirt that was barely covering my ass. "Go put on something warm, Mel."

Malik went down the hallway. I waited a moment until he was out of sight and then hurried to my room. I grabbed my plush robe and a thick pair of socks from the dresser drawer. I slipped off my shirt and slipped into the warmth of my robe. I sat on the edge of my bed and covered my frozen feet with my socks. I inhaled the atmosphere of my apartment—my bedroom—and felt a sense of tranquility and calm. The trek from Ellis's was harrowing and I was thankful to be safely settled in my own home.

I walked into the living room. Malik was sitting on the couch, pouring himself a drink. The lights were dim and jazz softly played in the background. I noticed he had a five o'clock shadow and his hair was a bit curlier than usual. He was wearing a wife beater and a pair of long basketball shorts.

"I put your bag over there." He motioned to the chair in the corner.

"Thank you." I went to dig my cell phone out and placed it on the coffee table. Two more missed calls from Ellis. I eased down on the sofa across from Malik with a long sigh.

"What are you doing out in this weather, Mel?"

I appreciated that he didn't take the direct approach. "I love the snow," I said with a sardonic chuckle that turned into a broken sob. I covered my mouth with my hand to stifle the crying. I wiped my eyes with my robe sleeve.

"You want me to make you some tea?" he asked.

I shook my head.

"You just came in covered with snow from head to toe. You need something to warm you up. I can see you shivering from here." Malik got up and went to the kitchen. He came back with a shot glass. He poured me a drink from his bottle, then handed it to me.

"What's this?" I smelled the contents of the glass, wrinkling my nose.

"It's tequila. Drink it. It'll warm you up."

I put the glass to my lips and tilted my head back. The tequila burned going down. I tapped my chest, coughing at the same time. I slid my glass over to Malik. "One more."

He raised his eyebrows but obliged. He handed me my shot before filling his glass again. We tapped glasses and then downed our shots together. I coughed. He didn't. Malik shook his head at me.

He leaned his head back against the couch. "I lost my job yesterday."

"Oh nooo," I said, dragging my second word out a little too long. Obviously, tequila works fast. "What happened?"

"I wish I could tell you. All I know is that I'm the fucking fall guy for some bullshit."

"That is some bullshit."

Malik laughed. "You better ease up on the tequila."

"Nope. Give me another."

He refilled my glass. "I busted my ass for that company. With less than two days before my campaign was supposed to go live, someone screwed me big time. I approved the final ads, but somehow an incorrect version got submitted. Of course, nobody knew shit."

"Not even Kai?"

"Don't even mention her to me. She was nowhere to be found and claimed she didn't know anything. I don't believe that shit one bit. Her ass is so tight with the boss; I know he told her what was going down."

"How could they do this to you right before the holidays?"

"Because they don't give a fuck, Mel. That's how. They don't care nothing about any fucking holiday."

"Some people only care about themselves."

Malik was quiet for a moment. "What are you doing home? Your parents are in town and you're out in a snowstorm. How did you even get here in this weather?"

"I had a horrible fight with Ellis about his mother." I banged my glass on the table for another shot. "That woman is a witch. I mean it." I swallowed the tequila. It was going down much easier. "There's something evil about her. The way she talked to my parents...she was so rude."

"So you left your parents over there?"

"I wasn't planning to leave them. They had already gone to bed and I just ran out of the house. I didn't know where I was going—I just had to get away from Ellis. No matter what his mother does, or says, he always has her back. Never mine. He *never* has my back," I said, emphatically shaking my head from side to side.

My cell phone started ringing. I leaned over and peeped at it. Ellis. I sent him to voicemail.

"Does he know where you are?"

"Nope."

"Ellis isn't one of my favorite people, but he's probably going crazy wondering where you are right now."

"Tough."

"Mel."

"I'm serious, Malik. That woman despises me and makes it clear that she doesn't think I'm good enough for her son."

No one had ever made me feel the way Bebe did. She never missed an opportunity to snub me or draw distinctions between our families, wealth or class. The fact that she felt she could drag my parents into her nonsense was crossing the line. We didn't have money like the Harlows, but we were hardworking, middle-class people that were proud of our accomplishments. I was running my own successful business. As a young African-American woman that was quite a feat. It meant nothing to Bebe. All she saw was a woman that didn't meet her standards. I didn't have the right breeding, upbringing, culture, financial resources or even friends.

I believed her when she said she could put a stop to our wedding. It seemed she could get Ellis to do anything that she wanted. It's a hard pill to swallow when the man you're marrying doesn't put you first. It makes you doubt the relationship you're supposed to have.

"Ellis doesn't do enough to put his mother in her place. He lets her go unchecked at my expense. He needs to tell her how much I mean to him. Let her know what a special person I am."

Malik leaned forward. "You are very special." He poured us both another tequila shot. "Any man should be able to see that. You're beautiful. Smart. Sexy…"

I studied him through the dimness in the room, trying to read his expression. He rubbed his hand over the beginnings of a beard and smiled. I threw back my shot. The room seemed awfully warm. I leaned back against the sofa cushion and put my feet up on the coffee table, crossing my ankles. My robe parted, exposing my leg up to my thigh.

Malik kept his eyes on me as he swigged his shot. He placed his glass on the table and then slowly moved his hand near my feet. Malik never took his gaze off of me. He gently tugged on the tip of my sock, easing it from my foot. He dangled the sock between his fingers for a few seconds, then dropped it on the table. He poured another shot, downed half of it, and then handed me the glass. I pressed the rim to my lips and watched him as he slipped off my other sock. Again, he let it dangle until I acknowledged that he was holding it. I finished his shot and he let the sock drop. He traced a finger along the instep of my foot. My breath caught in my throat. He took my foot in his hands and massaged his thumbs into the pressure point on the ball of my foot. I burrowed deeper into the sofa cushion. He worked his hands from my toes to my ankle and then gave my other foot the same attention.

Malik released my foot and slowly stood up. He didn't move from where he was standing. He just stared at me and I stared back at him. Malik licked his lips. I took my legs down from the table. With measured steps he came around to my side of the table and unhurriedly sat down on it in front of me. He positioned his knees on the outside of mine. He took the shot glass out of my hand and rested it on the table. "You're a special lady, Mel."

I swallowed hard, then exhaled a shaky breath. Malik put his right hand on my knee and lingeringly slid my robe away from my leg. He placed his left hand on my other leg and exposed it as well. He simultaneously rubbed both hands from my knees up to my hips and back again, applying more pressure with each motion. I placed my hands on top of Malik's as he massaged my inner thighs, smoothly parting my legs. He dropped to his knees between my legs. He reached for the sash on my robe and began to untie it little by little. I bit my bottom lip as his strong hands deftly loosened the knot.

Malik spread my robe, revealing my C's cradled in crimson lace. "Damn." A smile flitted across his lips before he leaned forward and kissed my stomach. Instinctively, my thighs tightened on his sides. He looked up at me with an intensity I had never seen before in his eyes. He traced his finger around my belly button, then bowed his head to kiss where he had just touched. His tongue darted in and out of my navel. I lifted my hand and ran my fingers through his curls. His kisses intensified as he inched his way up to my breasts. Malik paused when he reached the bottom of my bra. He leaned back, grasped the sides of my robe and pulled me forward until his lips touched mine. He sucked my bottom lip into his mouth. I pulled back. He tugged me forward again, pressing his mouth against mine, biting and sucking my lips. Malik grabbed me by the back of my head and pulled me into his kiss. His tongue entered my mouth, connecting with mine. They played a game of chase—where he led, I followed. He was hot, almost feverish. Malik kissed me like he was dying of thirst and I was his drink of water. I nibbled his lips and then licked them like a lollipop. He moaned and things stirred deep within me. He pulled away like he needed to catch his breath, his chest visibly rising and falling.

Malik pushed my robe away from my shoulders, caressing my arms along the way. He bowed his head forward and rubbed his face on the fleshy mounds of my breasts. I looked down at him as his cheek languidly stroked my softness, his eyes closed, head moving back and forth. Malik reached up and slipped his hand inside my bra, freeing my breast. His tongue circled my nipple. It instantly hardened. He flicked his tongue across it rapidly before sucking it into his mouth. I attempted to lean back, but he moved his hands behind me, keeping me in an upright position. He unhooked my bra, removing the obstacle that hindered him from having full access. "You are so beautiful," he said, his voice sounding raspy.

He reached for his own tank and pulled it over his head. He smiled when he saw my eyes travel from his chest to his stomach. His abs were chiseled perfection. I tentatively touched my hand to his pecs. Malik quivered. He eased me back and began kissing my stomach again. His hands found their way to my hips and with a nimble motion, Malik slipped his hands beneath my ass and slid my panties down to my knees.

My eyes went wide. "Malik—"

"Shhh," he whispered, without so much as a glance up. He planted tiny kisses on my stomach, venturing lower with each kiss. He slid my panties down my calves and over my feet. Malik spread my legs wide, licked his lips and then buried his face in my sunshine. His full, soft mouth covered my nani, the tip of his tongue sampling my nectar. He moaned and my kitty reacted. "You're so wet."

"Malik, stop," I said, my words breathy. "It feels too good." I tried to wriggle away.

Malik grabbed hold of my hips and pulled me into his face. His firm grip held me still as he drilled his tongue deeper into my center. The sensation sent a surge of electricity up my spine. "Mmmm, Malik…"

"You like that?" he asked. "Do you still want me to stop?"

"No."

"Should I stop?"

"No, don't stop."

He darted his tongue across my clit. "Ask me not to stop."

"Don't stop."

"Ask me not to stop, Mel," he said, kissing my inner thigh.

"Malik, don't stop."

"Say please."

"Please."

"Please what?"

"Malik, please don't stop."

He jerked me toward him, raising my legs over his shoulders. I gazed down my naked body at Malik's head between my legs. He feverishly licked around, up, down, inside and out like he was eating an ice cream cone and didn't want a single drop to drip. He sucked on my clit until my moans turned into one long, high-pitched note. Malik peered up at me. Our breathing was coming fast and heavy. He took my trembling legs off his shoulders. Still kneeling in front of me he pushed his basketball shorts down over his ass and thighs. I sat up on the couch, my feet on the floor, legs on either side of him. His penis was long, hard and standing straight up. Just like the rest of his body, it was smooth and beautiful. He looked down at it and then up at me. He leaned back into a sitting position, his ass on the heels of his feet. He wrapped one arm around my waist and slid me toward him. His other hand held his dick as he guided me onto his lap. I eased down onto his thickness and gasped. His hips jerked upward. We froze, his dick deep inside of me, and stared into each other's eyes. Malik's hands gripped the sofa cushion. I wrapped my arms around his neck. He thrust into me with a grunt. My arms tightened around him. He thrust again, harder and deeper. With the next thrust, I arched my back and rocked my hips down into him.

"Damn, Mel!"

I rolled my hips into his, my sunshine getting wetter with each gyration. Malik let go of the couch and wrapped his arms around my back, gripping my shoulders. He pushed until he filled me up, pulling me down onto his dick. I cried out.

"Let me hear you, Mel. Let go. How does it feel?"

I could hardly catch my breath and didn't answer.

He pumped more vigorously. "How...does...it...feel?" he asked between thrusts.

"Feels good," I barely managed to say.

He pumped faster. "Let...me...hear...you."

"So good."

In one quick maneuver Malik raised up, holding my body to

his, and laid me on my back. He planted his hands on the floor near my shoulders and held his body over me as if doing a push-up. He slowly pulled his penis from inside me and laid it heavily on top of my sunshine. It glistened from my juices. He moved his hips, sliding his dick back and forth, grinding on my clit.

"Talk to me, Mel. Let me hear you."

My kitty throbbed, craving to have him back inside me. I purred his name. "*Malik*."

"Do you want this?" He continued to stroke. "Look at it."

"I want it," I murmured.

"Tell me."

"I want it," I whined.

"Louder."

"It feels so good, Malik. I want you inside of me."

He rubbed his penis in my wetness. I wrapped my legs around his waist, drawing him closer. He pulled back, only allowing his tip to enter me. I squeezed with my legs; he resisted. Inch by inch, he slid inside. I lifted my hips, trying to coax him along.

"Give it to me, Malik."

"Yeah…talk to me."

"Give it to me." I propped up on my elbows, so my face was next to his. "I know you want it, too."

"Mmm…yes."

"Show me that you want it," I teased.

"You know I want it."

"Prove it," I said, licking my lips.

He pushed deep inside until our bodies bumped. In and out, over and over again. Malik growled with each long, forceful thrust. I was on the precipice of orgasm and the sweet friction had me about to explode. Malik was biting on my neck, caressing my body and playing in my sunshine.

I was singing his name as he handled my body right. "Right there, Malik."

"Oooo, you're so wet. Are you about to come?"

"Yes," I sang. "Yes."

"I want to feel you come. Make it rain all over me."

We moved together in sync, each movement intensifying the sensation. Malik grabbed my ass and raised it off the carpet. That was it. My pussy tightened around him and we both cried out. My juices poured all over him. He cried out again. "Mel! Damn!"

My sunshine contracted in waves. He pounded harder. "I'm coming!"

Malik pulled out and released his warm essence on my stomach. He collapsed next to me on the floor, panting loudly. "Damn, Mel."

CHAPTER THIRTY-NINE
MALIK

I turned on my side and propped myself up on an elbow, taking in the length of Melina's body. She lay on her back with one leg bent at the knee. There was a light sheen of sweat on her face, chest and between her breasts—she was glowing and simply gorgeous. I grabbed my tank and wiped my swimmers from her stomach.

"How much of that are we going to blame on the tequila?" I asked.

She brushed away the strands of hair that were clinging to her face. "Is that what you're planning to do? Say you got carried away because of the tequila?"

"I think we both know it would be a lie if we tried to blame it on the alcohol. There's been something brewing between us for a while now."

"As much as I would like to disagree with you, I can't. All I know is that I don't want to think right now. I don't want to question what happened between us or why. Because if I start thinking, I'll start panicking and I'm not ready to panic yet."

"I can respect that." I lay down next to Melina and pulled her close to me, wrapping her in my arms. She rested her head on my chest and draped her arm across my stomach. "I meant it when I said you're a special lady. And if you didn't know how sexy I thought you were before, you definitely know now."

"Malik, I know we have our differences, but I think you're special, too. You're handsome, intelligent, sexy—"

"Sounds like you're quoting me," I said with a laugh.

"Maybe I am, but I mean it."

"You forgot to add that I'm a good lover."

"Wow. You're going to go there?" she said, lifting her head off my chest.

"Yeah, I'm going there. You can't deny what just happened was amazing. It was intense. Hot. Sweaty. It was *nasty*…and you liked it nasty."

A sly smile spread across her lips. "Yes, I liked it."

"Your hair's a mess and you got loud. I liked *that*."

"That's what you like? That I look a mess?"

"Among other things, I liked that it was impulsive. I liked how you looked at my body with lust in your eyes. I liked how you kissed me like you meant it. I liked tasting you. I liked your hot pussy gripping my dick. I liked how you got so wet. I liked how you held onto me. I liked how you gave as good as you got. I like you laying in my arms right now."

"You're embarrassing me," she said, hiding her face in the crook of my neck.

"Why? There's something between us. You know it, and I know it."

She touched her finger to my lips. "Don't."

I sighed. "All right. You're right, but admit one thing, it felt natural."

"Malik—"

"All right."

Her phone vibrated on the coffee table. Melina sat up and grabbed it. She checked the display, then tossed it back on the table.

"How long are you going to ignore him?"

"I don't know."

"Mel, there's a storm outside."

"And?"

"Don't you think you should give him some peace of mind?"

"Since when do you care about Ellis's feelings?" She reached over and snatched her robe from the couch.

"I don't."

"Then leave it alone," she said.

"You're mad right now, but in the morning you'll see things differently."

"Let *me* worry about it in the morning." She pulled her robe on and clambered to her feet.

I stood in front of her. Melina's eyes were drawn downward to my hardhead. She caught herself and turned away. "I would think that after what we just did you wouldn't be uncomfortable with me."

"I'm not," she answered, avoiding my eyes.

"You can look all you want, Mel."

She pulled her robe tighter and then turned to leave the room, bumping into the sofa on her way out. "I need a shower."

I stepped into my shorts and sat on the edge of the couch. Melina's underwear, socks and my tank were strewn across the floor. The Patron bottle was nearly empty. I raised it to my lips and drained the remaining tequila. What had just happened? It almost felt like a dream. Maybe I was in a tequila haze. Did Melina and I really just have sex? Great fucking sex, at that.

I replayed everything in my mind. I was definitely the initiator. I pushed up on Melina. I wanted her. I had to have her. If I was being honest with myself I've wanted her for a long time. What I was having a problem processing was the way that Melina responded. She was as into me as I was into her. I understood being mad with her fiancé, but what happened between us had nothing to do with him. I felt it. It was in her kiss, the way her body reacted to mine.

I was trippin'. Maybe I was imagining a connection. Melina could've been taking revenge on her man and I was the easiest way to do it. Who knows? Instead of sitting there questioning her motives, I needed to consider my own. The tequila definitely didn't make me step to Melina—I've never needed liquid courage when it came to women. But my anger at Kai probably played a part in my actions. A small part. The real deal was that I wanted Melina and I went after what I wanted.

I rubbed my hands over my head, wondering if I had just fucked up. This woman was engaged. Without a doubt, I had complicated things for both of us, but something was burning in me and I couldn't help myself. I got up to turn off the music and pick up our clothes from the floor.

I heard the running water in the bathroom. I tossed the clothes on the couch and then wandered down the hallway, pausing outside the bathroom door. I turned the knob quietly and entered the steam-filled room, closing the door behind me. I pulled the shower curtain back and Melina startled. Her hair was wet and soap bubbles were streaming down her body. I shed my shorts and stepped into the shower behind her. I rubbed the front of my body against the back of hers, reaching around to squeeze her breasts.

I guided her hands to the shower tiles in front of her, gripped her hips and then entered her pussy from behind. I was in so deep, in more ways than one.

CHAPTER FORTY
MELINA

After my interlude with Malik in the shower, we went to our respective rooms. I lay across my bed in my robe, head wrapped in a towel. Every time I nodded off, my eyes popped back open. It was three-thirty in the morning and my mind raced. Guilt battled with disbelief, confusion and shame. My head throbbed and my stomach ached. It was the tequila having its revenge and I deserved it and more.

I had done the unthinkable. I recklessly cheated on Ellis. My fiancé. Nothing that had transpired between us gave me license to be with another man. Not just any man, but Malik. The man Ellis didn't want me living with in close quarters.

I placed my hand on my churning stomach, hoping to soothe it, but my thoughts drifted to Malik's hand pressed against my stomach as he sexed me from behind in the shower. My stomach lurched. I wasn't sure if repulsion or exhilaration was the culprit. I was so ashamed of what I had done, but it was impossible to ignore how good Malik made me feel. I fell asleep trying to figure out how I would face Ellis and Malik in light of what had transpired.

"Mel, wake up. Mel."

I roused to Malik calling my name from the doorway of my bedroom. The phone was ringing. My head…still pounding. "What?" I croaked.

"You need to answer that. Your boy has been ringing the phone nonstop for the past ten minutes. He lets it ring, gets the voicemail and then calls back." Malik turned and left, closing the door after him.

I rolled my head to the side to look at the clock. Five a.m. The ringing stopped and then immediately started again. I hadn't heard it in my comatose state. I reached over to the nightstand and picked it up. "Hello," I said in a voice that hardly sounded like my own.

"Lina? Is that you?"

As soon as I heard the fear in his voice, the guilt crashed down on me tenfold. "It's me, Ellis."

"I was so worried about you. Are you all right?"

"I'm fine."

"I have been calling you all night—ever since you left here. I was about to call the police."

"Thank goodness you didn't. I'm okay."

"I can't believe you would drive off in a snowstorm—"

"Not now, Ellis."

"Fine. I'm sending a car for you."

"No, I'll make my way back there in a few hours."

"I don't think so. The roads are terrible and I think you need to get here before your parents come down for breakfast. I didn't disturb them when you left. As far as they know, you're still here—you never left."

I knew he was right. I did not want to drag my parents into my drama. "I'll be ready."

"Good." He hung up without a good-bye.

I struggled to lift my body from the bed and over to my dresser.

I pulled out the most comfortable thing I could find to wear. An oversized sweatshirt and a pair of leggings. I sunk my feet into my Ugg boots and went about tackling my hair. It was damp and waving up on me. I pulled it back into a ponytail bun and threw on a knit hat. There was no help for the dark circles under my eyes.

I went into the bathroom and washed my face and brushed my teeth. I dotted on a bit of lip gloss, then went to the kitchen for a bottle of water. I needed to hydrate and to flush the tequila from my system.

Malik was stirring in his room, but he didn't come out. I spotted my bra and panties on the sofa next to his tank top that he used to wipe his semen from my stomach, and a fresh pang of guilt hit me. I tossed my underwear and my cell phone in my purse, then left the apartment to wait downstairs for the car to take me back to Long Island.

I dozed off on the ride. As the car pulled into the driveway I saw Ellis standing at the front door, still wearing his clothes from the day before. I took a deep breath and stepped out of the car.

Ellis held the door open for me as I entered the house. I removed my coat and boots with him looming over me. I shut the closet door and turned to see his outstretched hand. I paused a moment before grasping it. He headed toward the staircase, my hand in his. We went into his bedroom and closed the door.

Ellis released my hand and pulled me into an embrace. "I get it, Lina. I'm sorry."

I leaned back, so I could see his face. "Ellis—"

"I am sorry." He led me over to the settee at the end of the bed. "I know my mother can be difficult, but I honestly believe she has good intentions. Now before you say anything, let me finish. Obviously, there's a serious issue between the two of you. I intend to do everything I can to rectify the problem."

"Ellis, you're part of the problem. You facilitate your mother's behavior."

"She's my mother. She has such a different outlook on how to treat people. It's hard for me to admit this, but she's so accustomed to interacting with people of her own ilk, that sometimes she's a bit callous to others. I had hoped that she would see the beauty that I see in you and love you like a daughter."

"It's not likely."

"I think it would have been different if my father was still here. He loved you, Lina. He would have never abided by Mother treating you the way she does. He kept her grounded. She would've followed his example and truly welcomed you into this family."

"But your father isn't here."

His shoulders hunched. "I know. It's times like these when I miss him. There are so many days when I need to talk to him about work...about life...just about anything. There were so many things left unsaid between us." Ellis seemed to get lost in his thoughts for a minute. "He would know what to do about my mother—I don't."

"So what do you expect me to do?"

"Let me handle her."

"You have failed miserably in that department. If your father wouldn't have tolerated your mother's behavior, why do you?"

"I promise you, I will make things right."

"I want to believe you, but—"

"Last night, when I couldn't find you, it was unbearable. I didn't know if you were safe or not. The thought that I drove you from the house, and something could have happened to you, was maddening. The prospect of having to account to your parents and explain to your father that I didn't take care of his baby girl scared the hell out of me. I swore that if you returned safely that I would move heaven and earth to bring peace to our family. We *are* a family, Lina. You're my future wife. I love you."

I began fidgeting with my hands, turning my ring around my finger as I tried my hardest to hold back tears. "I love you," I whispered with a hoarse voice.

"I know we've discussed it before, but I want you here with me. There's no reason why we shouldn't be living together. We can start packing your things this week."

I nodded.

Ellis leaned over and kissed my cheek. "Things will get better." His kisses trailed down to my neck. "Trust me."

Trust. I had violated our trust. A tear rolled down my cheek. Ellis drew me onto his lap, planting kisses all over my face. He ended with a lingering kiss on my lips that nearly made me start bawling. Ellis led me over to the bed. We laid on top of the duvet, fully clothed, and spooned. Ellis on his bed with clothes on—I suppose people do change.

CHAPTER FORTY-ONE
MALIK

I was at the window, staring down at a snow plow boring a narrow path in the middle of the street, while burying the cars parked at the curb. There would be a lot of pissed people trying to dig their cars out later. The snow had stopped and the sun was shining bright, but it was cold, and the wind was still brutally whipping out there.

I heard Melina when she left the apartment at five-thirty a.m. obviously heading back to her fiancé. I knew she had to go back, but nevertheless it was fucking with me. She left without even speaking. What was I expecting? Some crazy shit went down last night. What was there to say about it?

I walked over to the couch and turned to the news on the television. The news anchor cautioned people to stay off the roads if they didn't need to travel. There were airport delays and many businesses were opening late. That was all I needed to hear. I would be cooped up in the apartment all day, but unlike yesterday, there would be no drinking. No more wallowing in anger. I'd spend my day working on my business plan. The first thing I needed was a hot cup of coffee. I hadn't slept much after I "showered" with Melina. I could still feel me inside of her; she covered me like a glove. I shook the thought from my head. It would be a long day if my mind kept wandering to what took place in here last night.

I couldn't explain it, but I wished she hadn't left. I wanted her near me. I understood it was improbable—her parents were in town. Melina was doing what she had to do and I needed to do the same. I went to the kitchen and brewed a pot of coffee. I set up shop at the kitchen table and got busy on my plan.

I got a text from Terrence at noon, saying that the snow couldn't stop him and he was on his way over. College football was on all day and my boy wanted to hang. I had put in two solid hours of work, so I was down.

I straightened up the living room and then made some hot wings to grub on while we watched the game. I was throwing some frozen fries in the oven when the buzzer rang. I gave Terrence a brotherly grip at the door. "Come on in and get comfortable, man. Make sure you kick off those snowy boots."

Leave it to my boy to tote cold beer in with him. "Put these in the fridge, Malik." He handed the beer to me, then got situated in front of the TV.

I returned from the kitchen with a tray of wings. "Man, Dru let you out of the house after the storm we just had?"

"C'mon, man. You know I call the shots," he said, laughing.

"Hold up. Let me get that on tape."

"Nah, man. You know what's said between brothers stays between brothers."

"Oh, no doubt. That's why I'll play the tape for her, instead of telling her."

He howled. "I'd have to revoke your players' card for that infraction."

"Man, your players' card disintegrated once you got engaged."

"You got jokes."

"All day."

"Well, you can take five while I go wash my hands." He left the room, laughing to himself.

I poked fun at him, but I was glad he found Dru. She made him a better man. We had been partners for a long time and got into lots of trouble together. I remember one time we went to Atlantic City for the weekend. We met a set of twins from A.C. at the casino. Sherri and Berri were their names. We argued over which one of us would get Berri. Never mind that they were identical and equally hot. We figured with a name like Berri, she had to be the freaky one. We spent the night gambling, drinking and getting to know the twins much better. They came up to our room and things happened. It was a wild Saturday night. We both had Berri. We both had Sherri. In the morning, the twins asked us to give them a lift home. They gave us directions, not to their house, but to their father's church. He was a minister. He was standing at the entrance to the church greeting his parishioners and saw us when we pulled up. He walked up to the car, scowling until Sherri and Berri introduced us as their college classmates that would be coming to service that morning. They dragged Terrence and me into the church. Four hours later, we were still sitting in the front pew, listening to their father's fire and brimstone sermon. At one point Terrence nodded off and the minister called him out from the pulpit. As soon as the benediction was read we shot out of there. Sherri and Berri were on our heels, but we were too fast for them. We jumped into the car like *Starsky and Hutch* and peeled out of there, tires screeching all the way down the street. We've got a million stories like that—and worse—that stay between us. At least Terrence had the good sense to change direction. I was still adding to the storybook collection.

I was chuckling when Terrence walked back into the living room. "What's funny?" he asked.

"Sherri and Berri."

"Aw, man. I let you get me into some situations back in the day."

"I got *you* into situations? We both know that ain't true. You corrupted my ass."

"I prefer to call it mentored." Terrence laughed. "But you took it to a new level."

"Man, go head. I'm not even trying to listen to you rewrite history."

"I know the truth hurts. I'm going to grab a beer. You want one?"

"Nah, I'm abstaining from the liquor today." I told Terrence about losing my job and Kai's disappearing act. "I put a hurting on the Patron yesterday. The bottle is as dry as a desert."

"Dude, you drank an entire bottle of tequila?"

"I had a little help."

"Kai stayed here drinking with your angry drunk ass?"

"Me and Mel."

"Me and *Mel?*"

"We had sex last night," I blurted out.

"Man, what the fuck? Tell me you didn't."

"I wish I could."

Terrence muted the television. "Malik, what are you doing, man?"

"I wanted her, T."

"Oh, you wanted her? Just like that. You couldn't control yourself?"

"Come on, man. Don't bust my chops. I'm wrestling with this shit. Last night things just happened. We were talking and I made a move."

"Malik…"

"I know, man. She was pissed at her man and came home. We both just got caught up in the moment. T, it was crazy. I started touching her and then we started kissing. We went at it raw, man. That's how crazy it got in here."

Terrence shook his head from side to side. "Now what?"

"I don't know," I mumbled.

"Where is she now?"

"She went back to Long Island."

"Back to dude."

"Her parents are in town. She had to go back." I wondered to myself whether she would've gone back to Ellis's if her parents weren't there.

"I don't know if you want my advice, but I'm going to give it to you anyway. Leave Melina alone. She's about to get married, man. Respect her situation."

I silently nodded. I didn't have a rebuttal for Terrence. I took the remote and unmuted the television. The referee was calling a play on the field. Offsides. I waited for the penalty.

CHAPTER FORTY-TWO
MELINA

When my mother and I returned from dress shopping, Daniella was at the house. She gave me a big hug when I came through the door. I introduced her to my mother and she bestowed her with the same effusive greeting. She was so sweet. I hoped Daniella would never become like her mother.

"Did you find a dress?" Daniella asked.

"Actually, we did," I responded.

"And it's beautiful," my mother said, beaming.

"I can't wait to see it. I know Melina is going to be a beautiful bride."

"I also found the bridesmaids' dresses. I'm going to coordinate a fitting for you, Charlee and Giselle, in a few weeks. So keep your calendar open."

"Just let me know when and I'm there. Everyone's in the sitting room," she said, rushing us along. "We were waiting for you to get back. Ellis said he wanted to share something with the family."

"Okay. I'll be there in a second. Mom, you can go with Daniella. I need to take a couple of aspirin for my headache." I wondered what was up. Ellis hadn't made me privy to any announcement he wanted to make.

I went up to Ellis's bathroom to get the pills from his medicine cabinet. My head had been aching all day. The tequila, combined with a lack of sleep, was taking its toll. Earlier, Ellis and I had dozed for about an hour before he got up. He practically had to use a cattle prod to get me up and running. After he left the bathroom to get dressed, I went in and closed the door behind me. I inspected my body from head to toe to make sure there was no physical evidence from my night with Malik. I checked for love bites, scratches or anything that wasn't supposed to be there. There was slight redness where Malik had repeatedly slapped my ass in the shower, but other than that, all was clear. I took a scalding hot shower, trying to let the lingering memory of the night before drain away. I just needed to get through the weekend with my family and then I could deal with what I had done. I wanted to ask my mother if we could cancel our plans to go dress shopping, but I knew she wouldn't understand. Hell, I didn't even understand. All I knew was that shopping for a dress after my night with Malik didn't feel right. When I finally went downstairs to meet my mother, she asked if everything was okay. Obviously the concealer I applied on the dark circles beneath my eyes wasn't covering up a thing. I assured her I was fine and we headed to the bridal shop. On the ride over, I caught her peeking at me. I could tell she wanted to ask me something, so I preemptively started a random discussion. Thankfully, by the time we began to look at dresses her concern had dissipated. I must have tried on at least twenty gowns before we settled on the very first one in which I had started. It was an organza A-line gown, with a fitted bodice, sweetheart neckline and a long, sweeping train. I knew it was the one. Posing in the mirror, I was picture-perfect. In reality—nothing was further from the truth.

I interrupted my father's entertaining recollection of how he used to chase my boyfriends off when I was younger. They were all laughing at his exaggerated tale of inciting fear in any guy that dared to ring his doorbell.

"Daddy, please. Are you telling those stories again?" I asked, as I came into the room and took a seat next to my mother.

"I'm glad I didn't meet you back then," Ellis joked.

"Something tells me that you wouldn't have had a problem with Mr. Bradford," my mother offered.

"Daddy had a problem with everyone. No exceptions."

Daniella looked from me to my father. "That's sweet."

"I'm keeping track of who Daniella brings around, too. They'll have to pass my inspection before she can go out with them."

Daniella laughed. "Oh goodness."

Ellis was doing his best to step up in Daniella's life since his father died. She may have been in college, but a girl always needs her father. If that's not possible, a loving big brother can make a world of difference.

"Face it, Daniella, I'm keeping tabs on you."

"Ellis, stop it," I said.

"Thank you," Daniella mouthed.

"All right. I do want to say a few things to everyone. The wedding is rapidly approaching and I'm embracing the prospect of being a married man. I have everything I could ever want, and more than I had ever imagined, both professionally and in my personal life. Lina is a remarkable woman. When I met Lina, I immediately wanted to know her better. She brought something to my life that I hadn't realized was missing. I spend so much time running my company and immersing myself in work. It's easy to allow work to control you, but Lina grounds me. She helps me to see that there's much more to life. I look at her and I envision our future together. I see a home filled with love, some children and plenty of family. Lawrence and Cynthia, I'm proud to have you as in-laws. Mother and Daniella—I'm thankful for both of you. This weekend has made me realize that we're all family. The holidays are here and it's wonderful that we can all be together as a family. We have to treat each other with love and respect one another. When I think about my future with Lina, I'm striving for a close-knit family. We have four months until the wedding, but I don't want to be apart from this woman. I know I'm getting a little long-winded, but I wanted to share my sentiments with you and to let you know that Lina is moving in next week."

"I'm sure I speak for myself and Melina's mother when I say it's about time," my father responded. "We prefer that she's here with you."

"That's wonderful," Bebe said, her lips pulled tight.

My mother knitted her brow at me. She had to be wondering why I didn't mentioned anything when we were together earlier.

"We're going to start *packing* this week. I've accumulated a lot of stuff over the years, so it will take me longer than a week to get it all done," I said, trying to save face with my mother.

"But even if we haven't completely packed everything, she'll still be moving in by week's end," Ellis quickly rebutted. "I want her moved in before Christmas."

A smirk settled on Bebe's lips. "Melina's right. These things can take time."

"We'll get it done," Ellis replied.

"Let me know if I can help,"

"Thanks, Daniella," I said.

Ellis clasped his hands together. "And with that being said, let's go have dinner."

CHAPTER FORTY-THREE
MELINA

I took the train from my office into the city. Much of the snow from the weekend had been cleared away, but there was plenty of slush and icy patches to navigate at the corners. I gingerly crossed Lexington Avenue to 42nd Street.

Giselle and Charlee were already seated when I arrived at The Capital Grille for lunch. My mouth was running before I was even situated in the chair. "Thank you for meeting me on such short notice."

"Your parents' visit didn't go well?" Charlee asked.

"It started off rocky, but it got better by the end of the weekend."

"Did they leave yet?" Giselle said.

"Last night. They're back home in Maryland. I'll tell you about that later." I sighed heavily. "I've got bigger problems than the Harlows."

"Is everything all right?"

"What's the matter?"

"I can't believe I'm about to say this."

Giselle's hand went up to her chest. "You're scaring me, Melina."

"I'm sorry," I said, reaching over to rub her baby bump. "It's hard for me to say this, but I cheated on Ellis."

"What!" Charlee said, her voice carrying to the surrounding tables. "With who?"

"I cheated with Malik."

There was chatter at all the other tables, except mine. My eyes shifted from Charlee to Giselle and back. "Say something. Please."

"How did this happen?" Giselle whispered.

"I know it's not an excuse, but I had a fight with Ellis. I was pissed off and Malik and I started talking about our problems. We had some shots of tequila. Malik massaged my feet and it was downhill from there."

"All I want to know is how was it?" Charlee asked.

"Charlee, how is that relevant?" Giselle said.

"Giselle, don't front. You want to know, too. Melina, answer the damn question."

I shrugged my shoulders. "It was the best I ever had. Malik put it down."

"I knew it!" Charlee threw her hand up for a high-five. Giselle swatted it down.

"I feel so guilty. I can't believe I did it. What's worse is that I enjoyed it so much."

"Did you think so many people cheat because it feels bad? Girl, you have been living like Pollyanna for so long that you don't have a clue. People cheat every day."

"I'm not *people*, Charlee."

"You are now. And guess what? It's not the end of the world. You're human like the rest of us."

"So you're saying I'm not supposed to feel bad about what I did?"

"Of course not. I'm saying don't beat yourself up over it."

"Melina, I agree with Charlee to a certain degree. God knows you can't change what happened." Giselle's voice cracked and her eyes got watery. "But you can make sure it never happens again."

"It won't. I'm moving in with Ellis this weekend."

"Wow, okay. So you're running from your situation with Malik?"

"Charlee, we don't have a situation and, no, I'm not running." I explained to my girls what happened between me and Bebe and then what followed with Ellis. Naturally, I had to give a play-by-play of my interlude with Malik. "When I went back to Ellis's, he offered the most sincere apology and promised he'd do better when it comes to managing his mother."

"Can't nobody manage that vicious pit bull," Charlee said.

"But he's trying. On Saturday he sat us all down and discussed how important it was that we treat each other like family."

"And you think that's going to work?"

"We're getting married, Charlee. I have to have faith that Bebe and I can have a civil relationship. Either way I can't stay in that small apartment with Malik. Not after what happened."

"You're doing the right thing. Wednesday is my day off, so if you need me, I'll be over to help you pack." Giselle signaled the waitress. "I've got to order something. The little one is hungry."

"I need all the help I can get."

"I can come on Thursday to do the real work. I don't think you and Giselle will accomplish much with her hormones making her cry every five minutes."

Giselle laughed. "I've been getting better with that."

"You could've fooled me. You were just tearing up a few minutes ago."

"I can't wait to see what you're like when you get pregnant."

"That is the furthest thing from my mind. I'm too busy trying to get it in like Melina."

"Shut up, Charlee," I said.

"I will. As soon as you tell me again what it was like being with fine-ass Malik."

I went back to the office after lunch with the girls. I could always depend on them not to be judgmental and to offer sound advice when I needed it. I knew in my heart it was time to move in with Ellis. My fear that I wouldn't be happy had kept me from moving forward. But no relationship is perfect. In time, I could get Ellis to slow down with work and to devote more time to family. I'd even try to spice it up in the bedroom. We were already working on the problem with Bebe, so things could only improve.

The staff had left for the evening and I was basically shuffling papers around my desk. I was nervous about going home and seeing Malik. There was so much to say; I didn't know where to begin. Charlee had asked if I was running and that hadn't left my mind all day. Malik and I had certainly crossed a line and there was no turning back. It was best for everyone involved if I moved out. I had to forget what happened. I needed to dismiss the remnant sensations of Malik's hands on my body, his lips touching my most intimate places and the feeling of him stroking me deep inside. I had to believe that out of sight meant out of mind, so I could purge those lingering thoughts. I expected it to be awkward between me and Malik when I got home. The last thing I wanted was to be having flashbacks of us together.

With the office locked up, I embarked on my commute home. The entire trip I kept telling myself to just act normal when I saw Malik. I was anxious to see how he would behave or hear what he'd say. I exited the train station and walked toward our street. As I neared the corner where I had parked my car all I saw was an empty space. "Oh shit," I mumbled to myself. My car had been towed. Not only had I left my car in front of a no parking sign, but today was alternate-side-of-the-street parking. "Shit. Shit. Shit," I said while marching down the block.

Malik was in the living room when I came in. "Hey."

He looked up from the file in his lap. "Hey."

I spoke over my shoulder as I hung up my coat. "My car must have gotten towed today. I left it at the corner Saturday night because of the snow."

"It's not towed. I moved it yesterday."

"Did you?" A smile flitted across my lips.

"I saw it on the corner when I went to the store yesterday. I used your spare key to move it. It's down the block."

I went into the room and sat next to him. "Thanks, Malik."

He tossed his folder on the table. "Listen, Mel. I feel like I should apologize for the other night. I don't know where that came from. I mean, I know where it came from, I just don't know what made me do that. I know you're with Ellis and it was wrong of me to… well…you know."

I was glad I wasn't the only one uncomfortable with our indiscretions. "I've been thinking about what I would say to you when I got home. Now that I'm here my words are falling short."

Malik looked good in his steel-blue V-neck sweater and dark-blue cargo pants. He was clean-shaven and his hair was shorter than when I last saw it.

He caught me giving him a once-over and smiled. "I can understand that."

"I don't want to pretend that nothing happened here on Saturday. In fact, I want to put my cards on the table. I loved what happened between us the other night. I'd be a liar if I said I didn't. But the guilt has been eating me up inside for two reasons. One, I cheated on Ellis, and two, because I enjoyed it so much. I can finally grasp what people mean when they say they knew they were doing wrong, but it felt so good.

"I am every bit as responsible as you for what happened. I would never let you think it was your fault. I should have stopped before things went too far, hell, before they got started. But I didn't. And that's my cross to bear."

"So I take it everything is back in order with Ellis?"

"We're working on it."

"Did you tell him about us?"

"No and I'm not going to."

"It's our dirty little secret, huh?"

"Malik."

"What if I told you that I want it to happen again?"

"It can't."

"Why not?" he asked, inching closer to me.

"Because it's not right."

He leaned over and kissed me on the neck. "No one can determine what's right or wrong but us."

I put my hand on his chest and pushed him back. "I'm confused. You just apologized for your behavior and said that you were wrong."

"I apologized because it was the *right* thing to do for putting you in a fucked-up situation. But if we're putting our cards on the table, the truth is, I want to be with you again."

I put some distance between us and went to sit across from him. "Malik, I think the best thing for me to do is to move out. We can't be roommates. Saturday never should have happened."

"It's no secret that I don't like Ellis. Even if I did like the brother, I'd still say he's not the man for you."

"And I suppose you are?"

"I'm not going to make this about whether it's me or him. It's about you. I know you, Mel. You won't be happy with that man."

"I don't need this right now," I said, shaking my head. "We were kidding ourselves thinking we could live in close quarters like this without something happening. You're a *single* man. I get that maybe I was the forbidden fruit. Well, now you've tasted the fruit and it was a big mistake. It's not going to happen again. I can't live in this apartment with you. We need to go our separate ways."

"That's it? Our friendship is over because of this?"

"How can we be friends when you're telling me you want to sleep with me again? I'm engaged, Malik."

"You were engaged two nights ago."

"That was a low blow."

"No, it's the truth."

"Well, what about your truth? Let's talk about you."

"Talk about me, what?" he said, tossing his hands up.

"What about Kai?"

"I don't know."

"That's a classic Malik answer. You throw my engagement in my face but get evasive when I bring up your relationship."

He nodded. "I'll give you that."

"So, answer the question."

"Okay. I like Kai. She has potential to become someone special, but right now our shit is broken."

"Well, I suggest you work on fixing your shit with Kai, instead of trying to tear apart my relationship." I got up and headed toward my room. "I'll be out by the end of the week."

CHAPTER FORTY-FOUR
MALIK

Melina got me thinking I needed to figure out my situation with Kai. I had never officially deemed her my girl, but since we started messing around I hadn't been seeing anyone else. We had spoken briefly earlier in the day and were meeting at her place when she got home from work.

I stepped off the elevator and began walking down the hallway to Kai's apartment. I caught a glimpse of someone heading into the stairwell at the end of the hall. I could've sworn it was the big dude we had bumped into on a previous occasion in the elevator. "What the fuck?" I muttered.

Kai's door was cracked open. I gently nudged it and stepped into the foyer. She was smoothing her hair and adjusting her shirt over her slacks. She spun around when she heard my footsteps. "Oh, Malik, you're here."

"It's seven o'clock." I loitered near the door, inspecting the room. A pillow from the sofa was on the floor and two glasses of water on the coffee table.

Her eyes were drawn to what had my attention. She bustled to replace the pillow and carry the glasses off to the kitchen. "Don't just stand there. Have a seat."

"Looks like you were doing a little entertaining."

"Don't beat around the bush, Malik," she shouted from the

kitchen. "If there's something you want to know, then ask." She came back into the living room, drying her hands on a dish towel.

"So dude was just in here?"

"If by dude you mean my neighbor, Gavin, then yes, he was here."

"Word? You want to fill me in on what was going on?"

Kai's hands immediately went to her hips. "You might want to rethink your tone, Malik."

"I see Big Boy sneaking into a staircase as I'm coming down the hall and then I walk up in here and you got shit thrown on the floor. You're over there fixing your hair and clothes, but you're worried about my tone."

"I think you need a reality check. You don't own any of this," Kai said, striking a pose. "I gave you multiple opportunities to make this an exclusive arrangement, but you kept side-stepping, probably too scared to be *locked* down. So now you come into my home acting like I'm your woman? I think we both know that's not the case. And just to set the record straight, though I don't owe you any explanations, Gavin and I are friends and nothing more. I don't appreciate your insinuation that he was sneaking off. That's my neighbor. He doesn't need to sneak from my apartment."

Women were notorious for mixing their messages. On the one hand, Kai wanted to make it known that I had no claim to her if she was fucking dude, but on the other hand, she said they were just friends. I knew I had probably hurt her ego by not saying either way whether I wanted a serious relationship with her. I had to admit that it was more of a stall tactic than a rejection. I didn't know what I wanted, so I left the issue hanging. I figured as long as we were spending time and having fun, then she was still getting what she wanted.

"That's cool, Kai. I'm just wondering why you didn't speak to your friend when we bumped into him months ago. Neither one of you uttered a single hello. It's funny. When I see my friends, we *speak* to each other."

"Really, Malik?" Her neck was rolling now. "Now you're just being an ass."

"I've been called worse."

"Not by me. At least not yet. Gavin and I met at a condo-owners meeting *after* we saw him on the elevator. I don't have to do this with you. You're not my man, so stop pretending to be."

I had to chill. My suspicions were just that. Suspicions. I didn't come over to anger Kai. I came over to discuss the one thing that had her pissed. Us. "Listen, when we first decided to mix business with pleasure, we both knew what it was. You knew the rules just like I did. We were keeping it light, so no one would get hurt, especially since we worked together. I'm not blind and I can hear. I know your feelings began to change toward our situation. I'm not gonna lie. I was cool with the way things were going."

"Don't you mean the way things *are* going?"

"That's what I said."

"No, it's not."

I released a stream of hot air. "Let me finish. I know you want more, but I'm asking you to be patient with me. I got a lot of balls up in the air right now. Getting fired thrust me into overdrive, trying to get my agency open earlier than planned. You know how important that is to me. But I do want to figure out where we're going with this, when the time is right."

"Okay. Let me see if I understand what you're saying. Basically, I shouldn't rock the boat and expect anything serious until, as you say, *the time is right*. Yet you can come in here and question what I do and with whom even though you and I aren't exclusive?"

"That's what you took away from what I said?"

"Yes, Malik."

This wasn't the time for tiptoeing around the issues. "Kai, I'm still feeling you out. Sometimes what you say and do don't quite match up. On more than one occasion you've gone missing, most recently last week when I got fired. And I'll admit that dude walking out of here right before I arrived pissed me off. You're right we aren't exclusive, but again, I need to be able to trust what you say and do. If you're telling me that Big Boy is just a friend I have to take it at face value, but that's not how it looked."

"You're doing an awful lot of speculating about what I do. What about you? I guess you're living the life of a saint. You're not with me twenty-four/seven. Am I supposed to believe that you're not involved with anyone else?"

"Exactly."

"Bullshit. I know how you are with the ladies and I know you're fucking someone other than me."

"You're wrong," I said without flinching. Technically, I wasn't lying. What occurred between me and Melina was a chance encounter. Melina had made it clear that there was no chance in hell of it happening again, no matter how much I wanted it to. She was moving to Long Island in a few days and planned to sign the lease to the apartment over to me. Ever since we slept together, I'd been trying not to think about Melina. Yet somehow she kept popping into my head. I knew she was getting married and would have been moving soon anyway, but I kept thinking how much I would miss seeing her and being around her and even how I enjoyed her company when we were out together. My feelings for Melina definitely had nothing to do with fucking.

Kai came over and planted herself directly in front of me. "It's written all over your face that I'm not wrong." She moved my arms out of the way and positioned herself on my lap. "But, like you, I have to take your word that it's the truth."

"Fine. Sounds like we're on the same page."

"Not quite. I like to get my way, Malik. Right now, you're getting your way."

"And I appreciate it, but think of it as my *agency* getting its way." I stood and lowered Kai onto the sofa.

"Where are you going?"

"Business is calling."

"You're not staying with me tonight?"

"Unfortunately, I can't. I have to be at the Gable Building in the morning to sign the lease on my office space."

Kai smiled up at me. "Well, kudos to you. It seems like you're going to get everything you deserve, after all."

As I left the building, I wondered whether Big Boy had already slipped back into Kai's apartment.

CHAPTER FORTY-FIVE
MALIK

I strolled through the main lobby in Grand Central Station on my way to the Gable Building on Lexington Avenue. The morning rush was like orchestrated chaos, people crisscrossing each other at varying paces, amazingly avoiding collisions. Had I not been on my way to sign the lease to my office, I would have been annoyed by the hustle and bustle. Somehow knowing that in a matter of minutes I'd be holding the keys to my own office suite helped me maintain my calm.

The receptionist led me to the waiting area and offered me a cup of coffee. Initially, I declined, but after fifteen minutes of waiting for the property manager I had a change of heart. I glanced at my watch for the tenth time in two minutes. My appointment was scheduled for nine a.m. It was nearing half past the hour.

Finally, the manager rushed into the room. "Mr. Denton, I'm Roger Gordon. I'm sorry to keep you waiting, but we seem to have a problem."

I stood, so we could speak eye to eye. "What sort of problem?"

"It seems the suite we were going to lease to you is no longer available."

Heat rushed up the back of my neck. "How is that possible?"

"I apologize. There must have been some sort of internal mix-up among our team, but that suite has already been leased."

"I spoke with your office two days ago and was assured that I could have that space."

"I apologize for this oversight, Mr. Denton," he said, his face reddening. He was repeatedly apologizing, but not offering any viable explanation.

"Well, what other suites can you show me in the building?"

"That was our last suite and we don't have any other offices available either."

"You mean to tell me that suite was the only available space in the building?"

"Again, I apologize, but we can add you to our waiting list. You'll be at the top position when a suite becomes available."

"You've got to be kidding me."

"I really wish there was more that I could do to rectify the situation. We have your information and will be in touch if anything opens up. Again, I'm really—"

I turned and left the office while he was still talking. I was seething. Perspiration had dampened the collar on my shirt. I headed into the bathroom across from the elevators. I snatched a few paper towels to blot around my neck. I threw the used paper towels toward the garbage and they missed, falling to the floor. I walked over and kicked the metal garbage can. I caught sight of myself in the mirror and my face was as red as Roger's. I took a deep breath to compose myself. I picked up my wad of towels from the floor and chucked it in the trash. I took another deep breath and then exited the bathroom. I stopped dead in my tracks. I'd know that comb-over anywhere.

Donner turned toward me. "Malik. I didn't think we'd be running into each other so soon."

"What the hell are you doing here?"

He pushed his glasses up the bridge of his nose. "It's a free world, isn't it?"

"For some."

"I've heard that you're planning to take over New York, but seems like you're getting off to a rocky start."

"Oh yeah, and where did you hear that?"

"I think you know it's not a coincidence I'm here."

My fist clenched. "Kai?"

"My people are loyal to a fault, Malik. Especially Kai. I have to commend you. This is a great find. I think this location will be perfect to set Kai up in a satellite office, which she'll head for Newport and Donner. You look surprised. Don't be. Kai's been keeping me posted on your plans for quite some time."

"Is that so?"

"Isn't it obvious?"

"So you fired me because you knew I wanted to start my own agency."

"I felt you were no longer an asset to Newport and Donner. I'm not going to hand my clients over to the competition. And you never quite fit into the team dynamic at Newport and Donner. For some reason you refused to accept the pecking order."

"Maybe because I was better than anyone you have employed there."

"That may be and I guess only time will tell. So here's some free advice for you. *If* you're ever going stand a chance in taking over New York, you better surround yourself with trustworthy people. It's one of the things I've prided myself on throughout my extremely successful career."

"It seems you're surrounded by lowlifes without an ounce of integrity, just like yourself. Do me a favor, keep your advice because just like you said, it's free and not worth a damn."

We rode the elevator down together in silence. When we reached the ground floor, I turned to Donner, and said, "Get ready for the takeover, Gerry."

CHAPTER FORTY-SIX
MELINA

Boxes cluttered the living room and part of the hallway. Packing was going exactly how I had expected—slowly. I felt as if I was walking in circles and not making any progress. I couldn't figure out what items to pack first, what should go or what should stay. Ellis encouraged me to leave everything, or throw it away, and buy whatever I needed. I wasn't raised that way and rejected the notion as soon as it left his mouth. I planned to leave the living room and kitchen furniture for Malik, since I would have no use for them at Ellis's place. My bedroom set I would donate to a shelter for women. There were single mothers that couldn't afford furniture and a free bedroom set could make life just a tad easier.

I squeezed through an opening in the boxes to get to the door. I let Giselle in and rubbed her swelling tummy with both hands. "Hi, mommy."

"I see who's going to get all the attention," she said, laughing. "Can I get some love, too?"

"I'm sorry, Gigi." I gave her a hug and a kiss on the cheek. "Come on in and watch out for the boxes."

"It seems like you're making progress. What do you want me to do?"

"Not much."

"Melina, I'm pregnant, not an invalid."

"I know that."

"Tell me what you need me to do."

"Okay. You can start bubble wrapping the picture frames over on the étagère."

Giselle stepped over a small box and went over to the shelves.

"Be careful."

"I'm fine." She picked up a picture of me, Ellis and his parents. It was from the night we went to the jazz benefit at Lincoln Center. Giselle traced her finger down the picture, then clutched it to her chest.

I paused, puzzled by her behavior.

She carried the picture over to the couch and sat down. "Melina…"

I put down the tape roll I was using. "Yes?"

Giselle was staring vacantly at the picture. "I wonder if my baby will look like him."

With deliberate steps, I moved closer. "Like who, Gigi?"

"His father." Her lips were trembling and tears formed in her eyes.

"You found out you're having a boy?"

"No…I mean…I wonder if my baby will look like Dr. Harlow—Ellis's father."

"What are you saying?" I heard what she said, but my mind wasn't comprehending or processing it correctly. "Giselle, why… why would the baby look like Dr. Harlow? What are you telling me right now?"

"We met at a medical conference about a year ago. When I saw him, I thought he looked familiar. I guess I knew his face from your pictures. I went over to introduce myself, just to say hello and to let him know that we knew someone in common. We started talking, but had to cut it short to attend our sessions. We ended up having dinner together the first night of the conference and then met for breakfast the next morning. It was strictly professional. I was in awe of his career in medicine. I asked him as many questions as I could about his experience in pediatric surgery. I wanted to know about some of the career choices he made along the way and any advice he could give me. On the second evening, we made plans to meet at the cocktail reception. We talked all night. About everything. He was so charming and engaging. We left together and went back to my room.

"Neither of us could explain why we were about to tempt fate, but we were like two magnets drawn together. Obviously, I knew he was married and he loved his wife. He told me the only reason Mrs. Harlow wasn't with him was because she had a bad cold and decided to stay home at the last minute. She usually attended the conferences with him because it gave her an opportunity to shop while he was preoccupied and couldn't halt her spending spree." She laughed to herself.

I eased down on the arm of the sofa, waiting for her to continue.

"We were in my room talking for hours and when he finally leaned over and kissed me, I knew there was no turning back. We made love—and that's what it was, Melina—it was tender and sweet. It was like he understood me and I understood him. I had never been with a mature man like Dr. Harlow. A man his age. Being with him made me realize that I wanted someone like him in my life. Not him necessarily, because I knew that could never be. You know me, Melina, I'm not a homewrecker. But after being with Dr. Harlow I knew I wanted an established man, in his prime, that had mellowed over the years and could appreciate the important things in life. If anything, that night with Dr. Harlow opened my eyes to what was missing in my life. When he was leaving my room the next morning, we handled our farewell with class and sophistication. Considering the delicate nature of the situation, and the parties involved, we swore never to speak of what transpired and agreed to never see each other again, not even during the remainder of the conference. He kissed me on the forehead before I closed the door behind him. I attended the rest of the conference and returned home three days later. A week later, a dozen roses were delivered to me at the hospital. He called. We had dinner. And so it began...

"He really loved his wife. I wrestled with that. I still do. When I think back to that first night, I wish that I could rewrite the past. I know it's foolish, but it's what I think about, alone at night, with this baby growing in my stomach."

I sat staring at Giselle, trying to make sense of the fact that Ellis's sister or brother was about to be born to one of my best friends. "Giselle—"

"I know you hate me because I hate me," she interrupted.

"You're pregnant with my fiancé's sibling. Why didn't you tell me any of this before?"

"How was I supposed to tell you that I was having an affair with Ellis's father? What would you have thought?"

"I don't know what I would have *thought*, but I would have told you that you'd lost your damn mind!"

"You don't think I know this sounds crazy?"

"Giselle, it doesn't *sound* crazy. It *is* crazy. Why didn't you tell me?"

"I don't know. I felt like I couldn't get you involved. We were together for seven months and every time we saw one another we swore it would be the last time. We just couldn't stay apart. After he died—" Her voice caught in her throat. "After he died, there was no way I could bring this to you during your time of grief. I mean, I was grieving, too, in my own way."

"This is unbelievable."

"There's something else you should know. We had been together the night before he died. We made love and when we said it was going to be the last time I sensed it was for real. The guilt had been getting to both of us and we realized it was time to truly end it. He had a heart attack the next night. Six weeks later, I found out I was pregnant. He never even knew. I must have gotten pregnant that last time we were together. That's fate for you."

"Oh God, Gigi." I moved next to her and hugged her. "Who else knows about this?"

"No one. Not even Charlee—you can't tell a soul. Promise me."

I leaned back, so I could see her face. "I can't make that promise."

"Melina—"

"You just told me that you're having a baby by my fiancé's dead father. As complicated as this is, I think Ellis would want to know that his father has another child. Your baby is his family, his brother or sister."

"Melina he *will* know this baby through you. You're going to be auntie, remember? I can make you and Ellis the godparents, so Ellis can have an active role in its life. But *please* don't say anything. I don't want to taint Dr. Harlow's legacy and destroy his family."

I could see the desperation in her eyes. It all made sense now. Why she was so down about the pregnancy and refused to share any details about the father. I shook my head. "Nothing has changed. I love you and I'm here for you just as I've always been. I'm in your corner and always will be, but I have to think about this. Ellis deserves to know."

She sighed heavily. "Who knows, maybe you're right. I've been carrying this secret around like a heavy weight. Maybe it's time to let it go and deal with the repercussions. Whatever you decide to do, I'll understand."

I did my best to assure Giselle that she would always be my sister and that I could never hate her, but I didn't hide my disappointment. On my way back from walking her to her car I started to replay so many things—past behaviors, conversations, and most importantly, our recent dinner at Ellis's. Giselle was actually with Bebe and Ellis discussing her pregnancy. She was supposed to be one of my bridesmaids. As much as I wanted to tell Giselle everything would be fine, I couldn't because that may have not been the truth.

CHAPTER FORTY-SEVEN
MALIK

Kai startled when she saw me standing outside of her apartment building. I quickly approached her, captured her by the arm and escorted her past the doorman. She pulled away once we got in the elevator, stealing glances at me from the corner of her eye. When the elevator stopped, she looked at me nervously. I followed her down the hall and inside her apartment.

"What are you drinking?" she asked.

"What are you serving, something laced with arsenic?"

"I'm trying to keep this civil."

"All right. I'll take a beer."

Kai handed me a Heineken and a bottle opener. "I figured you'd want to open it yourself."

"Can't be too safe with you around."

"It was business, Malik."

"I figured you'd say that."

"That's because it's true. I do what it takes to stay on top."

"Including screwing me. I guess that makes sense, since you love to screw."

"You were planning to leave Newport and Donner anyway. So they beat you to the punch. Is it really that big of a deal?" She walked over to where I was sitting. "The way I see it, in a few years your agency will be a goliath in the advertising industry. By then, I will have turned my division of Newport and Donner into the most profitable arm of the company. You and I will be the power couple of Manhattan."

"Are you smoking crack, Kai?"

"Why do you think I did this? You were an underling at Newport and Donner. I don't do underlings. I needed you to be the man...running your own agency...the man in charge."

"I bet that makes sense in your warped mind. What happened? Gerry got too old for you?"

"There's nothing between me and Gerry. Not now. Yes, I did sleep with him a few times when I first started at Newport and Donner, but that was years ago."

I laughed. "You're a piece of work."

"Gerry cultivated my career. I owe a lot to him."

"Right, like your new division in your satellite office."

"Exactly." She kneeled in front of me, placing her hand on my hardhead, rubbing gently. "Malik, I think we should start over. We're not colleagues anymore. We wouldn't have to hide our relationship. We could start fresh. We'll just start over from the beginning."

I stood up, pulling Kai along with me. "You know what? That's a great idea. Let's start over." She reached up to hug me, but I pushed her arms away. "In particular, let's start over with the reason why I came here. You know you threw quite a wrench in my day. After Gerry snatched up my office space I can admit I was feeling a little defeated. But I knocked the dirt off my shoulder and started making calls. The first call was to my dad to tell him about all this bullshit. He wasn't too happy, but I can always count on him to get me back on track. My next call was to Sphere Electronics. I spoke to Harv, the head of the video game division, to let him know I wouldn't be meeting him for lunch on Friday. Yeah, that's right, Harv and I had built a nice rapport while I spearheaded his account. He asked me to come to his office immediately because he wanted to share something with me. Can you imagine my surprise when Harv told me that Gerry slandered my name? Aside from telling Harv that I was an incompetent that botched his launch, he also let it be known that he fired me for it. I think he used a few colorful phrases that could undeniably be construed as discriminatory."

Kai's scowl was making it a momentous occasion.

"So guess what, Kai? Not only will Sphere Electronics be one of my top new clients—you ready because it gets better—I'll be suing all of your asses at Newport and Donner. It looks like I'll be having a happy holiday after all," I said with a flourish and a hearty laugh.

Kai smiled stiffly. "It won't stick, Malik. You have a lot to learn. Discrimination is difficult to prove."

"Not when you have a witness to testify on your behalf. Oh, make that four witnesses. Gerry made his comments to Harv's entire team."

Fear flashed across her face. "Wait a minute, Mal—"

"Thanks for the beer." I placed my empty bottle on the table and headed to the door. "I guess that's game," I said, with a wink.

CHAPTER FORTY-EIGHT
MELINA

Eleven p.m.

I was curled up on the bed, watching the news. Ellis had not yet come home from work. This was not a good start to the week, considering I moved in on Saturday and spent all day Sunday unpacking. I thought we would unwind together tonight. The commute from my office to Long Island took about an hour. Traffic wasn't bad and I made it home by seven. I came in and made dinner, ate by myself and then retired to the bedroom upstairs. I didn't like staying downstairs after dark—the house was too big to be sitting in alone. After I bathed, I slipped into a black lace negligee and waited. I had hoped that Ellis would be home at a decent hour, but when he called at nine to say he was running late, I pinned up my hair and put on an oversized sleep shirt.

Ellis eased between the sheets, waking me in the process. The clock on the nightstand read twelve-thirty. He wrapped his hand around my waist and pulled me close. He kissed my neck, then shoulder. I snuggled against him. Ten seconds later he was snoring in my ear. I don't know how long I lay awake listening to him. The next thing I felt was him kissing me on my forehead. One eye popped open to see him leaning over the bed, dressed for work and saying good-bye. It was five-thirty in the morning.

I got up at seven and took my time getting ready for work. Ellis had called while I was having my breakfast of toast and tea. He was all apologetic for coming home so late the night before and promised he'd be home early in the evening. I was thinking about making it a short day. Christmas was in two days and Ellis and I had barely discussed our plans. Aside from Bebe and Daniella coming over, I had no idea what we were going to do. Were we staying home for dinner? Were we going out? I had no clue. I was going to miss spending the holiday with my parents, but I was thankful they were able to visit two weeks ago.

I finished off my tea and cleaned the little bit of a mess that I made in the kitchen. I decided that I'd go in for a few hours and then leave at noon to do some last-minute Christmas shopping. I hadn't found the perfect gift for Ellis yet. I needed to get something for Charlee, too. Giselle was covered and I had already gone crazy buying gifts for the baby. The baby. My little niece or nephew that would actually be my brother or sister-in-law.

I needed to come to terms with what Giselle told me and determine how I would handle the information. How could something so potentially devastating be a blessing at the same time? I understood Giselle's position that it might be best not to tell Ellis about his father, but how could I look at myself in the mirror if I didn't let him know that he had another sibling in the world? I hated that I was now the beholder of Giselle's secret. If I told Ellis, nothing could or would be the same. Bebe would be devastated to know that Dr. Harlow was unfaithful. Finding out that he had a child as a result of his affair would probably kill her, especially considering her obsession with image. How would it look to others that Dr. Harlow left behind a dark secret? She'd die of shock and embarrassment on the spot. I couldn't even imagine how this could impact Daniella's perception of her father.

And as selfish as it may seem—what about my wedding? How could Giselle be a bridesmaid when she had an affair with my future mother-in-law's husband? I could strangle Giselle for putting not only herself, but all of us, in this predicament. The only reason I refrained from going ballistic when she told me was because I knew she was hurting and she wore her regret like an old, shabby coat. She was suffering enough and Dr. Harlow wasn't here to share the backlash. Giselle would have to bear it alone.

I grabbed my purse from the island and headed off to work. My assistant Nadia had been hinting that she wanted to go skiing upstate for the weekend, but her friends were leaving on Friday, the day after Christmas, and she had to work. It had been a good year for Trinity Accounting, so I planned to announce that I was letting the staff go at noon on Christmas Eve and the office would be closed until the following Monday.

When I arrived at the office, I let the holiday spirit overflow. I made my announcement to the staff and handed out holiday gift cards to everyone. Nadia had helped me find out what each person liked in advance, so we could personalize the gifts. Dave was raving over his Home Depot, Omaha Steaks and Land's End cards. Heather couldn't stop talking about what she already planned to get with her Banana Republic, Pottery Barn and Sony cards. Each card had a value of five hundred dollars. I had an incredible staff and it was the least I could do to spread some holiday cheer and put smiles on their faces.

I hugged everyone on my way out and wished them a happy holiday. I was off to complete my shopping. I hadn't figured out what to get a future mother-in-law that had everything. I searched for a one-way trip to hell, but apparently it wasn't available in stores.

I phoned Ellis to confirm that he would be home early because I was cooking dinner. He promised to be walking through the door no later than six o'clock. I hurried and won my fight with the holiday crowds, then made my way home to Long Island. I was still getting used to the idea of living in suburbia. The quiet and the isolation was a far cry from the buzz of Brooklyn. I drove past the circular driveway and pulled into the entrance to the estate that led into the garage. I disarmed the security system and then began bringing in the gifts. I placed the wrapped presents under the tree and immediately started dinner. Once I had the London broil and potatoes in the oven, I relaxed with a glass of Merlot.

Ellis entered the kitchen, loosening his tie. "Wait. Don't move. This is a sight I've wanted to see for a long time and I want to savor this moment."

"What are you talking about, Ellis?"

"Me coming in from a hard day of work and you in the kitchen, waiting for me to get home. It's like we're married already."

"You better be kidding."

"You know I am," he said, with a laugh. He planted a robust kiss on my lips. "I am elated that you're finally settled in here with me."

"And hopefully I'll be seeing a lot more of you."

"Now that's funny. Do I have time to get comfortable?"

"Dinner's in twenty minutes."

"I'll be back in fifteen."

Dinner was ready, the table set and I was on my third glass of wine. Ellis returned, wearing slacks and a merino wool crew neck sweater. I would have to work on his interpretation of casual lounge wear.

"You're on point tonight. I thought I'd have to come get you."

"Not tonight. I'm famished."

"Okay, let's eat." Ellis joined me at the table and I fixed our plates. It was nice to have dinner together. "I meant to ask you what you want to do about Christmas."

Ellis cut a piece of his meat. "Mother and Daniella will be here tomorrow night. We can have our annual Christmas Eve toast and open a few gifts, if you like. On Christmas Day, I thought Mother would prefer to stay home, instead of dining out. Chef will be here to prepare dinner. How does that sound?"

"That's fine. In my family we never go to a restaurant for Christmas dinner. Christmas has always been a time to stay home with loved ones." I reached out and grabbed his hand. "This will be your first Christmas without your dad. How are you feeling?"

He shrugged. "I worry more about Mother and Daniella."

Ellis rarely discussed Dr. Harlow. When he mentioned that he missed him the other day, it was the first time I had heard him say it. "I'm sure he'll be looking down on us."

"Or up."

"What? Why would you say that?"

He waved me off. "This is delicious. What's for dessert?"

"Me..." I said with an enticing smile.

We finished our dinner and Ellis left me with the dishes while he made a call. I cleaned the kitchen and then went upstairs to get ready. I was determined to spice it up between us.

I bathed and then rubbed my body with fragrant oil until every inch of my skin glistened. I removed the clip from my hair and tousled my curls, so they fell loosely around my shoulders. Last night I went for the negligee, but tonight I was going au naturel.

I dimmed the lights and a faint golden glow filled the room. I climbed onto the bed and fluffed a couple of pillows behind me. I curled my legs to the side and placed one arm above my head on the pillow. Ellis stepped into the room. I sat up slowly, seductively moving my shoulders. I crawled to the center of the bed and rose to my knees, legs apart. I ran my fingers through my hair, shaking my head from side to side, until it wildly framed my face. "Are you here for dessert?"

Ellis stopped in his tracks. I beckoned him toward the bed with my finger. He crossed the room and stood next to the bed. The phone was in his hand. "You look really delicious and I want dessert, but—"

"Shhhh." I crawled to the edge of the bed and slipped the phone out of his hand, letting it drop to the floor.

His eyes followed the phone. I reached up and jerked his chin until he was looking at me. I kissed my fingertip, then pressed it to his lips. He kissed it and I returned it to my mouth, gently sucking on it. He moaned and grabbed me around my waist, pulling me against his body. He rubbed his face against mine, his lips tickling my ear. "Just give me five minutes, honey. I have to call Beijing and then I'm all yours."

My arms dropped to my sides. "Really, Ellis?"

"I'll be right back." He bent down to pick up the phone, then left the room.

I plopped back against the pillows in disbelief. Ellis could have stayed at the office. When he did return to our bedroom, an hour later, he took off his clothes and hung them neatly on hangers, brushed his teeth and then finally came to bed. We kissed for a few minutes and then it was business as usual as he climbed on top. No sparks. No spice. I had planned to tear his clothes from his body, piece by piece, and explore every inch of him with my tongue along the way. I wanted to try a new position or two and see fireworks. I wanted to fill him up on my love until he couldn't take anymore. I wanted to feel the passion. As we lay together in the dark the only thing I felt was empty.

CHAPTER FORTY-NINE
MALIK

I thought for a moment as they all waited for me to answer. These were my boys—my partners—I didn't have to lie to them.

"Yeah, man, I miss having her here."

"Ohhh!" they yelled in unison, hands flying up in the air.

Drinks were flowing, food was on the table and my ass was in the hot seat. Terrence, Amir and Lex were over for our annual Christmas Eve Taste. The Taste was a gathering exclusively for the fellas. The ladies weren't allowed. No one usually complained about the men-only policy, since everyone would be together for Terrence's New Year's Eve party at Rituals.

"I saw it coming a long time ago," Terrence said.

"C'mon, man. Now you're making up stuff," I responded.

Lex chimed in. "Nah, he's not."

"And of course you saw something, too?" I asked Amir.

"I didn't see shit. I'm too busy trying to keep up with my own women. I don't have time to be worrying about what my little brother's doing."

"Have you spoken since she left?" Lex asked.

"Do I need to remind you brothers? This is *The Taste*, not *Dr. Phil*. Now change the damn subject!"

"I'll take that as a no." They howled.

I hadn't talked to Melina since she moved in with Ellis. I realized that I'd been hoping she would reach out to me to say Merry Christmas or even to say that she forgot something here, but so far no word. I just wanted to hear her voice. But as much as I wanted to talk to her, I refused to call. I had done enough damage and knew the best thing for me to do was to leave Melina alone and let her be with her fiancé.

"I'm with Malik. Leave it alone. I'm tired of hearing about his broke-down love life. My little bro lost two fine women in one week. He's setting new records. I'm about to call Guinness."

More laughter. It was going to be a long night if I didn't switch gears. "Yeah, I had a tough week, but you can't keep a good man down. That's why yesterday I signed the lease for my new office at the MetroTech Center right here in Brooklyn. Starting the first of the year, the M. Denton Agency will be open for business."

"Congrats, man," Terrence said.

Lex echoed his sentiments.

"That's a good look. So you took Dad's advice and set up shop in Brooklyn."

"Yup. I found a bigger space, for less money, with a cool view. I guess everything happens for a reason. It'll be hard work, but I'm used to that. Once I get my staff in place, I'll be on my way to the top."

Terrence stood. "Put those glasses up. Let's toast to this brother." He lifted his glass. "Malik, ever since I've known you, you've had a fire inside of you. You dream big and go after what you want, even when the odds are against you. You're full of determination and you never take no for an answer. You're destined for success. Let your vision be your guide."

"In all things…" Lex added.

I toasted with my partners. No truer words had been spoken. They knew me well.

CHAPTER FIFTY
MELINA

My cell phone had been vibrating all morning. Merry Christmas and happy holiday text messages from family and friends flooded my inbox. Among the messages was a text from Dru inviting me and Ellis to a New Year's Eve party at Rituals. I started to type my reply when Ellis entered the bedroom. He was already dressed and drinking a cup of tea.

"Merry Christmas, Lina."

I placed my phone on the nightstand. "Merry Christmas, Ellison."

He paused a moment, then slowly shook his head from side to side. "You sounded like Mother for a moment. She always called my father Ellison. Never Ellis. You'd always hear her say 'Good morning, Ellison. Did you do this, Ellison? Did you do that, Ellison? Where have you been, Ellison?' She was always so reserved with him—at least in front of others. I would imagine she had to be different when they were alone, but maybe not." He sat on the settee with his back to me. "I was just in the dining room having breakfast with Mother and she commented that it was interesting not having my father around for the holidays. She didn't say *sad* or *lonely* or even *strange*, she used the word *interesting*. It's as if she was weighing whether she preferred him not being here."

"Well, I certainly miss him." I went to sit next to Ellis.

He was hunched over, arms resting on his lap. He concentrated on repeatedly interlocking and unlocking his fingers. "You know, Lina, my father wasn't a perfect man. He had flaws like everybody else—maybe more than some."

"No one is perfect, Ellis."

"The night he died we had dinner at Peter Luger Steak House."

"I remember."

"It was just the two us. You know Mother would never allow him to consume that much red meat. We would go there from time to time without her knowing." He smiled at the memory and then took a deep breath. "Well, that night, he didn't seem like himself. He wasn't completely there with me. I asked if he was feeling all right and he said he felt like he was coming down with a cold. I could tell there was something bothering him. He ordered two scotches back to back and he relaxed a bit. I pressed a bit more to find out why he seemed out of sorts. That's when he confided in me. Why me, I still don't know. It must have been eating him up and he needed to tell someone."

My heartbeat quickened. "What did he tell you?"

He looked over at me. "That he was having an affair. He was in love and thinking about leaving my mother."

I hesitated, not knowing how to respond. "What did you say?"

"What didn't I say? We had a heated exchange at the table, struggling to keep our voices down. He kept trying to tell me that it wasn't his intention to hurt his family. I laughed at that. Apparently he was cheating with a younger woman. I accused him of being an old fool being led around by some bimbo. Now that pissed *him* off. He wouldn't say much about who this woman was, but he took offense at my assuming she was a classless degenerate. He kept saying she was an intelligent woman with a successful career, so she wasn't interested in his money. I figured it was a colleague, but he wouldn't say anymore about her. He wanted to keep the focus on himself. How he loved my mother, but he wasn't happy and hadn't been for years. He said he felt unfulfilled. That was the word he used repeatedly—unfulfilled. He said he'd been living my mother's life all those years and not his own. He said he was going home to tell my mother."

"Ellis, I—"

"At that moment, sitting across from him at the table, I hated him. I told him he was being a fool and then I got up and left the restaurant without another word. He died that night. I never asked Mother if he told her, but I assumed so. I felt she deserved the right to preserve the image of her marriage. No one needed to know that my father wanted to leave to start a new life with someone else."

"Did you ever try to find out who the woman was?"

"I thought about it, but I decided against it. He's gone. What's done is done. He didn't have the opportunity to leave this family to start another."

I thought about Giselle and the baby. "What if you found out he did have another family? I mean, what would you do?"

"He didn't mention a family, Lina. He only admitted to having an affair."

"I know," I said, tentatively, "but sometimes there are children, too."

"I don't even want to think about that. If my father does have some bastard children out there, they'll stay that way, out there as little bastards. They won't get a dime from me or my family. I wouldn't want anything to do with cleaning up his mess. As far as I'm concerned you let sleeping dogs lie."

I looked at the man sitting next to me and couldn't believe my ears. Just weeks ago Ellis talked about the importance of embracing family and yet he would be able to completely disregard his own flesh and blood. I squeezed his hand. "I suppose you're right. If there were any kids out there they'd be better off staying that way."

I went to get dressed, leaving Ellis alone with his thoughts, because I needed to be alone with mine.

We were all in the living room surrounding the tree. I handed Daniella her Christmas present. Ellis financed the gifts but had left the shopping to me.

She screeched when she opened the box. "This is the Louis Vuitton bag I've been looking at for months! Thank you, guys!"

"Ellison, you spoil her too much," Bebe said.

"This is for you, Bebe." I handed her a box.

"That's from me and Lina, Mother."

Bebe turned the box in her hands. "They say big things come in small packages." She stripped off the paper and opened the box. "This is nice. A cute little pendant," she said, using her manicured fingertip to move the pendant around the box.

Cute *little* pendant? That pendant was upwards of five thousand dollars. I would have never spent that much money on her, but Ellis insisted that nothing was too good for his mother. "It's Harry Winston," I said.

"Yes, dear, I read that on the box. Thank you, Ellison. Thank you, both. It's beautiful." Her mouth was puckered so severely, I was expecting her to spit out a lemon seed.

Ellis handed me my gift. "Merry Christmas."

I peeled back the paper, revealing a Rolex box. Nestled inside was a watch. Diamonds surrounded the face and also adorned the Roman numeral six.

"How do you like it?" he asked.

"I love it." I leaned over and kissed him.

"Ellis does have good taste," Daniella said, "but a watch? Where's the romance? Something to make her ooh and aah."

"It's not just a watch, Daniella. This watch represents the *time* Lina and I have been together, the *time* we'll spend with one another and the hope that *time* will always be on our side." He took the watch out of the box and put it on my wrist.

"Well, when you explain it that way, I guess it's a romantic notion," she said with a laugh. "All right, Lina, let's see what you got Ellis."

I reached under the tree and pulled out Ellis's gift. I handed him the rectangular box. Bebe watched like a hawk as he tore off the gift wrap. His eyes narrowed when he saw the iPad in the box.

"That's hot," Daniella commented. "As much as you're on the go, you need one of those."

"Lina, thank you. It's great." Ellis hugged me, kissed his mother on the cheek and then turned to his sister. "Daniella, how about you show me how to use this in my office?"

"Don't be long," Bebe said. "Dinner will be served at five."

They left the living room together with Daniella chattering about how much she loved her gifts. Their voices eventually trailed off and Bebe and I were left together in silence.

Bebe leaned back in her chair, crossing her legs. "You don't mind that I coordinated the dinner menu with Chef, do you?"

"Of course not. Why would I?"

"Well, you are the lady of the house now, aren't you?"

"Yes, I am."

"When do you plan to step up and act like it?"

I took a deep breath. "It's only Christmas dinner, Bebe."

"No, I believe it's more than that."

"Bebe, let's not—"

"A mother wants to feel that her son will be taken care of when he marries. She wants a wife for him that will treat him like a king."

"We're not going to do this again."

"We will do this again and again until you get it through your skull that Ellison deserves more in a wife. So either you will *be* more or you'll *be* gone."

"Excuse me? What gives you the right to dictate my relationship with Ellis? Yes, he's your son, but he's not a baby. He's a grown man that makes his own choices and he chose me."

"Yes, but we all make mistakes, dear."

"Bebe, you are a bitter woman. Just because your happiness was ruined doesn't mean you can destroy mine."

"What did you say to me?" she said, through gritted teeth.

Bebe rose from her chair and I stood up. She put her hand on my shoulder and pushed me back down into my seat, holding me there. "I want you to remember one thing." She leaned down and got all up in my face. "You're here now, but don't get comfortable. If I want you gone, then you're gone." She let go of me, pushing me back in the process.

"You're sick, Bebe."

She started toward the door. "Perhaps I am, dear, but it's astonishing what you can get your hands on when your son owns a pharmaceutical company—remedies for all sorts of *problems*. Don't be a problem."

Bebe left the living room and I could still see her contorted face next to mine. She was really insane.

Ellis came to the door with his iPad in hand, fiddling with the display. "Daniella's got me up and running. I came to get you for dinner."

I walked over to him and pulled him into the room. "Ellis, your mother has lost it and I'm not going to deal with her anymore. She just threatened me."

"What are you talking about?" he said, tapping the screen.

"Put that damn thing down. Did you hear what I said? Your mother put her hands on me and *threatened* me."

"Lina, you're not going to start this on Christmas, are you?"

I knocked the iPad out of his hands, sending it crashing to the floor.

Ellis took a step back. "What has gotten into you?"

"Your mother! She attacks me whenever we're alone, never when you're around, because she likes to put on this air that she would never say the venomous things she says." I began to pace back and forth. "It's becoming so clear to me. She knows I'll complain to you and it'll start to drive a wedge between us, because in your mind, your mother is not that type of person. Bebe knew this from the beginning. She *knew* this would happen."

"Listen to yourself. You're not making any sense."

"I am making sense, Ellis, and if you would listen you would see that. Your mother thinks you're making a mistake by marrying me. I'm not worthy. Not only that, she told me that if she wants me gone, she can make it happen. The best part of all of this is that she threatened to get her hands on some drugs from your company to do it."

"Lina, that's absurd. Mother cannot access anything from my company. You should know that."

"I don't know what she can or can't get, but that's not the point, Ellis. You don't see anything wrong with what your mother said to me? You don't have a problem with your mother threatening our relationship and what sounded like my life?"

Ellis took my hands in his. "Listen, I told you I would work on Mother. If she said these things—"

"*If?*"

"If she said these things I'll talk to her tonight. But right now they're waiting in the dining room. We don't have time for this."

I looked down at his hands holding mine. I didn't feel the warmth or protection that I got when holding my daddy's hands. I didn't feel safe or like Ellis would always take care of me. I gazed at the watch on my wrist and thought about what Ellis said it represented.

"You're right," I said, barely above a whisper. I swallowed hard, trying to keep my voice steady and holding back the tears. "We don't have time for this." I pulled my hands from his, unfastened the watch and handed it to him. "Our time is up."

"Lina, what are you doing?"

"Here's another gift you can give to Bebe." I slipped my engagement ring from my finger and pressed it in Ellis's palm. "Tell her the wedding is off."

"Lina…"

I slowly walked out of the room, listening to Ellis call my name while Bebe called to him from the dining room. He didn't come after me and I never looked back.

CHAPTER FIFTY-ONE
MELINA

I was lying on Giselle's living room couch, watching TV. I was wearing a pajama top, had rollers in my hair and floppy socks on my feet. She came in and stepped in front of the television, obscuring my view.

"Melina, you know I love you—"

"Prove it and kindly move your big belly out of the way."

"Oh, no you didn't," she said, laughing. "Okay, it's time to get tough. You've been in that funky pajama shirt for days. It's already after noon. Get your ass off the couch and get dressed."

"You don't even sound right trying to be tough. And my shirt isn't funky. I bathe every day."

"Fine, but I'm sick of looking at it. I know you're upset about Ellis, but you can't stay like this."

When I left Ellis's on Christmas night, I drove straight to Giselle's. She was in Connecticut with her family, but she had the doorman let me into her apartment. She came home later and found me with red, puffy eyes and a runny nose to boot. When the tears finally dried up, she made me eat something and tell her what happened. I told her everything and let her know that I didn't tell Ellis about the baby. It was her decision if and when she ever told him. She insisted I stay with her until I found a place. I had been holed up for days in her apartment.

"I'm missing the movie with you standing in my way."

"Just so you know, Charlee is on her way over and if she sees you like this, she will be all in your ass. How's that for tough?"

I sprung up. "I'm getting dressed now."

Giselle's doorbell rang. "Too late. She's here. Why don't you answer it, Melina?"

"Damn you, Gigi." I went to open the door for Charlee.

She looked me up and down. "Oh, hell no! What is going on up in here? We can't have this. Go shower, or do whatever you have to do, to not look so busted."

I started laughing at her dramatic entrance. "I don't look busted."

"There are lots of mirrors around here. Have you seen yourself in one? Because I'm looking at busted."

"Shut up, Charlee."

Charlee came into the living room and sat down. "So how are you feeling?"

"Better."

"That didn't sound too convincing."

"Giselle, please tell her that I'm okay."

"As long as she's lying on the couch, she's fine."

"Thanks a lot, Gigi."

"Tell me one thing," Charlee started. "Did you keep the ring?"

"Nope. I gave it back."

"Damn! Have I taught you nothing? Why would you give that rock back? He doesn't need it."

"Because I don't need it, either."

"This girl…"

I smiled. "I did keep the money though."

"That's my girl," she said, raising her hand for a high-five. "You did learn something."

"I've learned a lot," I responded with a hint of sadness.

Charlee leaned over and hugged me. "It's New Year's Eve. We are not staying here crying the blues tonight."

Leave it to Charlee to come in like a ball of energy and turn things upside down.

"Where are we going?" Giselle asked.

"All I have to do is make a call and we'll have our pick of the hottest parties tonight."

"I don't want to be out in the city with all of the crazies on New Year's Eve," she said, rubbing her stomach.

I remembered Dru's text message. "I was invited to a party at Rituals in Long Island if you want to go out there."

"It seems the dead has arisen and with a great suggestion."

"Who's throwing the party?"

"Terrence and Dru."

Giselle exchanged a glance with Charlee. "Malik's friend, Terrence?"

"And so?"

"So nothing," Charlee said. "I'll be back at nine to pick you two up. Lose the blues and be ready for some fun."

Giselle closed the door behind Charlee. "Are you all right to go out tonight?"

"I'll be fine. I think it'll do me some good."

"Well, let's get you ready."

"Giselle, I want you to know that I'm putting the money I got from Ellis in a fund for your baby. All of it. Every last dime."

"Melina, no."

"It's not up for debate. I'm not going to keep Ellis's money for myself, but I have no problem giving it to his family—whether he knows about it or not."

Giselle's eyes welled up. "Thank you, Melina."

I put my arms around her shoulders. "You should also know

that Dr. Harlow loved you very much and wanted to be with you. He told Ellis so."

Giselle lost it. I think she needed to know that. I hugged her tight until she exhausted her tears. And when she was all cried out, we were both ready to welcome in the New Year.

A live band was playing in the lounge when we walked into Rituals. There was a nice crowd jamming to the R&B they were performing. Everyone was dressed in their best, looking grown and sexy. I hadn't gotten my things from Ellis's yet, so I borrowed a tight, black bandage dress from Giselle. She wouldn't be wearing it anytime soon, so I was working it for the night. It was sleeveless, mid-thigh and clinging to my curves. My hair was full of bouncy curls that I had to keep pushing away from my face. Giselle was wearing a one-sleeved, gold dress that silhouetted her body and accentuated her baby bump. Charlee was in a red, backless jumpsuit, and the color was a perfect match for her fiery spirit.

We strolled into the lounge and managed to find an open booth. Charlee immediately ordered a bottle of champagne. Giselle ordered sparkling water with lemon and lime.

"This is a nice spot," Charlee said.

"Terrence's sister owns it. She has a nice clientele."

"Impressive," Giselle added.

"I'll be right back. I think I see Dru and I want to say hello."

I set off in the direction of the bar. Dru was standing with a familiar face. I walked up and tapped her on the shoulder.

"Heeey, I'm glad you made it." She kissed me on the cheek. "You remember Terrence's sister, Jade?"

"I do," I said as we hugged our hellos.

"Where are you sitting? I'll come over and join you in a minute."

"I'm here with my two girlfriends." I pointed out Charlee and Giselle.

"You didn't bring Ellis tonight?"

"Long story, girl. Let's just say your advice came in handy."

"Okay, I'll be over."

I was heading back to the table when someone grabbed my hand. I knew the touch before I turned around. Malik held my hand firmly in his as he peered down at me. My pulse sped up at the sight of him. His café au lait skin contrasted perfectly with the cream sweater and slacks he was wearing.

"I didn't know you would be here tonight, Mel."

"Dru invited me."

"I'm glad she did."

"I came with Charlee and Giselle."

"No Ellis?" he asked, the makings of a smile playing on his lips.

I pulled my hand from his grasp and wriggled my naked finger. "No Ellis."

"Do you think Charlee and Giselle will mind if I steal you for a minute?"

I shook my head. He led me into the main dining room of the restaurant to a quiet table in the corner. He pulled out my chair, then sat across from me. He just stared at me for a good minute before he uttered a word.

"I knew." He paused. "It had been a long time, but I still knew."

"Knew what, Malik?"

"I had been running from feeling something real for so long. Running from relationships, from love. The fact that you were spoken for made it easier for me to keep running. But I knew what I was feeling and it was getting more difficult to contain. The night of the snowstorm I stopped running and all my pent-up feelings for you broke loose. The passion between us was crazy, but the *echo* I felt after was stronger, and I knew. I realize you may not feel the same right now, but I'm willing to wait for—"

"I think I know too, Malik. I've known for a while. I kept thinking that I needed to stay away from you because I was curious and curiosity could get me in trouble. But the night of the storm I didn't care about the repercussions. All along you'd been showing me glimpses of what I was missing and that night I *wanted* to be with you. I felt our connection, the passion."

"We're good together, Mel."

"Malik, I don't want to rush into—"

"Don't worry, we'll take it slow."

"I'd like that."

He got up from his chair and reached out for my hand. I stood in front of him.

"Let's start with a kiss and see how that goes," he said.

I tilted my head to meet his kiss. His lips gently parted mine and our tongues intertwined. His arms tightened around me, holding me firmly, securely. When we pulled apart, I felt lightheaded.

Malik smiled. "That was nice. Next maybe we can share a dance or two."

He guided me on to the dance floor where we grooved to the music and when he held me, I felt a warmth that made my body melt into his.

I saw my girls and his boys pointing and smiling when they saw us together. I guess they all knew, too.

At midnight we toasted in the New Year together, as one big boisterous group, celebrating new beginnings.

Malik leaned over and whispered in my ear. "And finally you can come home with me where you belong."

"But I don't have my bed anymore, remember?"

Malik wrapped his arms around my waist, pulling me to him.

"I guess that means you'll have to sleep close to me each and every night."

"How close?"

"*Real* close."

"As close as we can get?"

"Even closer."

"You win...let's go home."

ACKNOWLEDGMENTS

The moment you realize how blessed you are, is the moment when you should begin to give thanks. This is my moment. I want to thank everyone who picked up this book to spend a little time in *Close Quarters* with me. I appreciate you and hope that you enjoyed it.

To my family, your support has been amazing. You never let me down, always lift me up and I thank you for having my back then, now and always. I love you guys!

Lots of love to the Old School Crew…you know who you are. And where would I be without my sisters? DST for life!

Zane, you are an inspiration! I'm truly thankful to be a part of the Strebor family. Charmaine, you're an absolute joy to work with and I thank you for all you do. Keith, thanks for bringing sexy to the cover—it's hot, hot, hot! Sara Camilli, thank you for being an amazing agent.

Thanks to all for your encouragement. You motivate me to keep creating.

Stay tuned…

ABOUT THE AUTHOR

Shamara Ray is a graduate of Syracuse University. She first enticed readers with her debut novel, *Recipe for Love*. Shamara has a penchant for the culinary arts and enjoys entertaining friends and family in her Long Island home. She is currently working on her next novel.

Visit the author at www.ShamaraRay.com, www.facebook.com/pages/Shamara-Ray, or via Twitter: @ShamaraRay